A Week *to* Remember

A Week *to* Remember

RUTH O'LEARY

POOLBEG

This book is a work of fiction. References to real people, events, establishments, organisations, or locales are intended only to provide a sense of authenticity, and are used fictitiously. All other characters, and all incidents and dialogue, are drawn from the author's imagination and are not to be construed as real.

Published 2025
by Poolbeg Press Ltd.
123 Grange Hill, Baldoyle,
Dublin 13, Ireland
Email: poolbeg@poolbeg.com

© Ruth O'Leary 2025

© Poolbeg Press Ltd. 2025, copyright for editing, typesetting, layout, design, ebook and cover image.

The moral right of the author has been asserted.
A catalogue record for this book is available from the British Library.

ISBN 978-1-78199-678-2

All rights reserved. No part of this publication may be reproduced or transmitted in any form or by any means, electronic or mechanical, including photography, recording, or any information storage or retrieval system, without permission in writing from the publisher. The book is sold subject to the condition that it shall not, by way of trade or otherwise, be lent, resold or otherwise circulated without the publisher's prior consent in any form of binding or cover other than that in which it is published and without a similar condition, including this condition, being imposed on the subsequent purchaser.

www.poolbeg.com

ABOUT THE AUTHOR

Ruth O'Leary lives in Dublin with her family and Golden Retriever, Rusky. She works as a freelance movie extra, playing various roles in TV dramas and movies.

Ruth's short stories have been published many times online and in two of Ireland's national publications, *Woman's Way* and *Ireland's Own*. She also writes a monthly travel blog called *Rambling Ruth*, combining her passions for writing and travelling, which can be found on her website.

She is active on social media and you can find her on Facebook, Instagram, Threads, X, and Bluesky under rutholearywriter.

Her debut novel *The Weekend Break* was an Irish Times Bestseller.

A Week to Remember is her second novel.

ACKNOWLEDGEMENTS

This book led me on a physical journey over the hills of Galicia in Northern Spain on one of the many traditional Camino routes, with very little preparation. If my characters were arriving solo and unprepared then I had to do the same. It was an amazing experience and I want to start by thanking everyone who wished me a *'Buen Camino'* along my Sarria to Santiago path. I particularly want to thank Michelle Byrne from Dublin, who I met in a forest on my first day, for our hours of chats and laughs along the way. To Miyuki Yoshida from Mount Koyasan, Japan, who made a five-hour walk to Palas de Rei feel like half that. Thank you also to Sheila Fitzgerald, founder of EVA-ethical volunteering adventures, for agreeing to appear in the book.

For their help and guidance, I would like to thank my agent Kate Nash, Paula Campbell of Poolbeg Books, my editor Gaye Shortland, and David Prendergast for my wonderful book cover.

Thank you to every member of my online writer group Writers Ink under the leadership of Vanessa Fox O'Loughlin aka crime writer Sam Blake and business mentor and journalist Maria McHale with contributions from literary agent Simon Trewin. Because of them, I continue to learn about this writing life and the publishing industry. Writers Ink really is 'my tribe', a place to find writing support and advice from the kindest, nicest, book-mad people!

I would like to thank my fellow Poolbeg writers Lucy O'Callaghan and Sharon Black, and the very supportive Irish branch of the Romantic Novelists Association and The Society of Authors for the great chats and information-swapping meet-ups.

Thank you to bestselling author Faith Hogan for your lovely review of my book. You are so kind and generous.

I would like to thank the staff of the Tyrone Guthrie Centre for looking after me so well when I spent a week there finalising my edits. It truly is a magical place.

Thank you to the booksellers for stocking my books and to you, the reader, for purchasing them. I am so grateful every single day that I get to do this.

Finally, thank you to my mum and dad, my sister Barbra and my brother Peter for their support. And to my husband Hughy and my sons Jack, Michael, and Tim – let's keep the adventure going.

DEDICATION

To Camino Dreamers Everywhere:
Whether it takes days or weeks,
Remember
—Your Camino Your Way—
One step at a time.

CHAPTER 1

Friday 30 June 2023

Dublin Airport

Paula sat at Gate 302 in Dublin Airport, with loads of time to spare. She was three hours early. Having woken up nearly every hour throughout the night, she decided she might as well get up and hang around the airport – that way she couldn't back out. The kids had texted to wish her good luck and Kevin had sent a voice message from his hiking trip, but she'd felt so jumpy alone in the empty house that she couldn't wait to leave it.

You wanted to do this, she reminded herself, nervously fiddling with her new pixie haircut, you wanted adventure, sixty is the new forty and all that.

She did want adventure but, as she had left all the organising to her best friend Jill, she hardly knew where she was going and had no idea what to expect.

This would have been Jill's third Camino trip but, just two days ago, they were exchanging texts on whether to bring conditioner or not when Jill's mother had a terrible fall. She lost her balance when her beloved Jack Russell jumped up to bark furiously at a political canvasser at the door. Ironically, she had trained him to do that, but this time she wasn't expecting it and fell over with the fright. She was taken to the hospital where, following an X-ray, they confirmed she had fractured her hip. So Jill had to back out of the trip to spend time at her mother's bedside.

Paula remembered how stressed she sounded when she rang her with the news. She became even more stressed when Paula said she too would cancel.

"You have to go!" Jill had pleaded.

"But I've hardly even looked at your emails! I had planned on just following your lead on this trip."

"You'll be fine."

"But will everyone else be in groups?"

"No, this is the one place where a lot of people travel solo and, besides, you're not completely on your own. *Follow the Camino* has booked all your accommodation, and a driver will collect you from the airport. He picks up your luggage every morning and delivers it to your next hotel. Trust me, all you have to do is walk. You'll be following the pack, and you'll meet so many people doing the same."

Looking around now, Paula could see what she meant by "the pack". As more people arrived, they were dressed just like she was, in outdoorsy hiking gear. Hiking trousers with multiple pockets (which Paula had to admit were very practical) and zip-up fleece tops very much like her own, seemed to be the uniform.

Most were around her age too. Except for one. A tall, stylish young woman turned a few heads when she walked through the busy airport, with a coffee in one hand, duty-free bag in the other, and her long red hair bouncing loosely down her back. Stopping near Paula, she checked her boarding card and, after a quick look around, plonked herself down a few seats away, letting out a loud sigh.

She must be at the wrong gate, thought Paula. Although she was wearing casual gear and had a small rucksack with her, she also had a full face of make-up on and looked like she was about to go on location to model for a nature lovers' magazine.

As more people arrived at the gate, many seemed to be in groups with matching luggage labels. The downside of travelling solo now was that she had to figure things out for herself. Opening her carry-on backpack, she checked her documents for the twentieth time. Jill had booked them on the Camino Frances, a famous route of the Camino de Santiago that officially starts in France. However, they would begin their journey in Sarria, Spain, a popular choice for those with only a week to spare. Sarria, being 115 kilometres from Santiago's Cathedral, meant that walkers would cover the final 100 kilometres that qualifies pilgrims for the Compostela certificate, confirming you had walked the Camino. Since Sarria was a small town in the Galician mountains of northwest Spain, it was necessary to fly into Santiago Airport. Upon arrival, a driver named Carlos would pick her up and take her to Sarria, where she would spend her first night before starting the walk tomorrow.

Dinner out on my own tonight, she thought. She sighed as she put the itinerary back in her backpack. When was the last time I did that? She couldn't remember.

"Are Lingus Flight 742 to Santiago de Compostela is now departing from Gate 302."

Taking a deep breath, Paula gathered her things and stood up. The good-looking redhead was sitting completely still, staring in front of her.

She's definitely at the wrong gate, Paula thought as she nervously joined the line of happy hikers.

What on earth am I doing here? Rachel looked around at the people queuing up excitedly to board the Aer Lingus flight. It's like I'm trapped in some awful outdoor adventure movie.

Some men, some couples but mostly groups of women over forty, it seemed, were chatting, comparing itineraries and looking very excited.

What is everyone so happy about? It's just a walking trip. She didn't get it. She was here to get away, somewhere Craig would never think of looking for her. She needed to clear her head and try to think what her next step could be after the most humiliating episode of her life.

But these people chose to be here, she thought, and some had done this before judging by the Camino badges on their backpacks, and the shells with red crosses tied on to their bags with red string. One big group seemed particularly excited, laughing and chatting animatedly about the routes they were taking. She made a mental note to avoid them.

Crossing her long legs, she looked down at what she was wearing. She had literally googled **what to wear on the Camino** and ordered everything online from Decathlon with next-day delivery. She had to admit that the hiking trousers and tops were very comfortable and it was a while since she spent a whole day in flats, but it was not the type of clothing she would choose to wear full-time at home or anywhere else.

Finishing her iced coffee, she shook her head. How had it come to this? She sat staring ahead of her as the flight attendant called the flight for boarding. She felt sick.

I don't have to do this. I could just get up and leave the airport right now.

But go where? She was on four weeks' leave from work so she couldn't return there. She had hoped that a week walking would give her the space to think clearly about what had happened and help her plan her next move. But, looking around now, she wished she had done more research on the Camino.

She knew that "El Camino" meant "The Way" and that "Santiago" meant "Saint James" – one of the Apostles – and that the different walking routes, starting in France, Spain and Portugal were ancient pilgrimage routes but that nowadays religious and non-religious walked the route that fitted the amount of time they had. She didn't want to know any more about the history of it. The travel agent assured her that all she had to do was follow the yellow arrows on the route and that was all the information she needed.

"Could the final passengers for Aer Lingus Flight EI742 to Santiago de Compostela board now at Gate 302."

Rachel looked around. Just a handful of people remained. One woman was in total panic as an Aer Lingus gate agent helped her look for something in her upturned handbag. Maybe I should offer to help, she wondered as she picked up her passport and stood up. Feck it, I don't need any more drama in my life, she decided as she walked past them to board the flight.

"I'm so sorry, I'm sure I had it a minute ago."

"Don't panic, we'll find it." The gate agent sat down beside Cathy and helped her go through the contents of her bag, upturned on the empty table beside her, as the other passengers lined up to board the plane.

Cathy felt such a fool. She had arrived at the airport hours before to avoid this type of panic. She hadn't slept much the night before, knowing she had to be up so early to catch the airport bus from Mullingar, so that hadn't helped. It would have been quicker to drive but Ted always said she was such a nervous driver and that she'd never manage Dublin traffic. He was probably right, so she didn't chance it.

"I'm such an idiot." Cathy nervously twisted a strand of her thin brown hair which had slipped out of her ponytail.

"Now don't say that. It must be here."

"I'm in such a tizzy now!" Cathy was sweating. She was overheating in her large hiking top and wished now that she had taken the adventure shop assistant's advice on buying a smaller size.

"Ah, here it is!" the agent said, holding up Cathy's copy of *The Weekend Break*, the novel she had just started reading on the bus. The corner of her boarding pass was sticking out from the pages.

"Oh, thank you so much! I forgot I was using my boarding card as a bookmark. I'm so sorry!"

"Honestly, there's no need to apologise." The young agent smiled and helped her put everything back into her bag. "People get very stressed when flying – it happens all the time."

"You're very kind – it's just that I haven't flown in years – nearly thirty years – and I never travel alone so this is all ... new to me."

"Well, you're sorted now and you are going to a beautiful place so let's get you on board."

Cathy felt so stupid. What if Ted was right? What if she wasn't able to manage without him? A worry wart, that's what he used to call her. But she wasn't always like that, and she knew it.

No. Ted was wrong. I know I can do this, she said to herself. Gathering up her things, she took a deep breath and set off to board the plane.

CHAPTER 2

SANTIAGO AIRPORT

SPAIN

A blast of hot Spanish air greeted the passengers as they disembarked from the flight. It was twenty-five degrees in Santiago de Compostela, a nice contrast to the grey day they left behind in Dublin. Being a small airport, going through passport control was quick, and they were through to the baggage carousels in no time.

Paula spotted her backpack immediately and threw it over her shoulder. It was one of Kevin's. He had about four different types of backpacks of different sizes and lengths, hung up in the garage.

"It's important to get the length right," he'd said, measuring one up against her back.

Paula had made interested sounds but really she didn't care as long as she could carry it. She was taking very little with her. The advantage of this type of walking holiday was that there was no dressing up. It was hiking gear during the day and comfortable clothes, with a change of shoes or sandals for the evening. After Jill pulled out of the trip, Paula watched some YouTube videos on packing for the Camino and reduced her clothes pile to the bare minimum. One of the things she was looking forward to was not caring about how she looked for a week. Her new comfortable hiking clothes made her less conscious of her menopausal spare tyre which had appeared around her waist ten years ago and refused to leave. She hated it.

Rachel stood at the carousel. She had managed to get through the two-hour flight without speaking to anyone. The two women beside her talked nonstop about their Camino plans but Rachel kept her headphones on, happy to have a window seat as she listened to a Mel Robbins podcast about restarting your life and building yourself back up after a huge life change.

Being single at thirty-nine was certainly a curveball she hadn't seen coming. Picking up her bag, she checked her notes and headed out into arrivals to look for a driver called Carlos.

In the arrivals area, a tall, tanned man who looked to be in his early sixties stood with a sign that had CARLOS written in capitals on it. His wavy silver-grey hair was held back from his face by the sunglasses on his head as he greeted the Irish group he was meeting from the flight.

He certainly is fit for an older guy, Rachel noticed, remembering what her best pal Charley said to her when she rang to wish her bon voyage: "The best way to get over one man, is to get under another one!"

Rachel brushed that thought aside. He might look like a silver-haired Antonio Banderas, but even the thought of going near another man again made her nauseous. Male company was the last thing she needed on this trip.

Carlos ticked everyone's name off a list.

"I am just missing one person, a lady called Cathy Kinsella. Does anyone know her?"

Everyone in the group of about ten people shook their heads.

Just then, a stressed-looking woman with a huge suitcase came through arrivals, looking around frantically.

That's the same woman who was panicking in Dublin airport, Rachel noted.

"*Cathy?*" Carlos called out.

The woman nodded and came over. She went to shake his hand and dropped her passport.

"Oh, I'm so sorry, my case was last to come out and then I couldn't find my passport," she said, bending down to pick it up. Her shoulder-length brown hair was tied back loosely with an elastic band and loose strands had fallen around her face.

"It is not a problem," Carlos said kindly. "Follow me, everyone!"

Carlos's minibus was just outside the door. He opened the back for everyone to put their backpacks in. Rachel leaned her bag beside the bus and went to climb in.

"Excuse me? Everybody puts their own bag in the back," he said with a smile.

Rachel did not return his smile but quickly placed her bag in the back of the van before getting in.

Cathy struggled with her case, so Carlos helped her lift it in.

"I'm so silly to bring a suitcase," she said, embarrassed when she saw everyone else had a backpack. "It's just I couldn't decide ... there was so much choice ..."

"Please, don't worry. We will manage," Carlos reassured her.

"So sorry," Cathy said to the other passengers as she boarded the minibus last and took her seat before letting out a long sigh.

Before they left the airport, Carlos stood at the front of the minibus and welcomed everyone to Spain. He informed them that the bus journey would take one hour and thirty minutes. The Cathedral in Santiago was the end point of their Camino pilgrimage so the transfer would take them 115 kilometres east of the city to their starting point – Sarria in the Galician hills.

"Galicia is often referred to as the Ireland or Scotland of Spain," he said, "but not just for the amount of rainfall we get here, making everything very green, but because the influence of the Celts has endured the longest in this region. And, would you believe, the bagpipes are a very popular instrument here!" He smiled. "Also, the Galicians have their own language. Spanish will be understood, but you may hear Galician spoken amongst the locals. This is a reminder that Galicia is autonomous and therefore a nation within a nation. As you probably already know, it is said that the body of St James is buried in the Cathedral de Santiago. Today, some people walk the Way of St James for their own religious reason but for others it is an adventure and an escape from busy everyday lives. So sit back and relax and, if you look out the window on our way, you will see some pilgrims along the road."

And with that he sat into the driving seat and they were on their way.

Some of the people on the bus were discussing their previous trips on the Camino and Paula was eager to chat to them and hear their advice.

"Am I naive in thinking I can just follow the yellow arrows and the people in front of me?" she asked one of the more experienced walkers.

"No, not at all – it is that straightforward. But don't try to keep up with anyone," he advised. "Walk at your own pace. If you try to keep up with people or race ahead, you could end up with nasty blisters or, even worse, an injury – it does happen. So go at your own pace and enjoy it.

The scenery is beautiful and there are loads of places to stop and have a coffee – so make use of them. That would be my advice."

Paula felt better after hearing that. She'd never walked more than ten kilometres in one go and she certainly didn't want any blisters, so she would gladly take his advice.

The bus passed through some small towns as it went further into the hills and the countryside. Open fields and forests stretched out for miles as they headed towards the mountains in the distance.

Cathy was sitting at the back, staring out the window, taking in the scenery. She could hardly believe that she was here in Spain and doing it by herself.

Rachel relaxed a little. She put her headphones on and closed her eyes. She wasn't listening to anything; she put them on to prevent people from talking to her. She wondered how many of the group were here for the same reason she was: to think, to walk and sort things out in their heads and maybe, like her, to find a new direction in their lives. A bit much to ask for in one week but, hey, *"The Camino provides"*. This was the phrase she had seen many times on the Camino Facebook pages she joined for information.

It was also the phrase used by the pension manager when they arrived in Sarria to find that there was a problem with the room allocations.

After the ninety-minute transfer Rachel, Paula and Cathy were the last people to be dropped off at their pension. The guesthouse at the end of town was made of local sand-coloured stone with blue wooden shutters on the windows and wisteria creeping up the outside walls. It was very pretty but there was a problem. Instead of three single rooms, the pension had booked one room with three single beds.

"Three beds!" Rachel sighed loudly, dropping her bag on the floor and leaning over the reception desk. "If I'd wanted to share with other people I would have booked an albergue for half the price and bunked in with forty sweaty hikers! No offence," she said, turning to Cathy and Paula, "but I'm sure these ladies feel the same. I booked a single room, I paid for a single room, and I *want* a single room."

As it was popular for hikers to stay in albergues – special hostels for pilgrims – the manager, when realising there was a room shortage, didn't see any problem in putting the three women in a room together.

Rachel, however, did not share his view. Her 5-foot-8 height had her towering over the manager who, in his late sixties, had seen many pilgrims arrive wound up on their first day and was not a bit fazed by Rachel's demands.

"As I said, this is a problem only for this one night, all other nights are okay, but a pilgrim was injured and could not leave his room today and there was confusion and cancellation and a late booking. These things happen," he shrugged, "but remember – '*The Camino provides*'."

"What does that even mean –" Rachel began.

"Excuse me."

Everyone turned to Cathy who spoke in a voice just a little louder than a whisper.

"I'm happy to sleep anywhere tonight. It's getting late and I just want to drop my bag and get something to eat."

"Me too," added Paula. She could tell from the look on the manager's face that the tall redhead who seemed used to getting her way wasn't going to get anywhere with this guy. "I'm happy to share for just tonight. As you say, these things happen." She lowered her voice and leaned in close to Rachel. "I don't think you're going to get anywhere here. It's a small town and there won't be many other options."

Rachel looked from Paula to Cathy and back to the manager who was yawning now. She wanted to tear a strip off him for yawning in front of her, but she conceded that it would get her nowhere.

Patience, Rachel, maybe this is your first lesson on this Camino.

"Fine, we'll take the room," she said.

As if there was ever any other option, thought Paula.

When they carried their bags upstairs to room Number 3, they were pleasantly surprised. The room was huge, and the beds were far apart from each other. The exposed brickwork was beautiful and each bed had a lace eiderdown which matched the lace curtains.

"Okay, this room is beautiful," Rachel had to admit. "Sorry if I was a bit cranky down there but it's been a long day in a horrible week."

"No need to apologise," Paula said as she started to unpack her bag. "I'm starving. Would you guys like to join me for dinner?"

"Absolutely. I definitely need a glass of wine," Rachel said, taking out her packing cubes. Everything she'd brought was in its own special pack, Paula noticed – she must be well used to travelling.

"I think I'll just grab a snack from the shop," Cathy said, sitting on her bed beside her unopened suitcase.

"Are you sure? It's going to be an early start tomorrow and we have a long day of walking ahead." Paula didn't want to force the issue, but this shy woman looked so thin and pale. A good feed might help.

"*Em*, well, maybe you're right, yes. I will come with you if that's alright. I'm very tired but I should eat something. Thank you."

"Great, let's go," said Paula. "I think most places close early in these mountain towns. The pension owner recommended a place called Roberto's."

It was still bright outside and the walk to the restaurant was by the town's river.

"I recognise that river from brochure pictures," Cathy said, smiling. She could hardly believe she was seeing it in real life.

The mountain air smelt so clean and fresh and, although the sun had gone down behind the mountains, it was still warm and many people were dining outside.

They passed their first Camino sign, a large stone bollard with the famous blue-and-yellow scallop-shell symbol on it, above a yellow arrow pointing the way and, underneath that, the distance to the Cathedral in Santiago, 114.539 km engraved in the stone.

"Almost one hundred and fifteen kilometres to Santiago," said Paula. "Do you mind if I take a photo of us at the sign?"

The others agreed and let Paula take a selfie which she then sent to her friend Jill and to her family WhatsApp group to let Kevin and the kids know she'd arrived.

"If you give me your numbers later I can send it to you," said Paula, putting her phone away.

"Oh, that would be lovely!" Cathy said. "I can send it to my daughter then."

Rachel agreed, to be polite.

When they arrived at Roberto's, they were lucky to get a table outside, overlooking the river.

"It's a busy town," Paula said, looking around. "And aren't the railings so pretty?"

The riverside railings had the famous Camino scallop-shell design in the ironwork.

"I believe that Sarria is one of more popular starting points for people," said Cathy, "because it's just over one hundred kilometres, which is the minimum requirement you need in order to receive the Compostela."

"What's the Compostela?" Rachel said, looking around for a waiter.

"It's the Camino Certificate of Completion," said Cathy, surprised that Rachel didn't know this. Cathy had dreamed of one day receiving hers and now it was going to happen.

"Well, I need a glass of wine," Rachel said, changing the subject as she raised her hand for the waiter. "Anyone else?"

"I'll join you," Paula said, sitting back and taking in her surroundings. She recognised some people from their flight sitting nearby with delicious platters of meats and cheeses in front of them. Other tables seemed to be occupied by Camino walkers too. Everyone looked so relaxed.

"Water for me, please," Cathy said, nervously running her Miraculous Medal back and forth on its chain.

"Is that a Miraculous Medal?" Rachel asked, noticing the image of Our Lady on it.

Cathy nodded.

Rachel leaned forward to look at it. "My mother used to slip one into my handbag when I went home for a visit. She said it would keep me safe in the big city of Dublin."

"It was a present from a friend," said Cathy.

The waiter returned with their drinks and the menus.

Paula held her glass up. "*To a great week!*"

"*A great week!*" the others responded, raising their glasses and then taking a sip.

"I can't believe it's almost one hundred and fifteen kilometres from here," said Paula. "I'm feeling a little nervous now."

"Me too," said Cathy.

"So how much training have you guys done?" Paula asked, taking a sip of her wine.

Cathy and Rachel looked at each other.

"None!" they said together, as they laughed and shook their heads.

"Well, I walk five kilometres every day to and from work," Cathy said.

"That's a lot, you'll be fine," Rachel answered. "I don't walk much but I work out three times a week in the gym early mornings so I'm hoping that will help."

"Okay, now I feel completely inadequate," Paula said. "I walk a little bit but I should have put more thought into this. My friend Jill organised everything. I was just planning on following her but she had to pull out to take care of her mother who fractured her hip so I'm completely underprepared. I know people book months, even years in advance to go on the Camino but I only booked this two weeks ago."

"So did I," Cathy answered.

"So did I," said Rachel.

The three women looked at each other.

"Oh God, what are we like!" said Paula.

And the three of them burst out laughing.

CHAPTER 3

Day 1 of Walking

SARRIA

It was five-thirty when Paula woke and decided to get up. She found it hard to sleep in a strange bed the first night and had got up three times in the middle of the night to use the bathroom.

How am I going to cope with having a new bed every night, she wondered. Hopefully I'll be too tired from walking to care. Twenty-two kilometres today! She sighed. I just hope I make it before nightfall.

Moving as quietly as possible, so as not to wake the other two women, she picked up her underwear and the walking clothes she had left out from the night before and tip-toed to the bathroom. A shower would be too noisy, so she ran a flannel under the cold water tap and wiped it over her face to wake herself up. Following this with her 50 SPF moisturiser and some roll-on deodorant, she pulled on her underwear, the black three-quarter-length walking trousers she had bought just the week before and a bright pink walking T-shirt. After rubbing Vaseline on her feet, a tip her husband Kevin had given her to avoid blisters, she put on her Merino-wool walking socks and her trainers. She had packed up her backpack the night before and left it close to the door so that now she just needed put her toiletries and pyjamas into the top of it, grab her fleece and her small backpack for the day ahead and she was ready.

Wide awake now, she planned on sitting outside in the charming garden seating area at the back of the pension, which she had noticed the previous night, and wait for dawn to break.

Using the light from her phone, she manoeuvred around Cathy's open suitcase on the floor and unlocked the bedroom door. She pulled her backpack up onto her shoulder and left the room quietly, closing the door behind her.

The pension was very quiet but as she reached reception she saw that an early walker had left a bag there and presumably had left already. She had heard that some pilgrims brought head-torches as they liked to leave in the dark before dawn, to walk alone.

Leaving her main backpack in the collection area, she pushed her small backpack up onto her shoulder, opened the front door as quietly as she could and walked around the side of the building that led to the garden. The sky was starting to brighten and a light from the kitchen helped her see where she was going.

Kitchen staff must be in early, she thought as she sat down on a garden chair and zipped up her fleece. The air was warm and in the distance she could see the early-morning fog hanging around to tops of the forest trees. Behind her, the warm morning air enhanced the scent of the nearby jasmine trailing up the old stone walls of the building.

She closed her eyes and inhaled the sweet smell.

"Ah, an early bird!"

Sitting up straight, she turned around to see Carlos the bus driver walk out from the kitchen. He was barefoot, wearing jeans and a hoody, looking more relaxed and casual than the day before. The smell of the coffee he was carrying made her stomach rumble.

"Oh, good morning," she whispered, not wanting to wake the other pilgrims. "I hope it's okay to sit here. I woke early and decided to get up and see the morning in."

"Of course, you are excited for your first day?" he said as he approached.

"Yes, possibly, or nervous more likely, I haven't a clue what I'm doing."

Carlos nodded. "Let me get you a coffee." He put his cup down and walked back towards the kitchen before she could reply.

"Milk?" he called from the kitchen door.

"Just a little, thank you."

"Sugar?"

"No, thank you."

Carlos returned and handed her a cup of coffee.

"*Gracias*," Paula said with a smile.

He sat down on the chair beside hers and ran his toes through the damp grass, not saying anything, just looking at the trees ahead.

"I didn't realise the kitchen opened this early," Paula said to break the silence.

"It's doesn't, I get special privileges," he said, smiling as he looked over at her.

"I see ... so what has you up this early?"

"I love this time of the day before the world awakes," he replied. "I feel this is when my brain calms the thoughts in my head."

Paula just nodded. How do you answer that, she wondered. She wasn't sure whether to stay or go but then the birds started singing and a gentle breeze rustled through the tall trees surrounding the property. She felt relaxed and Carlos didn't seem to mind her sitting there in silence.

Maybe this is my first lesson on the Camino, she thought. I don't have to fill the gaps in conversation all the time. Maybe I need to practise just sitting in the silence.

She sipped her coffee and listened to the birds.

Rachel had tossed and turned all night. She hadn't shared a room with other women since her college days. Lying on her back with her hands behind her head, she thought about her first day here. The two women seemed nice enough, and their dinner together was actually a nice distraction, but she wasn't here to make friends or take on anyone else's woes. Thankfully neither of them suggested that they walk together today.

The older one, Paula, seemed nice but a little too excited for Rachel's liking. She spent half the bus trip asking the driver about the area and the history of the different Camino routes. Rachel was sure he was bored with her questioning but too polite not to answer her. Paula did relax over dinner though and it was funny to find out that each of them had booked only two weeks ago.

The other one, Cathy, well, it was clear that she was a very nervous type. She seemed quite jumpy but maybe she had a lot going on in her life. And it took ages for her to decide what to eat in the restaurant and then she just ordered what Paula had ordered. What was that all about? I can't figure her out at all, thought Rachel.

On the bus drive, she noticed Cathy staring out the window with her shoulders curved as if trying to make herself as small as possible. Rachel had no intention of asking why either woman came on the trip. She had her own shit to sort out.

Getting out of bed, she used her phone torch to light the way to the bathroom. Passing Paula's bed she noticed that she wasn't there. She's eager to get going, she thought.

Breakfast here was from 6 to 7.30 but Rachel planned on starting her walk and getting breakfast on the way. She never ate breakfast at home and usually survived purely on coffee until lunchtime. Glancing over at the other bed, she could see that Cathy was still asleep. Strange way to sleep, she thought as she noticed Cathy was curled up in a ball right at the very edge of the bed even though there was plenty of space. She needs to unwind, literally, she said to herself as she shut the bathroom door.

After showering and dressing, she ran her fingers through her long red hair and twisted it in a long roll, pulling it through the hole in the back of her baseball cap and securing it with a scrunchie. She would normally blow-dry her hair straight, but for this trip, she was going to let it dry naturally and wavy.

Leaning into the mirror, she applied some sunblock. No make-up either for this trip. It will do my skin a world of good, she thought, fixing the peak on her cap. She sprayed sunblock on her arms and her ankles. She couldn't take any chances with her whiter-than-white skin. Even living through the long sunny summers in New York she never tanned – the most she got were extra freckles. A tan was never something she could pull off so, instead, she protected her skin by wearing the highest SPF every day summer or winter.

Placing the last of her toiletries in her main backpack, she packed up her small day pack and quietly left the room.

I presume Cathy set an alarm for herself, she thought just as she was leaving. Ah well, not my problem.

Dropping her bag at reception, she opened the front door. The mountain air was warm for this hour and the morning fog hung on the treetops. It was bright now although the sun hadn't come up yet. A group of about five people passed her, all heading in the one direction. Dressed in hiking gear just like she was, it was clear that everyone in Sarria was here to walk this part of the Camino.

"*Buen Camino!*" one said, nodding in her direction.

"*Buen Camino*," she replied.

They all seemed to be using walking poles. Although she had not trained for this trip, she scoffed at the idea of using poles. Three mornings a week in the gym had to account for something.

Today's walk was twenty-two kilometres. Piece of cake, she said to herself as she stepped out into the quiet street and followed the pilgrims up ahead and across the bridge to start her Camino.

CHAPTER 4

Cathy rolled over and rubbed her eyes. The sunlight was shining through a gap in the curtains. For a moment she wasn't sure where she was. Looking around the room, she saw that she was alone and that the other women's belongings were gone.

"Oh my god!" She sat up abruptly, grabbing her watch. It was 7.45. "Oh no!"

The backpacks and cases had to be down at reception before 8 am for Carlos to collect them and deliver them to their next destination. Today that would be Portomarin, twenty-two kilometres away.

Cathy swung her legs out of bed and rummaged through her suitcase which was open on the floor from last night.

"I brought way too much," she said aloud as she pulled out a pair of leggings and a top. She didn't bother changing her underwear, no time. Stuffing everything back into her suitcase, she hurried to the bathroom to wash her face and teeth and have a wee before racing back to put her toiletries in too. Luckily she had taken her small backpack out with her to dinner last night so that was ready. She took some arnica cream from her backpack and rubbed it gently on her right hip. She had heard it was good for bruising but hadn't noticed any difference yet.

Grabbing her hoodie, she took one last look around the room before heading down the stairs. Relieved to see other bags there, she left hers where Carlos had told them and headed out the door. She had missed breakfast so would just have to stop for something along the way.

Standing at the front of the pension, she looked around and took a deep breath. They were in the mountains and the air was clean and fresh. Luckily Paula had taken a picture last night beside the first marker leaving Sarria. It was just before the river so Cathy knew which direction to go and started walking.

It was so great to meet Paula and Rachel last night, she reflected. Not having to eat or sleep alone was an unexpected bonus. I probably wouldn't have slept a wink in a strange place by myself. They have no idea that the last time I went out to dinner with women, apart from family, was maybe thirty years ago. They have no idea what my life has been like and how much of a big deal it was for me to go out with strangers and order my own food. No idea at all.

"*Buen Camino!*" someone called out as they passed her.

"*Buen Camino!*" she replied with a smile.

I can do this, she said to herself.

She stopped when she got to the bridge. Reaching into her backpack, she took out the rosary beads that Father John had given her. Whenever she felt overwhelmed and her mind was racing, she said a decade of the rosary. It was her mantra and helped calm her mind. She knew she might feel lonely on this trip, so she wound it around her wrist and pulled the sleeve of her hoodie down over it to keep it in place. She felt reassured just having it there. In her pocket she carried a smooth round stone. She had taken it from her own garden at home. She had read that people sometimes carried stones to represent emotional baggage that they were carrying and when they forgave themselves or resolved an issue on the Camino, they left the stone behind them. Rubbing the stone in her pocket, she started walking.

It felt good to be out in the fresh morning air. She walked over the bridge, climbed up a very steep set of steps, and then up a narrow street where the smell of coffee from the cafés made her stomach rumble. She was hungry but didn't want to stop until she had walked for at least an hour. Google Maps had said it was a five-hour walk so stopping early would just drag that out.

When she reached the top of the road she heard singing. Looking around, she saw that it was coming from a small church up ahead. Ignoring the yellow arrow pointing to the Camino route, she walked towards the sound. The decorative wooden door was slightly ajar, so she pushed it open and walked through the arched doorway. The church was tiny with no windows so she squinted until her eyes adjusted to the darkness. An electric chandelier hung over a small altar at the top of the church. The only other light came from the open door and the lit candlesticks around the church.

As her eyes adjusted to the dim light, she saw a group of about twenty people facing the altar. One woman was singing so beautifully it brought tears to Cathy's eyes so she turned away to light some candles and get herself together. The group then prayed aloud in Spanish. Moving to the back of the church, she lit a candle and said a short prayer. The familiar smell of the candles and incense calmed her.

When she was about to leave, the group blessed themselves, picked up their walking poles, and turned to leave the church.

They smiled and some greeted her with a *'Buen Camino'* as they passed and she replied.

A young man of about thirty nodded for her to go ahead of him.

"Have a good Camino," he said in English with a smile, presumably noting her accent.

"Thank you – you too. I'd better get going," she said, checking to make sure she had everything with her.

"First time?" he said, holding the door open for her.

"Yes, I don't know what I'm doing really," she said, flustered.

"I lead a group every year – you can walk a bit with us if you like," he suggested.

"Could I?"

"Yes, of course," he said as they stepped out of the church.

They followed the small stream of pilgrims up the path back to the route.

"We start as a group but people find their own pace and eventually we all walk on our own, but we are not far from each other if someone wants to talk. We also try to visit a church and light a candle along the way."

"That sounds lovely. I'm Cathy, by the way."

"I'm Eduardo," he said and then pulled at the neck of his jacket to reveal a white collar, "Father Eduardo," he said with a grin.

"Oh, I would never have guessed," Cathy said, smiling. "You're very young. Where I come from most of the priests are elderly."

"You are from Ireland, yes?"

"Yes."

"We have many pilgrims and walkers on the Camino from Ireland. Some for the pilgrimage and some just for the walking."

Cathy smiled. She felt relaxed now. She was very comfortable in the company of priests. They were the only men Ted didn't feel threatened by. She had to be so careful at home not to be seen chatting to any man or Ted would go off on one. A memory came to mind of him not speaking to her for a whole weekend because he had seen her laugh at something Sophie's football coach had said. Other mums were laughing too at his joke, but Ted only saw her making a show of herself and of him, by laughing along. He banned her from taking Sophie to practice for the next two weeks which caused embarrassment for Cathy as she had to fake illness to ask other mums to give Sophie a lift.

That seemed like a lifetime ago now as she walked in comfortable silence with Father Eduardo through beautiful green fields with only the sound of cows in the fields and the footsteps of the pilgrims crunching on the path.

Although she was hungry and her body was tired, she waited until Father Eduardo and the others stopped so that she could eat with them. Her right hip was stiff and still bruised from the last incident with Ted, but she didn't want to stop and possibly have to speak to strangers.

It was the fridge door that time. He waited until she was walking past it and then flung it open, banging the door against her hip. "*You stupid woman!*" he shouted. "*Will you watch where you're going? This fridge cost money, you know!*"

For years he made her feel clumsy, coming up behind her and shouting when she was carrying glasses or dishes, making her almost drop them. She knew now that none of it was her fault but in the early days she believed what he told her because he was so concerned for her afterwards. He told her she had a problem with her nerves, convincing her to give up driving by telling her she was too nervous on the road and would cause an accident. So she ended up walking five kilometres each way to her job as a receptionist in a nursing home, every day. Sometimes in winter she took the bus but the fresh morning air on her walk cleared her head and it was the only exercise she got.

Father Eduardo introduced her to three other women in his group as they shared a table for lunch. Cathy didn't know what to order so she let them order first and then copied them. On the rare occasions that she and Ted had gone anywhere for food, he ordered for her. She used to order for herself but grew weary of him criticising whatever she chose. "Pasta again? Jesus, that's so boring. You could make that yourself at home for half the price." And if she ordered steak, he would have something to say about that too. "I hope you're going to chip in for that – do you think I'm made of money?" So to avoid a ruined evening it was easier for her to say, "Why don't you order for the both of us." It kept him happy to have control over the situation and so she got used to him ordering for her without asking her what she wanted.

As a result, she found it difficult, when looking at a menu, to decide for herself. It was an element of this trip that she never considered before coming out.

I need to remind myself that I can order what I like and it's nobody's business, she told herself as her food arrived.

"This is delicious," she said, tucking into a chorizo tortilla and fresh bread.

"We make this all the time at home," one of the women, Carlita, said, "but it is always nice when someone else is doing the cooking. And, in my house, it is my husband who is the cook!"

"Lucky woman!" said Marta, her friend, laughing.

Cathy smiled and nodded to join in. The only time Ted ever made anything was tea and toast when she was bedridden with the flu. She thought it was funny at first, that he had reached thirty years of age without ever cooking for himself and he had no intention of changing that. And yet he was obsessive about cleaning. As part of his need to control, he cleaned obsessively most days, getting up at 6 am to clean before going to work. He expected everything to remain spotless all day which was so unrealistic, especially when baby Sophie came along, and his cleaning obsession added greatly to Cathy's stress levels.

His strict religious views of not living together before marriage seemed respectful if not old-fashioned but Cathy realised a few months into her marriage what a mistake that had been. If she had lived with Ted Kinsella even for one month before their marriage, she would never have walked down that aisle.

"Café for everyone?" Marta asked, standing up.

"Oh, sorry, I was miles away. Yes, please."

Marta took the coffee order for their table and refused any payment for it. "It is my pleasure," she said with a smile.

Cathy liked this group. They spoke in English when talking to her, but she was also happy to hear them speak in Spanish to each other. She was enjoying being in their undemanding company and she felt Father Eduardo recognised that too.

"After lunch, we will walk to the next church on the route and say the Rosary," he said. "You are welcome to join us or go your own way – that is also okay."

"I don't want to intrude."

"We are all one family on the Camino, on the one road. You are welcome always."

Cathy's eyes filled up. Everyone she had met so far had been so nice to her. These strangers and their kindness to include her, moved her. If strangers can like me, maybe I'm not a bad person. I need to remember that, she thought, wiping a tear away.

CHAPTER 5

PORTOMARIN

Rachel stood with her hands on her hips, looking up at the steep old Roman steps that had to be climbed to enter the town of Portomarin.

"Are you kidding me?"

"Fifty-two," a man said, arriving over the bridge behind her.

"Excuse me?"

"Fifty-two steps, in case you were wondering," he said with a smile.

"Well, I wasn't but thanks anyway."

"There is another way if you follow the road around to the right. It's longer but not so steep."

"*Hmm* ..." She stood watching as other people took their time climbing the steps.

Her legs were already burning, having completed the twenty-two kilometres. The walk had been fine at the start, through an oak wood that smelled so good, and then through small hamlets with farmhouses in traditional yellow brick with red geraniums growing out of every window box.

But she had started too fast, walking at her usual Dublin pace for the first few hours. The competitive spirit in her made her march ahead. She decided not to look at her watch or her phone while she walked and just let hunger and tiredness guide her. This turned out to be a good idea because when she did stop for food, she realised that she had walked for three hours.

The mountaintop café where she stopped for breakfast had wonderful views of the golden valley below it. The fields, in an orderly patchwork, went from the top of the valley to the bottom and up the other side. Some fields had cattle but most seemed to have some type of crop growing in them, the pattern interrupted every now and then by forest trails.

When it arrived, the smell of the chorizo tortilla and a coffee she ordered made her stomach rumble. Resting her legs on a free chair opposite, she tucked in hungrily. All around her, people sat enjoying their well-earned breakfast while taking in the beauty of the golden fields around them.

When was the last time I stopped and enjoyed the quiet like this? she wondered. Most of the last two years were spent working late at the office and then working at home, making plans with Craig for the opening of their new business. They were so excited. Her dream of having her own legal agency was about to come true and in partnership with the man she loved. It seemed so perfect. They were such a power couple. They worked hard and they played hard. They ate out in Dublin's trendiest restaurants and jetting off to New York for the weekend or Paris for an overnight was not unusual.

Maybe if I had sat still for one moment and taken time to look at the bigger picture, I might have seen that Craig was not the man I thought he was, she thought as her mind wandered back to the day that changed everything, four weeks ago.

Rachel had been sitting in her sixth-floor office overlooking Dublin Port, ready to put into action her surprise for Craig. She had checked her watch, pushed back her chair and, kicking off her high heels, slipped her feet into the Sketchers she kept under her desk.

"Emily, I'll be back by two," she said to the company receptionist as she passed her on the way to the lift. "I don't think anyone will be looking for me."

Once inside the lift, she smiled to herself. On the ground floor of Troy & O'Doherty Associates was a small shopping centre with a supermarket, coffee shop, two restaurants and a florist's, which was where Rachel was headed today. She had rung ahead first thing this morning and ordered one dozen roses and extra rose petals. She nearly got dizzy at the cost, but it was something she wanted to do.

She knew it was silly, but she loved the movies where the main character, usually female, came home to find a trail of rose petals leading from the door to the bedroom and she wanted to recreate that scene in Craig's apartment.

After picking up the flowers, she popped into Dunnes Stores and bought two bottles of Moet champagne. They were celebrating tonight, and she knew Craig would never think of doing something like this. Anyway, he had back-to-back meetings in his office in Blackrock this morning, finalising accounts before their three o'clock appointment with the bank, to set up a business account for their new firm.

It was such an exciting time for them, starting a business together and moving in together. Was it a crazy idea or a brilliant idea? Only time would tell. But they were both excited about this new venture and spent many nights planning every aspect of the new business.

Walking quickly over the East Link Bridge that spanned Dublin's River Liffey, she glanced up at the huge modern apartment block overlooking the river where Craig's apartment was located. With ceiling-to-floor windows, you could see all the way to O'Connell Bridge in one direction and the whole dock area out to the Irish Sea in the other. She pulled the collar of her trench coat up to block out the breeze coming up off the water. Trucks and juggernauts rattled over the bridge as they headed for the port. Glad to get to the other side with the bouquet of roses intact, she let herself into the apartment block and took the lift to the sixth floor.

Reaching Craig's apartment, she was taken aback on hearing the sound of the hoover inside. He must have come home for lunch. Well, so much for her surprise!

She knocked before letting herself in.

"Craig?"

The hoover kept going and she followed the sound into the open-plan living room and kitchen.

"Oh, Miss Rachel!"

Marlena jumped in surprise when she turned around and saw Rachel standing there. She put her hand to her chest, shaking her head and smiling as she turned off the machine with her foot.

"I didn't mean to startle you, Marlena, sorry," Rachel said, smiling at Craig's cleaner. Marlena was well into her seventies and Rachel didn't want to give her a heart attack. "I didn't know you came on Thursdays?"

"No, I don't. Mister Craig messaged me last night to ask if I can come today for an extra clean."

"Oh, I see," Rachel said, looking around at the empty pizza box on the counter and some dirty dishes and glasses in the sink.

I hope he doesn't expect me to clean up after him when he moves in with me, she thought briefly as she looked around. She hadn't been to his apartment in weeks as it was more convenient for Craig to stay at hers. They planned to start their business together from her house. Already her spare bedroom had been turned into a home office with two desks and some filing cabinets installed. Boxes of their new stationary had just arrived this week. It was a temporary arrangement while they looked for a suitable office to entertain clients in.

"I won't disturb you, Marlena – I just want to put these in the bedroom," she said, checking her watch. She needed to get back to the office and double-check that she had all her documents in order before meeting Craig at the bank.

Stepping into the bedroom, she paused. Her eyes scanned the room.

Something was off. The duvet was scrunched up. Pillows and cushions were thrown around the room.

"Sorry, Miss Rachel, I have not cleaned in here yet," said Marlena, appearing behind her.

"*Eh*, that's okay," Rachel replied, walking slowly towards the top of the bed. Her heart pounded in her chest. Something was not right here.

She stood at the bedside table and placed the shopping bag on the floor. A glass of water ... on my side of the bed? Leaning forward, with her free right hand she pulled back the crumpled duvet just as she heard a key turn in the apartment door.

"Just me, Marlena!"

Rachel heard his footsteps on the wooden parquet floor as he entered the hall.

"We're in here, Mister Craig!" Marlena answered him, walking out to the hall.

His footsteps stopped.

"We?"

"Yes. Miss Rachel is here."

Rachel heard him let out a deep breath before he started to walk again and she knew, right there in that hesitation, that he was guilty.

"Hey, babe!" He smiled as he entered the bedroom, and then stopped.

"*Who the FUCK owns this!*" shouted Rachel as she stood back to reveal a red thong under the duvet, in its perfect triangle shape.

"I ... I don't know ... I ..."

She felt the blood rush to her head. She felt repulsed as she looked at Craig standing there pathetically searching around for an excuse.

"*YOU BASTARD!*" she roared as she ran at him, bashing the bouquet of roses into his face.

"*Ahhh!*" screamed Marlena as she looked on from the hall.

Craig covered his face with his arms as she continued to beat him with the roses.

"Jesus Christ, Rachel! Will you .... just ... listen ..."

When Rachel was finished she threw the roses on the floor, walked passed him, out the door, and into the lift. It wasn't until the doors shut and the lift moved that she noticed she was shaking and she could not control the tears that came.

Running out of the apartment building, she turned right, and very soon she was in Thorncastle Street in Ringsend. She knew if she just kept walking past the bridge and along the river, she would be home in ten minutes.

And then what, she asked herself. But she didn't know. She was due back in the office at two and the big meeting with the bank was at three. She quickened her pace. Her breathing was quick and shallow.

I just need to get home.

She could see Marian College.

Almost there.

Turning left she ran across the street of her small estate and let herself into her house. Shutting the hall door with her back, she stayed there leaning against it. Relief flooded over her.

Thank god. I'm home.

She stayed leaning against the door until her breathing calmed down.

What the fuck do I do now?

Her phone rang in her handbag. She let it ring out. Easing her feet out of her trainers, she hung her coat over the bottom banister and dragged her bag behind her as she walked to the kitchen. Plonking her bag on the table, she opened a cabinet, took down a large glass, and filled it with cold tap water. Her hands were shaking. Her phone rang again, vibrating in her bag on the kitchen table. She glanced over at it.

What am I going to do?

Sitting down at the kitchen table, she tried to remember Craig's face. Did he deny it? She remembered how he paused when he heard she was there and by the look on his face it was clear he was guilty. But did he deny it? No, he didn't – he'd mumbled, 'I don't know'.

She was stunned. How could this happen, today of all days? They had both handed in their notice at work, they had a meeting in – she checked her watch – in less than an hour that would lock them in legally to opening a business together. A legal practice, her own legal company, everything she dreamed of.

And Craig, she had believed that he was everything she wanted. She thought this was her happy ever after. But now?

"How could this happen?" she whispered to herself, shaking her head. "How could this happen *again*?"

A sharp knock on the door made her jump. *Craig.* It had to be him. She sat still. She did not want to talk to him right now.

Oh no, her heart dropped and she placed her head in her hands when she heard a key in the door. Of course, he had his own key – she gave it to him on its own keyring with a capital C for Craig. He was supposed to be moving into her house tomorrow.

"*Rachel?*" he called out as he came down the hallway.

She straightened herself up and took a deep breath.

"What do you want?" she said calmly, not turning around.

She could feel him moving nearer and could smell the expensive Tom Ford cologne he always wore. He stopped for a second behind her and then moved to the other side of the table. Pulling out a chair, he sat down opposite her, putting his car keys and the house key on the table.

Rachel raised her head and looked him straight in the eye.

"Look, I know you're angry with me right now," he said, leaning forward, putting his forearms on the table, "and you have every right to be. I can explain everything later, but we need to put our personal issues aside and get to this meeting." His hands opened and closed as he spoke, as if he was negotiating a deal. "Can we do this? Can we put things aside for the sake of the business?"

Is he for real? He's not denying it. He's not apologising. What is this?

"What's going on here, Craig?"

He shifted uncomfortably and she could see a bead of sweat forming on his forehead like a boil.

"Rachel, don't overreact is what I'm saying. Whatever you saw or thought you saw, can be sorted out later ... this meeting is too important."

"Whatever I *thought* I saw?"

Craig dipped his head to the side, looked up, and held her stare with the same piercing blue eyes she fell for over two years ago.

"Rachel, I am so, so sorry. I messed up and I'll do anything to fix this but can we talk about this later? What we have is so great. We are about to open a business that will be the best in Dublin. Don't ... don't ruin everything now."

"Me? Ruin everything? *Are you for fucking real?*"

"I'm sorry," Craig said, putting both hands up in defence, "wrong choice of words, I didn't mean that ... I admit it. It is all my fault but I love you so much and I will make it up to you ... just don't ... don't throw it all away. I love you. And yes, I made this awful mistake but we have such a great future together."

"How did this happen?"

"Look, I slipped up, plain and simple. There were some impromptu leaving drinks after work and someone came on to me and I don't know ... it's been such a stressful week, and I drank too much, and it went to my head. I'm a dickhead. I'm sorry ... it was just a stupid mistake that I barely remember. I take full responsibility, and I'll do anything to fix this."

"Oh god!" Rachel turned away. She couldn't look at him, she felt sick.

"Look, we're both adults here," Craig said, reaching across the table. "I want to be with you. I want to run a business with you. We are amazing together! Yes, I strayed last night, but it meant nothing, *absolutely nothing*."

"I can't just forget this and move on, Craig. I feel so hurt and betrayed and I am so angry. Because, yes, I thought we were amazing together and, yes, I believed we had a great future together – but how can I trust you now?"

She couldn't believe this was happening. She felt so angry she wanted to reach over and slap his face hard. She dug her nails into her seat to help control her temper.

"I love you, Rachel, and I love our life. I will do whatever it takes to make you trust me again."

"People warned me about you. He's a womaniser, they said, watch yourself there, they said."

"You changed all that, Rachel. Last night meant nothing to me." He leant forward across the table. "You and me – that's what's important here. We work well together, Rachel, we make a great team, you know that."

Rachel swallowed hard. Yes, he admitted it, but was he genuinely sorry he did it or more upset about missing the meeting? She had thought his coolness was attractive, she had thought it gave him a cutting edge around the negotiation table, but now that skill meant that she couldn't read him.

I let him in, I took down the walls I had built up over the years to protect me from being hurt like this again. How could this have happened?

Craig looked at his watch.

"Am I keeping you?" she said.

"Rachel, we have to go. We need to get the documents before the meeting." He was sweating more now and loosening his tie.

"Do you need a glass of water?" she asked, raising an eyebrow.

"I can't read you, Rachel. I am so, so sorry. I was an idiot and I don't expect you to forgive me straight away but we have too much together to throw away. I promise you nothing like that will ever happen again. But ..."

"*But what?*"

"We really have to go – honestly, darling, we can't miss this meeting." He stood up, picking up his keys. "Can we put everything aside until after the meeting?"

"I'll follow you out," Rachel said, standing up.

A look of relief flooded over him.

"Oh, thank god! You had me worried there," he said, grinning nervously as he approached her for an embrace.

"*Don't touch me!*" Rachel said, walking down the hall ahead of him.

"Okay, okay, we'll sort this out later," he said.

She opened the door.

"We'll take my car," he said as he stepped outside.

Rachel reached out, took his hand and smiled.

Craig smiled back and moved closer.

"I'll take this!" she said, grabbing the front door key from his hand. "You won't be needing it. You have fucked everything up, you have ruined everything!"

"What? What the ...?"

"How can I ever trust you again?"

"Rachel, please, calm down and we will deal with this after the meeting? I will make it up to you, I promise you that," he pleaded.

"You don't get it, do you? It's over. *The dream, my dream, your dream, you just ruined everything!*"

"Are you serious?" he said, raising his eyebrows in disbelief. "Oh, come on! It was a mistake. Have you never regretted anything in your life? You call me a womaniser? I seem to remember the night we met it was you who came after me. We're the same, Rachel, that's why it works."

Rachel felt like she'd been slapped in the face.

"How dare you! We were two years together!"

"You can't do this over ..." Craig stopped as neighbours were walking by, having collected their kids from school. "Rachel, think about this!"

"Don't you get it, Craig? I can't trust you. You've blown it. If I can't trust you I can't go into business with you and I certainly can't be with you. It's over, everything is over. You did this. All by yourself, you fucked everything up!"

Rachel went to shut the door, but he blocked it with his foot.

"If I didn't love you, would I have given up my job? My flat? I have to move out tomorrow," he said. "I've said I was in the wrong, I've apologised, and I know we can sort this out, just not now."

Rachel leaned in close to his face. "If you don't leave now I will scream and every yummy mummy on this street will come running. If you come here again I'll call the Guards."

Craig stepped back as if he'd been punched and Rachel slammed the door. She could see through the stained glass that he was still standing there so she bolted the door.

"Rachel? Rachel? It's okay, I know you've had a shock. I'll ring the bank and change the appointment, okay?" He was pacing up and down now. "Let's take a few days and sort this out. I'll stay in Roger's and we'll talk tomorrow, yeah? Rachel? I'll text you the rearranged meeting details. Everything will be fine."

And with that, he got into his car and drove away.

Rachel walked back into the kitchen and collapsed into a chair.

It's so quiet, she thought, looking around. Everything feels so still, as if time has stopped. How could my life change in such a short space of time? One minute going one way and the next a complete detour. What if I hadn't called over to his flat? I would be none the wiser. The thought shocked her. She looked at the clock. Three o'clock. If she hadn't gone to his apartment, she would be at the bank now signing her life away and then going back to his to have celebration sex on the clean sheets that Marlena was employed to put on and drinking champagne to celebrate their amazing future together.

And now? Sitting in her dark kitchen Rachel was horrified at the situation she was in.

Oh my god, I would never have known!

She felt lightheaded. Was this a once off or had he done it before? What if he had cheated in a month or two from now? By then they would be locked together legally as business partners and partners in life with him living here with her. She felt nauseous now, the shock of the whole situation hitting her.

She'd known he had a reputation when she met him but they were seeing so much of each other she never doubted that he was only with her. In fact, six months after they started dating he introduced her to his boss who shook her hand and said, "I am delighted to meet the woman who has tamed Craig Callaghan. He's a different man now."

She had felt ridiculously proud that it was clear he was with her and nobody else. When he worked away he phoned every night and always got a taxi straight from the airport to her house on his return. They made love so many times in the hall or on the stairs as they couldn't wait to get to the bedroom before ripping each other's clothes off.

Craig had a strong sex drive and his lust for her turned her on and made her feel like she was the sexiest woman in the world. There was only one time four months ago that he rang from the airport saying he was going straight home and not to hers as he was exhausted. She was so secure in their relationship that she didn't think for a second that he might have strayed while away. But now she wasn't sure. She hated this. She loved him and he had said he loved her but now everything was ruined. Even if she wanted to forgive him, she did not want to live her life feeling insecure and suspicious. No, she couldn't do that.

Sitting at her kitchen table, she rested her forehead against the palms of her hands as the tears came. "What the fuck do I do now?"

Taking her phone from her bag on the table, she saw that she had three text messages. One from Craig: **Meeting postponed until Monday at two. We'll sort this out x**

Another from her secretary: **Sorry, Rachel, Helen was asking if you were coming back to sign some exit forms.**

And one from her boss Helen Troy: **Are we still on for 5.30? Your secretary hasn't a clue where you are.**

Helen had a way of letting you know she was pissed off with you, even by text.

Shit! Rachel had forgotten that she had told Helen she'd pop by her office and sign the exit forms today. *Exit forms.* She was supposed to be leaving on Friday. A leaving dinner had been organised in the nearby Gibson Hotel. There's no way she could go to that now. She and Craig were supposed to go together.

She had imagined them there, all dressed up and smiling, as they talked about their new business, and how everyone would be jealous that she had broken away and become her own boss. But now she had to put a halt to the dinner and the leaving party. She could fake illness and just disappear, but it wouldn't be fair to leave the company with a going-away bill.

She sat up straight in her chair.

No, I need to get my job back or extend my leaving date, or something. I have a mortgage to pay. I need to buy myself some more time.

Feeling calmer, she reached for her phone and dialled Helen's number. Her boss was not a warm woman. She was ambitious and outspoken. She didn't break through the glass ceiling, she smashed through it, scattering anyone in her way. She pushed people and most people hated her for it. But her high standards made Rachel work harder to impress her and working under Helen enabled her to handle any case that came her way.

I'll tell her the loan fell through and ask for more time, Rachel thought as she nervously bit her bottom lip, waiting for Helen to answer.

"Rachel, why are you ringing me? Are you coming or not?" Never a polite hello from Helen.

"No, I got delayed and I need to ask a favour." Taking a deep breath, she continued. "There is a problem with the business loan. It hasn't been approved. It's going to take more time and ... I was wondering if I could delay my departure from the company. Would it be possible to stay on a bit longer until this is sorted?"

Silence.

Rachel could hear Helen thinking on the other end of the phone.

"You handed in your notice."

"I know."

"Your leaving dinner is this Friday."

Rachel took a deep breath. She didn't have the energy to lie or play games.

"Okay," she sighed. "I'm sorry, it's not that. Everything is ruined. The deal is off. Craig and I are no longer partners in any sense."

"Oh, I see. Since when?"

"Since ... today when I found out ... he was cheating."

"I see."

Silence again.

Rachel sighed. "I need a job and I'd really like to keep the one I have."

"We have already interviewed for your job, Rachel. Three rounds of interviews."

"I know and I'm sorry. Believe me, this is not a phone call I ever thought I'd have to make."

Silence again. Then a deep sigh.

"Who knows about this?"

"Nobody. Even Craig thinks it's still going ahead and that I'll come to my senses."

"And will you?"

"*No!*" she shouted. "Sorry, no. Even if I wanted to I can never trust him again."

"This could get messy for you."

"Like I said, I wish I wasn't making this call ..."

"No, I mean he could make things difficult for you. A man like Craig doesn't give up easily. I think you need to take some time off, some time away where that player can't come crawling back."

Player? Did everyone see Craig as a player, even Helen?

"You mean you're advising me to leave immediately, go quietly."

"No. I think you should take annual leave. Get away for a few weeks. I will tell everyone your original story – that the loan was delayed so you are not leaving us yet – and you go away, somewhere where he won't be able to contact you."

"But ... you'd do that?"

"Men like Craig ... well, I know his type. They hate to lose. Getting some distance from him will help you see things for what they are. You are way more talented than he is, everyone knows that. So do you want to take the leave or what?"

"Yes, oh God, thank you, Helen."

"I'll put you in for four weeks of paid leave. Come in early tomorrow and sort out any files outstanding and leave them on my desk. He will try to change your mind so if you want my advice, I would go away soon. And no five-star resorts. Do something he'd never expect."

"Like what?"

"I don't know. Maybe a walking holiday?"

"A walking holiday ... I don't think so."

"Don't knock it until you try it. It's the best way to clear your head and get perspective on the world."

"You're not a ..."

"Walker? Yes, I am. But don't tell anyone. I don't want the staff to think I'm human."

Rachel laughed at this. She never knew Helen had a sense of humour, despite working with her all this time.

"He'll never think to look for me on a walking trip, that's for sure."

"And if you want to make sure he won't find you, then walk the Camino. He'd never follow you there and you'd be moving to a new place every day so you'd be harder to keep track of."

"The Camino? What's the Camino?"

"Look it up." Helen was back to her gruff self. "Do we have a deal? I can't stay talking here all day."

"Yes, yes, thank you so much."

"Okay. It's just a one-month extension. Sort out your files and get back to me in a month."

"I'll keep in touch."

"No need. Ring me in three weeks with an update. Good luck."

And then she hung up.

Rachel sat, looking at the phone in her hand.

Did that actually happen? Helen Troy, the coldest woman in business, just threw me a lifeline? Well, miracles really do happen. What crazy day!

Getting up from the table, she walked across the kitchen to the fridge. Taking out a half bottle of Mateus Rosé, she took the bottle and a wine glass upstairs to the box room that she and Craig had converted into a small office. Ignoring the boxes of newly ordered stationary around the place, she sat down at one of the new built-in desks and opened her laptop. She poured herself a glass of wine and sipped while she waited for the screen to open up, the ice-cold wine giving her some comfort.

"*Now – google*," she said as she typed in her password and waited for the search box to come up. "What on earth is the Camino?"

A shiver ran through Rachel now as she recalled that day. *I was so close to the life I thought was perfect for me.* Her heart still hurt when she thought of him. A single tear rolled down her cheek. She couldn't just switch off her feelings for him. She missed him but he had turned her life upside down.

And what was worse, she sighed, *was I never saw it coming.*

Sitting at the top of a mountain now looking out on the wide open Spanish countryside with only the sound of a few cows in the distance, she took a deep breath. *This is what I need*, she thought, *peace and quiet and no drama.*

After she finished her food, she decided to slow down a little to take in her surroundings and appreciate them. She spoke to nobody while walking, except for a polite *"Buen Camino"* as she passed fellow walkers. The only sound when walking through the fields and forests were other walkers' footsteps and walking poles. The rhythm, almost like a mantra, was very soothing. She could see the attraction: all you had to do was walk. Everyone was going in the same direction and the way was marked clearly by yellow arrows spray-painted on the sides of farmhouses or village walls. Also, it was reassuring to see the kilometre numbers going down every time you passed the '*mojones*', the metre-high stone markers like the one they took a photo of last night going out to dinner. She also enjoyed walking with no music or podcasts. She needed to give her busy brain a break.

When she left the café, she reckoned she had an hour and a half of walking left and, although she passed a few break stops and small cafés along the way, she decided just to plod on till the end. But now, looking at these ancient steps of Portomarin before her, she was beginning to regret that decision.

"Ah, well, it has to be done," she said as she started to climb them.

Keeping her head down, she concentrated on one step at a time. No peloton can compete with this, she thought as her thighs burned. Once she reached the top, she turned around and was rewarded with a beautiful view over the river. The river was so still that it reflected the forest she had just walked from, which stretched down to its shore.

I did it. Day One done, she said to herself as she took out her phone to take a photo and then look up the directions to tonight's pension.

Cathy and Paula were staying in the same accommodation. They realised this last night as they had all booked through the same company, *Follow the Camino*. They had no plans to meet up tonight and Rachel was happy about that. She planned to get an early bite to eat and then go to her room. She had brought a new journal with her and wanted to use this time to get her thoughts down on paper and hopefully make sense of them.

Casa do Maestro was located right beside a huge church on the main street of this very pretty town. It was half past one and other walkers who had already arrived were having an afternoon beer in the sun, but Rachel was eager to have a shower and a siesta.

Pushing the door open, she was delighted to see that her bag had already arrived. The receptionist checked her in and then began to show her around.

"Here we have a small kitchen for guests and a room to relax," she said, directing Rachel to a beautiful colourful room with glass doors leading out to a garden.

"*Rachel?* Rachel O'Brien, I don't believe it!"

Rachel turned around to see someone she hadn't seen in years.

"Mrs Molloy?"

Although she looked very thin and frail and her curly red hair, which Rachel remembered so well, was now replaced by a colourful turban, she recognised her ex-boyfriend's mother and went over to hug her. She had spent her teenage and college years in and out of Mrs Molloy's house and always enjoyed a chat and a cuppa with her, but she hadn't seen her in years as some memories were just too painful.

"I don't believe it!" Bernie Molloy held Rachel at arm's length to have a good look at her. "You haven't changed a bit – you look fabulous."

"I don't think so after that walk!" laughed Rachel. "But what are you doing here? Are you walking the Camino?"

"Yes. I walked this route before, years ago, and I wanted to do it one last time. But I'm taking my time, taking rest days in between walk days."

"I see. Are you with a group?"

"No, dear, I'm with Simon."

Rachel stepped back in shock as if she'd been slapped in the face.

"Simon is here?"

"Yes, love, he moved home to look after me, and now ..."

"*Rachel?*"

Rachel froze. That voice. The way he said her name ... she didn't want to turn around. Her heart was pounding.

Swallowing hard, she turned around. And there he was, just a few feet away from her. Simon Molloy, the love of her life who broke her heart in a million pieces fifteen years ago.

"Simon ... I ..."

Before she could say anything else Paula arrived in the door, panting, and held on to the reception desk to catch her breath.

"Oh my goodness, I thought I'd never get here," she gasped. "God, those steps were torture!"

"Paula, this is Bernie Molloy and her son Simon from Cork," Rachel said, relieved that Paula provided a distraction. "They are ... old friends of mine."

"Oh hello! Excuse the state of me but those steps nearly killed me." Paula smiled, wiping her brow with the back of her hand. "Have you checked in yet, Rachel?"

"Yes, and I'm going straight to the shower and then to bed. We'll catch up later, yeah?" she said, looking at Paula pleadingly.

"Yes ... yes, of course."

Turning to Mrs Molloy but avoiding looking at Simon, Rachel said, "Okay, lovely to see you both again. I'm sure I'll see you along the way."

"I'm sure you will, love," said Bernie.

Walking back to reception, Rachel picked up her backpack and calmly walked up the stairs to her room. Once inside, she dropped her bag on the floor and fell backward onto her bed. Grabbing a pillow, she screamed into it until she had no breath left.

CHAPTER 6

Paula checked in, dragged her bag up the stairs and let herself into her room which was at the corner of the building. This meant that she had two windows, one overlooking the back garden and the other facing the side of the church and main street below which was lined with cafés and outdoor seating areas.

The whitewashed buildings with their colourful geranium-filled window baskets and the paved paths of Portomarin made for a very pretty picture with the town's church and main square at the centre of it. The church bell rang, announcing it was two o'clock.

Exhausted and sore, she was looking forward to climbing into the double bed but needed to shower first. The dust from the forest paths had kicked up onto the back of her legs and her feet were hot and swollen.

Just then her phone buzzed. It was a WhatsApp message from Jessica.

Hi Mum, how was your first day? J

Paula was too tired to type so she called her instead.

"Hello, love."

"Hi, Mum! I was just wondering how you got on."

"Not too bad, I think. I'm sore and tired and dusty but I did it. Day One done."

"Was it hard?"

"There were more hills than I thought so my knees are screaming at me right now. And, at the start you have to climb steep steps before leaving the town of Sarria and at the end you have to climb steep steps to enter Portomarin. They do like their steps!"

"But you did it, Mum. Take lots of painkillers and try to put your feet up, if you can."

"Oh, I have loads of painkillers with me, don't you worry about that. I'm going to take some anti-inflammatory tablets now and then have a hot shower. I tell you what, though, those cheap walking poles I bought last week are lifesavers! I would have been lost without them."

"It wasn't all hills, was it?"

"No, thank God. Lots of open fields and it's lovely walking through tiny hamlets and farmlands."

"So you're enjoying it?"

"Yes! Don't worry about me, love. And I've met lovely people already." Jessica was such a worrier and, as this was Paula's first time to travel anywhere abroad on her own, she was conscious of the need to keep everything light-hearted.

"Okay, I'd better go, Mum. I just wanted to check in on you."

"Thank you, pet. I'll send more photos tomorrow."

"Bye, Mum."

"Bye, love."

That was a hard morning but so rewarding, Paula thought as she ran the water in the shower, letting it heat up while she undressed. I am so proud of myself and I'm so glad I took Jill's advice to start early. Poor Jill, she would have loved the walk today and this had been her idea after all.

As she stepped into the shower, Paula recalled how she had scoffed at the idea of walking the Camino when Jill suggested it.

Jill and Paula had been friends for years. They met in teacher-training college and, after going their separate ways, met again when Paula applied for a job as a resource teacher in a local school where Jill was the principal. After years of working as a primary school teacher, she had fancied a change and retrained as a resource teacher. She loved her new role and, having worked in many schools around the city, was delighted when this vacancy came up in her local school.

That was ten years ago. They had picked up their friendship where they'd left off but didn't want to be too pally in front of the other teachers. So every Monday morning before school, they met in Howth for a walk. Then they caught up with each other's news and gossiped about school issues and some of the staff members.

So it was on a Monday four weeks ago that Paula arrived in the car park to meet Jill. She turned off her engine and sat looking out over Dublin Bay. This lookout point at the Summit car park in Howth was stunning. Pulling down the car visor, she slid across the mirror cover to check that she didn't have sleep in her eyes. These early Monday morning walks were sometimes hard to get out of bed for, but always worth it.

Ten years, she thought, as she ran her finger over the laughter lines around her eyes. Did I have these lines ten years ago? A knock on the window jolted her out of her thoughts.

"You wagon, you frightened the life out of me!" Paula said, opening the door and shaking her head as Jill stood there laughing.

"You were miles away!"

"Just counting my wrinkles. They're gathering around my eyes now like spider's legs. Why do we never appreciate how we look when we're younger?" she said, locking the car and zipping up her hoody.

"Come on, stop moaning, you look great ... for an aul' wan!" said Jill as she linked her friend.

Turning left, they walked towards the sunrise that had come up over Ireland's Eye, an island very close to Howth Harbour. There was a light breeze and the early morning sea air was invigorating.

"So, how are your party plans going?"

"Oh god, I am getting more and more stressed about it," Paula said. "You know I never wanted a 60th party. My idea of hell. But, oh no, Kevin went ahead and bloody well booked it in the same place as he had his, of course, because he had a wonderful night there. I told him I didn't want a party at all but he said if he didn't organise it then it would look bad or, worse, one of the gang would organise something. So what choice did I have? God forbid people would just leave me alone!"

"Okay, tell me how you really feel," said Jill, smiling.

"Oh, I'm sorry – and I'm ruining your walk, but it infuriates me. I just want to tell them all to feck off!"

"It must be awful to have so many friends who want to celebrate you."

"Yes, I know, I'm an ungrateful cow. But now it's taken legs, foreign legs!"

"What do you mean?"

"Well, we went out to dinner on Saturday night – just a quick bite in Casa Clontarf – and, of course, there was talk about the party and then Fiona asked me about retirement again. I've told them before that I have no intention of retiring and they all think I'm mad. They love retirement and I'm happy for them, honestly I am. They're busy with their golf and their Pilates, but it's just not for me. Emily even asked me when I was taking up bridge! Bridge, Jill!"

"Well, it is supposed to be very good for your cognitive brain."

"So is working."

"I'm not sure about that. These sixth years are eroding the last of my brain cells at the moment."

"Oh, sorry to whine on but – and I know this is going to sound terrible – when I looked around that table I just felt sad. These are my friends and I feel like I have very little in common with them anymore. They want to sit back and move slower through life. I want to jump up and plan adventures before my body won't let me do those things anymore."

"Well, Kevin's a hiker, he hasn't thrown in the towel yet. He's very adventurous, isn't he?"

"Yes, thank god, and I love that he is always planning and looking for another mountain to climb."

"Would you take up hiking and go with him on his adventures?"

"But that's just it, they're his adventures, not mine. And, anyway, walking up the side of a mountain in our Irish weather getting soaked to the skin is my idea of torture, not adventure."

"What about Aileen and Danny – are they still moving to Spain?"

"Yes, they bought a place and plan on spending half the year there and good luck to them. I'm genuinely happy for them. But that's the other problem. They want to throw another party for me in their new place in Spain."

"How horrible of them!" mocked Jill.

"Stop," said Paula, laughing. "It's not funny. They waited until I went to the bathroom on Saturday night and told the rest of them about it. When I got back to the table, everyone was looking at me and they announced it like it was a done deal! They got all excited about it and I just froze. Then they started checking dates on their phones and I know it's a lovely idea but it just made me feel claustrophobic, being put on the spot like that."

"What did you say?"

"I mumbled something about having to check the dates for the Leaving Cert and school holidays and then ... well, I threw you under the bus ..." Paula winced and looked at Jill as they both stopped walking.

"*Me?*"

"Yes. I had to. I was feeling so anxious that everyone was planning my life for me. So, I pretended that you had asked me to go on one of your walking trips and that I had agreed but I wasn't sure of the dates." She grimaced. "Sorry."

"That's okay."

"But, then that sparked a whole conversation about walking trips and Kevin asked if the trip with you was a couples thing and I may have answered no a little too loudly!"

Jill laughed.

"Anyway, sorry for dragging you into it but I just felt trapped."

"That's okay."

"And, what's worse is that I had to carry on the story at home, with Kevin asking all kinds of questions."

"Well, he *is* a hiker."

"Exactly. He just kept going on about hiking poles and correct footwear and he was excited that this might be my new hobby because I told him I wanted something new in my life. Anyway, after a lifetime of me not going on even one of his hiking trips and enjoying having the house to myself when he's gone, he's now delighted thinking I've turned."

Jill just laughed and shook her head. "It must be awful to be you, being invited to a party in your honour in a villa in Spain and having a husband supportive of your new hobby!"

"*Feck off!* Anyway, it's my pretend hobby. And I would love to go to Aileen's villa but only if I could be there by myself."

The women walked to their usual spot and, turning around, stopped to take in the view along the coast. The sun was now high in the sky, glistening over the Irish sea.

"I don't want to sound like your husband, but walking can give you all the headspace you need, even in a group. I met a group of strangers last weekend through an Instagram post. We met in a carpark in Wicklow. It was an all-female hike and after a little talk at the start, the leader led the way. I chatted with a few women at the start and then just walked by myself in the group until we got back two hours later. You could go for coffee with the group after or just head home. It might be worth thinking about."

"Yeah, maybe. I just feel so restless. And this bloody party is not helping."

"Is it too late to back out of it?"

"Yes. Everyone in our group has had a sixtieth party and if I pull out now someone could arrange a surprise and that would be my worst nightmare. Remember Alison Moran's?"

"Oh my god, that poor woman. I will never forget her big red face walking in from her spin class and the sweat marks under her armpits. She was horrified!"

"What a dickhead Des was! Surely he knew she was coming from a class?"

"She had to hop in the shower while everyone stood around feeling embarrassed for her."

"And then she had to clean up after the party the next day because her idiot husband had arranged a golf day!"

"Poor cow."

They walked on, saying hello to other early risers on the route.

"So what *did* you want to do for your birthday?" Jill said, walking ahead as the path narrowed.

"I wanted to wake up in a different country in peace and quiet and wander about with no specific plan. But my birthday falls during term time so I couldn't really take time off then Kevin said the kids would want to be there so that takes organising and ... oh ... ignore me. I will grin and bear it and count down the minutes until I can go home."

"Think about the presents you'll get."

"Exactly, that is a positive," said Paula with a smile, "but if anyone gifts me a candle I will hit them with it. I have enough candle presents from the school kids to open my own church."

"The Church of Cranky Old Women! I'd go to that," said Jill. "Look, hopefully you will enjoy it on the night. And if you want to come on one of my weekend walks in the Dublin Mountains just give me a call – I promise to not speak to you. In fact, I'd be very happy to completely ignore you."

"I don't know about that, but I need something. I feel so uptight all the time. Honestly, I'm annoying myself! Some days I want to run away and open a café in Santorini and on other days I want to sell up and move to the Aran Islands."

Paula stopped and put her hands on her hips.

"I'm not ready for retirement. I want new experiences, in new places. There are so many places to see, and we don't know how much time we have left."

"Okay, now you're getting morbid. We better get going." Jill pulled out her car keys as they reached the carpark. "And you're very welcome to join me on the Camino, you know? I'm leaving on the thirtieth."

"Oh, I think that's a bit drastic," Paula said, opening her car door.

"And opening a café in Santorini isn't?"

Paula shrugged.

"Why don't I email you my itinerary from *Follow the Camino*, the people I booked with, and that way if Kevin asks you about your pretend walking trip, at least you'll have the information about it."

"Good idea, thanks! You are still coming to the party, aren't you? Not the foreign one!"

"Absolutely. How could I miss the most uncomfortable night of your life!" Jill laughed as she got into her car.

"*Very funny!*" Paula shouted after her.

Jill waved, reversed her two-seater BMW and drove out of the Summit car park.

Paula sat into her Toyota Corolla and opened the glove compartment where she kept her work make-up. Just tinted moisturiser, some eyeliner, and the same Max Factor lip colour she had been wearing for over twenty years. Carefully applying her eyeliner, she wondered why at this early hour she felt so frustrated. Was it part of the menopause? Was it empty nest syndrome? The kids had moved out now and her sense of purpose went with them. The house was so quiet sometimes. And what about herself and Kevin? Could they really spend the rest of their lives together, just the two of them in that house now?

It wasn't just the party or turning sixty, it was the feeling that the future was pre-set, marked out. She felt a sense of panic when she thought about it. She knew friends who never made it to sixty, so she understood how lucky she was. Was she being ungrateful?

Why can't I be happy with my lot? she thought and sighed.

And poor Jill, not a relaxing walk for her hearing me vent my ungratefulness.

Starting the engine, she decided to google the Camino as soon as she got to work, just in case.

CHAPTER 7

Paula stepped into the shower, letting the hot water heal her tired body as she thought about how much ground she had covered on the way to Portomarin and all the people she had met. It was a wonderful feeling being part of a movement of people with a common goal but everyone doing it at their own pace.

She smiled when she remembered the big Spanish family getting their photo taken at the big white Sarria sign at the top of the town. An older man, maybe a grandfather, had balloons tied to his small backpack. It looked like it was his birthday and his whole family young and old were making the journey with him. At least he got to do what he wanted for his birthday, she thought, waving to him as she passed.

After passing a railway line, the trail headed up steeply through some woods. She paced herself so she wouldn't overdo it at the start, taking small steps and stopping to enjoy the view back down the valley as the path rose through the forest. All the time, whenever a pilgrim passed her, they wished her a "*Buen Camino*" which gave her a feeling of camaraderie and encouraged her to keep going.

At the top, the path widened out onto open fields. This was much better for walking as it was flat. You could see for miles over the fields. The path led pilgrims through green fields and small farmlands while cows looked on disinterested. Even sleeping dogs barely raised their heads at walkers passing by. The rhythm of other walkers and the sound of their boots and poles was comforting. Everyone was in this together, putting one foot in front of the other, following the yellow arrows.

Most walkers that passed her had a shell, with a red St James' cross on it, tied to their backpack, so when she saw a farm building turned Camino shop in the first village she came to, she bought a shell. The owner of the shop gave her a marker and told her to put her name and the date on the inside of the shell and he then tied it to her backpack with red string.

"*Buen Camino!*" he said as he waved her off back on the track.

The pension owner in Sarria had given them all their pilgrim passports when they arrived last night and had put their first stamp in it.

"To receive the Compostela Certificate confirming that you walked the last 100 kilometres of the Camino, you have to collect two stamps a day in your pilgrim passport and date them," he explained. "Without these stamps, you cannot receive your Compostela. The stamped pilgrim passport is your only proof."

The man in the shell shop had given her a second stamp and she was delighted with that, but there was space in the passport for eight a day so Paula decided to make it her goal to try to get eight if possible. She got another one when she stopped for breakfast and another one when she stopped for coffee and a baked Basque cheesecake that was so delicious it made her lightheaded with delight.

The nicest stamp was one she picked up in the forest. In the middle of nowhere along the forest trail an elderly Spanish man with long grey hair had a little table with stamps and beaded bracelets. There was a donation box on the table too. He smiled as she approached while he was stamping another woman's passport.

"You like a stamp?" he asked.

"Oh, I'm sorry but I have no donation," Paula explained. "No coins."

"It is not necessary. I will stamp for you."

"Thank you so much."

As she took out her pilgrim passport from her backpack, the other woman turned around and smiled.

"I'll put it in for you," she said as she threw in an extra euro.

"Oh, thank you so much!"

"You're from Dublin too?" the young woman asked.

"Yes, I am," answered Paula.

"I'm Michelle."

She was younger than Paula but was carrying a big bag on her back.

"I'm Paula, and these stamps are gorgeous." Paula folded her pilgrim passport and returned it to her small backpack.

They said goodbye to the man and started walking together, keeping pace.

"So where are you from?"

"Raheny," Paula answered.

"That's gas! I live near Malahide."

"A ten-minute drive from me!" said Paula, laughing.

"The Camino is funny like that – you can travel from afar to come out here and end up meeting a neighbour," Michelle said with a smile.

For the next two hours, they kept pace with each other as they walked through forests and over streams while the sunlight dappled the ground through the canopy of trees. Paula learned that Michelle had started at the very beginning of the Camino Frances in St Jean four weeks before, walking most days, staying in albergues, the pilgrim hostels, and carrying her full backpack on her back.

"That's incredible," said Paula. "I'm in awe of you, walking for weeks with your bag on your back. I don't think that I could do that."

"Well, there are probably people at home who are in awe of you for being here, thinking the same thing," replied Michelle with a smile.

The walking and talking made the time fly until Paula had to stop for breakfast and Michelle carried on.

"I might see you on the road!" said Michelle as she left.

Paula hoped their paths would cross again. She was fascinated by the length of the journey Michelle had taken on.

It really had been a lovely day, she thought as she turned off the shower. She wrapped herself in a big towel and lay on top of the bedcovers. Picking up her phone, she saw that her pacer app said she had walked 21.9 kilometres and, including breaks, it had taken her six hours. She was delighted that the pension was in the middle of town because she didn't fancy doing much more walking around today.

But she hadn't expected to arrive and find Rachel looking so stressed and in a very awkward situation. How strange, she thought, to come all this way and find an ex-boyfriend and his mother sitting in the kitchen, here on the Camino! Rachel seemed very anxious and couldn't wait to rush to her room.

She wondered what the story there was. They seemed very nice, and Paula was delighted when the son Simon offered to make her a cup of tea in the kitchen.

"Here, Simon, use my tea bags," his mother had said, taking a Ziplock bag out from her small backpack. "I never go anywhere without some Barry's tea bags."

"You're dead right. A nice cup of Irish tea is exactly what I need," Paula had said, happy to take her up on her offer.

Simon made the tea and Paula was very grateful for it.

"Now I feel human again!"

He seemed like a lovely man and so attentive to his mother. It was clear that she was not well, God love her. They didn't elaborate on their relationship with Rachel, but Bernie said that Simon and Rachel had dated when they were in school and college, that they hadn't seen her in years and that Simon had been living in Australia but was home now working remotely and looking after her.

"And did you and Rachel keep in touch all this time?" Paula had asked him.

"No," Simon said, shifting uncomfortably "but that was my fault."

Bernie broke the awkward silence by saying she was off for a nap.

"Me too," said Paula, finishing her last drop of tea. "And thank you for the tea. We'll probably see you later."

"I do hope so, it's been lovely talking to you," Bernie said as she got up from her seat very slowly.

"It's a slightly longer walk tomorrow – twenty-four kilometres, I think," Paula said, gathering her things.

"Yes, it is, but we will only do part of it," Bernie said. "I love the early mornings so we will walk early for as long as I can and then we'll get a taxi to the next pension. We're spending one night in the next town – what's it called, Simon?"

"Palas de Rei."

"Yes, that's it. We mix it up. Some days we walk a bit and then take a taxi and we take some days off completely and have a rest. I'm just happy to be here."

"'*Your Camino Your Way*', I believe they say," said Paula. "Well, if I don't see you later I might see you in Palas de Rei."

Paula meant that too. She had warmed to Bernie, and Simon seemed like a lovely son – but it was clear that he felt a bit shaken at seeing Rachel again and Rachel was definitely in shock after seeing him.

Getting into bed, she checked her phone: two WhatsApp messages from Kevin asking how she got on. I'd better reply, she thought, typing a brief message to let him know that she had survived Day One. I don't want him to suspect anything. Today had been a great distraction from the sadness she had felt over the past week. I need to know the truth, she sighed, but not until I can talk to him face to face. There will be plenty of time to deal with him when I get back, so for now I'm going to try to put those thoughts behind me and enjoy my own adventure this week.

CHAPTER 8

Paula stretched out fully in her bed. Feeling energised after her afternoon siesta, she got dressed to go out and find somewhere for dinner. She was about to leave her room when she heard a knock on her door.

"Rachel?" she said, opening it to find Rachel standing there, wringing her hands nervously.

"I was wondering if you were going out to dinner?" Rachel said.

"Yes, I was just about to leave."

"May I join you?"

"Of course – just let me grab my bag."

Picking up her bag and her key, Paula shut the door and they both headed downstairs. Rachel hesitated when they got to the last step and stuck her head out, looking around the reception area.

"Everything okay?"

"Yes. Fine. Let's go."

They walked out onto the main street into the early-evening sunshine.

"Oh, hi!" Cathy waved to them as she approached.

"We were just going out to dinner – do you want to join us?"

"*Em*," Cathy said, looking at her watch, "yes, that would be lovely. I was just in the supermarket getting some bananas and snacks for tomorrow."

"Good thinking, I might do the same," said Paula. "I could've done with an energy boost along the route today. You just don't know where your next café will be, do you?"

"Actually, I have an app I can show you. It lists every stop on the route," Cathy said excitedly. "The people I was with today showed me. It's called *Camino Ninja*. She showed Paula the icon on her phone.

"I'm definitely downloading that," said Paula.

Rachel was quiet but, even behind her big sunglasses, Paula could tell she was scanning the outdoor seating area of the restaurants on the main street, either looking for or trying to avoid her friends from the past.

"Where do you want to eat?" Paula asked, looking around. There was plenty of choice.

The main street's cafés and restaurants were full of hikers. Some had arrived late and were still in their walking gear. Most were sitting in the evening sun enjoying a glass of Spanish wine or a well-deserved cold beer.

"Let's try down at the end," Rachel said, quickening her step.

"No problem," Paula said, turning her face up to enjoy the sunshine.

Down at the quieter end of the main street, Rachel picked a café and they sat down at an outdoor table. Two older women in hiking gear were sitting at a table near them, speaking what seemed to be Dutch and tucking into their dinner of lasagne and salad.

"Oh, that looks good. I'm hungry now. So how was your day?" Paula asked Cathy.

"Wonderful, actually. I woke late and nearly missed Carlos and I missed breakfast too so I was a bit all over the place at the start but I met the loveliest of people, a Spanish group led by a priest."

"Lovely. Do you speak any Spanish?"

"No, but their English is very good. They are a church group and I volunteer in my local church at home, so I felt very comfortable around them. They were kind enough to let me tag along. I'm sure I would still be walking if I hadn't met them."

"I know what you mean," agreed Paula. "It's nice to walk alone but the time goes quicker when you are chatting, and everyone is so nice. The first person I met was a woman from Dublin called Michelle, can you believe that? Her house is ten minutes away from where I live!"

"That's incredible. I haven't heard any Irish accents except ours."

"What about you?" Paula asked, turning to Rachel.

"What? Sorry, I was miles away."

"We were just saying we both met lovely people today and how that really helped our walk."

"No, I didn't meet anyone on the walk, didn't talk to anyone, and then my past hit me right in the face when I got here."

"*What?* What happened?" Cathy asked, concerned, but the waiter arrived before Rachel could answer.

"Now what can I get for you?" he asked, taking out his notebook.

"I think I'll have the lasagne and salad and a beer, please," Paula said.

"Me too, but with water instead of beer, please," said Cathy.

"I'll have the burger and a very large beer," Rachel said.

After the waiter left, Cathy turned to Rachel. "Are you okay?" she asked anxiously. "What happened?"

Rachel sighed. "When I arrived at the pension, the mother of my ex-boyfriend was sitting there. I nearly died. It was a huge shock as I hadn't seen her in years. She is a lovely woman but ..." She took her sunglasses off and shook her head. "Her son Simon, my first boyfriend, who broke my heart fifteen years ago, is here with her. I mean what are the chances of that?" She laughed nervously. "And what can I do about it? Absolutely nothing."

Cathy and Paula looked at each other.

The waiter arrived back with their drinks and Rachel waited until he had placed them on the table and left before continuing.

"I came here to get away from one man who has just ruined my life and then I go and bump into another!" She shook her head and took a big gulp of her beer.

"It is unbelievable really to come somewhere like this and for that to happen," said Paula. "His mother doesn't look well – is she ill?"

"Yes, that's what makes it harder. I don't want to be rude to Bernie because she is such a lovely woman. I went out with Simon in school and all through college, so I was always in her house. I don't know what her illness is, but I get the feeling this is a bucket-list trip."

"Yes, she told me she wanted to walk this route one last time. She did it before with friends five years ago."

"I'm sorry I ran off and left you with them," Rachel said. "I just couldn't face him."

"I understand. He seems like a nice guy but, of course, I don't know anything about him. He made me a cup of tea and I know he came home to look after his mum during the pandemic."

Their food arrived and they all started to eat.

"You've obviously had a shock," Cathy said, reaching over and squeezing Rachel's arm. "Is there anything we can do?"

"I don't know. I just don't want to be left alone with him."

"How is his mum walking the route if she is that unwell?" asked Cathy.

"She told me that the five walking days we are doing, they are doing in ten days," said Paula, "so they are spending two nights here and in some other places, and sometimes they walk for a bit in the morning and then take taxis when Bernie gets tired."

"What are the chances they'll be in our accommodation tomorrow night?" asked Rachel.

"They are heading for Palas de Rei tomorrow but they didn't mention where they were staying."

"I think I'll leave super-early tomorrow and get to the pension before them. That way I can ask if they are staying there and, if they are, I'll stay somewhere else."

"You shouldn't have to do that," Paula said, feeling sorry for Rachel as she looked so stressed about the situation.

"I have to," sighed Rachel, pushing her plate away. "I haven't seen him in fifteen years. He broke up with me but, afterwards, when he tried to contact me, I blocked him. I've worked really hard to stop thinking about him over the years, to stop wondering where he is and if he ever thinks of me, and I thought I had succeeded." Rachel hesitated and looked down, wringing her hands. "But when I saw him today some old feelings came back," she said almost in a whisper as a tear ran down her cheek.

"Oh, Rachel!" Paula said, leaning over and putting her arm around her shoulder.

"I'm sorry. You don't know me, and I didn't mean to say all this. I'm probably just tired from today and I came here because my life was turned upside down at home. And now Simon is here and these old feelings … I don't know what to do. Maybe I should just get a taxi to Santiago and go home. Everything is a mess."

"Rachel, listen to me," Cathy said, leaning across the table, "you came here for a reason. You wanted to walk and sort things out. So don't let this man or the man at home or any man change your mind about that. Stay, please stay."

Something in the forceful way Cathy spoke made both Rachel and Paula sit up and take notice of this quiet woman.

"You have our phone numbers from last night, so if you need us we can be there for you," Paula suggested, taking out her phone. "And Cathy is right – you came here for you, so fuck 'em. *Fuck the lot of them!*"

At the next table, the older Dutch couple tutted in disgust at Paula's language so she said, "*Fuck the lot of them!*" again even louder, which made the three new friends crack up laughing.

CHAPTER 9

The three women finished dinner and headed back to the pension. The main street was still busy as bottles of wine and big pans of paella were delivered to tables of hungry hikers.

"Thank you so much for tonight, I needed the company. But can you do me a favour?" asked Rachel when they reached the door of Casa do Maestro.

"Of course," said Paula. "What is it?".

"Can you check that Simon and his mum aren't sitting in the lounge?"

"No problem," Paula said and went in.

"And thank you for your kind words," Rachel said to Cathy. "I'm sorry to burden you and Paula with my troubles but it's great to be able to talk about it."

"I know we've only met, but we're here for you. It's a funny thing, this Camino. You get to know people so quickly. Maybe it's because we are all walking in the same direction with one goal in mind. It really is a unique situation."

"I didn't talk to anyone. I was walking off my anger about a man back home but it's not a good plan as I only ended up thinking about him for most of my walk. They say the Camino sends you messages – well, I won't be thinking of Craig anymore now that Simon is here to wreck my head."

"Don't change your plans to avoid him either, Rachel. We only have one week here – take it for yourself."

"You're right. I need to stop and smell the roses as they say and stop thinking about either man."

"All clear!" Paula said, popping her head out.

They went inside.

"Okay, see you tomorrow at some stage," Rachel said, running up the stairs.

"I'm meeting some people at Mass," Cathy said to Paula, looking at her watch. "It's starting now, so I'll see you tomorrow."

"Handy having the church right beside us," Paula said with a smile, as the bells chimed for the evening Mass. "Goodnight. I'm going to grab a quick cuppa and then go to bed. Have a great day tomorrow if I don't see you."

Paula walked to the small kitchen for guests and put some water into the kettle. While waiting for it to boil, she peeked out to see if he was still there. She had spotted Carlos in the garden through the sliding doors when she was checking the lounge for Rachel. She had enjoyed his calm company this morning and their encounter crossed her mind a few times today. She made a small cup of tea for herself and headed towards the garden.

"Oh, hello again," she said, stepping out through the sliding doors.

Carlos, who had been lying back taking in the last of the evening sun, looked up. He was barefoot again and looked so well in his faded jeans and tight white T-shirt. She hadn't noticed his fit muscular arms in the dark this morning, but she noticed them now.

Carlos sat up, pushed his sunglasses onto the top of his head and smiled.

"Come," he said, patting the empty seat beside him.

Feeling a bit giddy, Paula sat down. The view from the back garden was of the side of the church and they both sat side by side, looking at it.

"How was your day?" he asked.

She could smell his musky cologne as he turned to talk to her.

"Really lovely. I met some very interesting people, walked through some lovely countryside and had a delicious meal tonight. I can't ask for more than that."

"Very good."

"And, as you said on the minibus, you must get similar rainfall levels to us because the colours, the fields and hills – honestly, it looks very like Wicklow at home."

"Maybe that's why we see a lot of Irish here," he said, "and of course we also have a strong Catholic people here too and a shared Celtic history and, yes, we have a lot of green fields!"

"That is true. I passed some lovely old churches today too. It's great to see them maintained. Some of them are tiny but still open to go in and light a candle. And I can see the attraction of the Camino. It's the simplicity. You collect our bags and just have to walk – nothing else. I got my Camino shell today too. I should know this but why is the scallop shell such a feature of the Camino?"

"There are so many stories but the scallop shell was originally given to pilgrims when they arrived in Santiago as a sign of the completion of their journey. This was before the certificate, the Compostela. Another story is that when St James' body was being transferred from Jerusalem to

Spain, after his martyrdom, the boat sank but his body remained intact as it was covered in scallop shells. But, for whatever reason, the symbol stuck and is used to guide the way on the Camino. And you can see it over the door of the albergues that welcome pilgrims on the route and almost everywhere else."

"Very interesting. The scallop shell and yellow arrows certainly helped me today," Paula said with a smile.

Carlos nodded. "Tomorrow will be a little longer and steeper hills, so take your time and enjoy, yes?"

"Good advice. I may have walked too quickly this morning from excitement, so tomorrow I will pace myself better."

The two sat in silence, comfortable in each other's company. Although she loved talking to people, she wouldn't usually spend time talking with men at home but she felt very comfortable with Carlos. And, of course, she now knew that her husband had no problem interacting with female hikers on his trips away.

"Do you work at home?"

"Yes, I work in a school as a resource teacher, assisting students who need a little extra help. It is a busy job but I'm off for the summer now."

"Very nice."

"My ... husband is semi-retired. Hiking is his hobby, so he is away a lot."

Why did I say that? 'He is away a lot.' Did that sound suggestive? Like, 'Come up and see me sometime?' Paula felt a bit flustered as she sipped the last of her tea.

Just then the bells of the church chimed.

"Okay, that's my cue to go," she said, standing up. "Early start tomorrow and I need to rest these legs."

"Sleep well," Carlos said.

"I will," she replied, glad that she'd brought her earplugs in case those bells were ringing on the hour all night.

"And if you want a coffee before you start tomorrow, I will be here," he said, pointing to his seat and holding her gaze.

Paula smiled and turned to leave before he saw her blushing.

As she walked up the stairs, her phone buzzed. It was Kevin sending her some photos from his hiking trip in South America. He's sending photos while I'm having a flirty chat with a good-looking Spanish man, she thought. Maybe he's telepathic. She refused to feel guilty. Had he felt guilty after his last hiking weekend in Killarney? He certainly showed no signs of it when he came back.

Brushing those thoughts aside, she got to her room just as Simon passed her on his way downstairs.

"Goodnight. *Buen Camino* for tomorrow!"

"You too. Goodnight," replied Paula.

Once inside her room she searched her phone for some photos from her walk today to send back to Kevin. He would be expecting some photos from her and even though she was furious with him she didn't want to confront him over the phone while he was in South America so she picked a few shots and pressed send with no message.

CHAPTER 10

Rachel had everything laid out for an early start tomorrow. They had copied Cathy's idea – so on the way home from the restaurant, the three of them had popped into the supermarket and bought some snacks for the morning. A banana and yogurt drink would do as breakfast on the road and save her time stopping at a café.

"Damn, I forgot to put the yogurt drink in the fridge," she mumbled to herself when she spotted it on her locker. She looked down. She was wearing a pyjama set of shorts and a top in white broderie anglaise, a very expensive present to herself she'd bought, from the White Company, on her last business trip to London.

She had packed everything else up and wasn't about to open the bag again for a sweatshirt so she opened her door and listened. Everything was quiet. Most people went to bed early on the Camino because of the early starts. Slipping out of her room, she tip-toed down the stairs to the small kitchen and put her drink in the fridge.

"Rachel."

She jumped in fright.

"Sorry, I didn't mean to startle you."

She turned around to find Simon standing in the kitchen, his tall frame making it feel even smaller. His eyes scanned her as she stood with her back against the fridge.

"Having a good look, are you?" Rachel flicked her hair back, stood up tall, and met his gaze directly as she spoke. She felt as though she was standing there naked, the way he looked at her.

"I'm sorry," he said, looking away, sounding flustered. "I didn't mean to ... can we talk?"

"Talk?"

"Yes. Please?"

This is ridiculous, she thought, but better to get it over and done with. "Okay," she said, sighing loudly.

Walking past him, she sat down on the couch in the guest living area. This was going to happen sooner or later so they might as well do it now so she could enjoy the rest of her trip.

Simon hesitated, looking from the couch to the free chair opposite it, before choosing to sit on the couch beside her. Rachel curled her legs under her. Her stomach was doing somersaults, sitting so close to him, but she couldn't let him see that, so she held her head high and stared at him.

"What do you want to say?"

Simon took a deep breath. "I want to say ... that I'm sorry." He paused and lowered his head.

His long fringe fell over his face and Rachel had to stop herself from reaching out and moving it out of his eyes. She moved slightly to sit on both of her hands so she wouldn't be tempted.

"I'm sorry for the way things ended with us. I was in a panic, and I was confused, but I shouldn't have ended things like that. I tried to contact you over the years to explain but –"

"Yes, it was awful," Rachel interrupted him. "It was the worst time of my life, Simon. I avoided going back home to Cork for years because of the looks of pity people gave me. Oh, there's poor Rachel who Simon dumped and then did a runner on!"

"I'm sure they didn't think that –"

"*You weren't there!*" she said, raising her voice. "You were too busy living it up in Australia to give two hoots about what was happening back in Cork!"

"You're right. I'm sorry. I'm sorry for all of it."

Rachel took a deep breath. She could feel her anger rising, remembering those early days.

"Like I said, I am truly sorry and I just want you to know that and I hope we can maybe be friends or –"

"No. No, we can't be friends, Simon. I can't be friends with you."

Because I still have feelings for you, she said to herself, looking into his eyes.

Simon held her gaze, his eyes wounded.

"I gotta go." She uncurled her legs and stood up.

Simon didn't move.

She didn't look back. She was exhausted and this was all just too much.

Rachel lay in bed looking at the ceiling. She was so tired physically and emotionally but her mind was too busy to sleep. Simon feckin' Molloy. How could this happen? How could he be here? How come, after fifteen years of avoiding any contact with him, he walks in here? She was flabbergasted.

He hadn't changed either. Older now, with a few lines on his face and tanned from the Australian sun. But that light brown sun-streaked hair still flopped over one eye ... just like it did the first night she turned around and caught him looking at her at the under-18s disco in her local rugby club.

Rachel and her friends had spent hours getting ready that night, in her best friend Charley's house. The objective at the under-18 disco was to kiss as many boys as you could in a night and Rachel had just complained to Charley that, as usual, even at sixteen years of age, she stood head and shoulders over most of the boys their age. Charley, at five foot two, never had that problem.

"There's a tall boyo for you now!" Charley had shouted over the loud music the DJ was blasting out.

Just as Rachel turned around to see who she was talking about, Simon nodded a hello in her direction. She nodded back and continued chatting to her friends who told her who he was, where he lived and what school he went to.

As he later told her, at seventeen and over six feet tall, Simon felt too old for these discos and usually preferred to go see local live bands – if the pub owners let him in. But tonight there was nothing on, so he'd tagged along with his cousins instead.

When the slow set came on, Rachel told Charley that she was going out for air but, as she passed Simon and his friends, he stepped forward and asked her to dance. She said yes. It felt great dancing with someone taller than her for a change. They didn't speak much and, unlike the other boys, he didn't try to kiss her. Instead, he just asked if he could meet her the next day at a café in the English Market in Cork City Centre. She said yes immediately and that was their first date.

They went out with each other for the last two years of secondary school and both were accepted into University College Cork where their relationship took off.

As Simon lived in a house opposite the college, Rachel spent a lot of time there and often popped in for a cup of tea and a chat with his mum Bernie when she had a long break between lectures.

It was shortly before graduation that everything fell apart. They had been planning a gap year travelling through Asia before working in Australia for nine months. Everything was organised. But then two weeks before their college graduation and four weeks before they were due to travel, Simon said he needed a break. He was desperately sorry but he had changed his mind about their trip and needed time on his own to figure out what he wanted to do and where he was going with his life.

Rachel's world collapsed. Everything she thought was certain was pulled away from her. Their relationship, their travels and their future disappeared overnight. Everyone in their social circle, who knew them as a couple and knew about their travel plans, was shocked. Rachel felt humiliated. Even his mother rang, crying, because she couldn't understand it herself.

Her graduation was ruined. She felt too embarrassed and humiliated to go alone, but her friend Charley made her see that none of this was her fault and she deserved to enjoy her graduation like everyone else. To save her embarrassment, Simon changed the date of his flight and left for Asia days before the graduation took place. As he would not be there, Rachel could hold her head high and graduate alongside her friends.

Charley was going to America for the summer, so Rachel changed her ticket to go with her and they both stayed with Rachel's sister Clare, who was working and living there. As a law student graduate, Rachel very quickly found a job and worked long hours to distract herself from her heartache. The company rewarded her by sponsoring her and organising a work visa which allowed her to stay on in New York and make a life for herself. She stayed for five years, only going home once.

During that time, Simon tried to contact her, but she blocked him. It was too painful to ever think of him as a friend. After a year she heard through friends that he was staying in Australia and had got engaged. Two years after he had broken her heart, he got married to an Australian girl.

After five years in New York, she took a position in London which meant she could go back to Cork to visit her family more. She dated other men, but nobody made her feel like Simon had.

She was still searching for that special connection when she was approached by Craig Callaghan at a legal conference in Chicago. Even though she found him attractive, she had turned down his many offers to take her out to dinner in the past because of his reputation as a ladies' man. But this time Rachel had just delivered a speech to a room full of top lawyers from legal companies all over the States and it had gone very well. She was on a high when he came up to congratulate her and this time she offered to buy him a drink. He accepted straight away and was even more delighted when she took him to her room later that night.

The next morning she left while he was sleeping, to get an early flight home. Playing him at his own game just made him pursue her more and she liked it. She was also surprised by how much she liked his company and her thoughts often returned to the amazing sex they had in Chicago, so she agreed to go to dinner with him back in Dublin. She was happy to find that there was more to the man than his good looks and fit body. He was intelligent and he made her laugh with his courtroom stories and, despite her best intentions, she took him back to her bed again.

A highly successful solicitor, he matched her drive and ambition. They were a power couple about town, building their reputations in the legal field. Socially, they were invited to restaurant openings and high-profile charity events in Dublin and were often photographed for the social pages of magazines. She really believed that Craig was everything she was looking for, but now she felt foolish for trusting him and planning a life with him.

And now, emotionally drained from dealing with Craig and the events of the past few weeks, Simon bloody Molloy shows up and is staying in this pension!

I will have to ring Charley – she will not believe this is happening, she thought.

Charley, who still lived in Cork, had mentioned that Simon's mum was ill but whenever his name came up Rachel shut her down. She missed the chats she used to have with his mother, but she had to cut herself off from her too. When Charley messaged her to say, '**Guess who's divorced now?**' Rachel realised she was truly over Simon Molloy as she didn't care what he was up to now or who he was with.

So why, in a pension, at the top of a mountain in Spain, did her heart do a somersault and her knees go weak when she looked into his eyes? He felt it too, she knew it. He was taken aback as much as she was, she could see it in his eyes.

"What the hell do I do now?" Rachel cried out loud as she hugged her pillow and pulled the blankets over her head.

CHAPTER 11

Rachel sat up straight as soon as her alarm went off at 6 am. She had slept really badly, tossing and turning all night. Her bag was ready, and her clothes were laid out. She washed and dressed quickly and put her hair up into a ponytail. It was still dark out, but she was determined to leave early. Even if Simon and Bernie walked halfway and got a taxi, she reckoned she could still beat them to Palas de Rei and book alternative accommodation if need be.

It was a slightly longer walk today, twenty-four kilometres. Google Maps said it would take six hours but that was the most direct route. The Camino route was very different, taking you over the mountains, so you could add on at least another hour. She had downloaded the Camino Ninja app Cathy had told them about that listed all the cafés and eateries along the route and the distances between them. Today the first stop would be Gonzar which was about eight kilometres from Portomarin but Rachel reckoned she could skip this one and keep going to Ligonde which was sixteen kilometres away. She guessed it would take her three hours to get there and that the banana and yoghurt drink she had bought in the supermarket should keep her going till then.

Moving as quietly as possible, she left her bag at reception, collected her yogurt drink from the fridge and stepped outside just as the sky was brightening. A single figure was walking ahead with poles so she knew she was heading in the right direction. Walking to the end of main street, she turned a corner as the river came into sight. She stopped for a moment to take in the view. It was beautiful at this time of the day. Early morning mist rose from the water and hung in the air, covering the tops of the trees around the lake and on into the woods

Two bridges spanned the wide river, one that she came over when she walked from Sarria, and the other that she must cross to leave Portomarin for the Camino path.

Having googled the route and checked the Facebook Camino pages, she knew to turn right when she got over the bridge. The path rose steeply from this point through the woods. She could see the lone walker with the poles up ahead, a blonde female with her hair in a high ponytail. She was glad that she was there to lead the way but happy to keep her distance and enjoy the quiet of the woods, the only sound being her footsteps and the birds waking up.

As she continued uphill, she felt the warmth of the sun on her back, and her shadow stretched longer in front of her as the sunlight filtered through the trees. Stopping to take a photo of her shadow on the forest floor, she paused and took a deep breath, filling her lungs with the fresh mountain air. The scent was a mixture of damp forest leaves and oak.

Moving on, the path evened out after fifteen minutes and she stopped to catch her breath. The sun had risen above the trees now and burned off the mist, allowing for a beautiful view from the treetops down to the river and back to the town. She took a photo of the valley, rich with colours of gold and green, then quickly moved on. She needed to focus on her pace today and keep moving to get to Palais de Rei as quickly as she could.

Paula heard a door shut at 6.15. She was awake now so she got up and opened the wooden shutters of the two windows in her room, letting the natural light in. Getting back into bed, she propped herself up with an extra pillow. It was dark outside and the moon was still up but she could see the sky lightening in the distance. She hadn't slept well at all. In Kevin's photos from South America, he looked elated. This annoyed her so much. She knew he was doing exactly what he loved – he could happily spend the rest of his life hiking great heights, but was he completely unaffected by their conversation the night before he left?

She knew she had been moody and disgruntled this past year as she approached sixty. I probably wasn't the easiest person to live with, she thought. Was I so engrossed in my own unease that I failed to notice that maybe Kevin was getting fed up of listening to me?

Although she had no interest in going hiking with him, she had tried to keep the romantic spark alive. Just a few months ago she had tried to interest him in a romantic night away. She had spotted a deal in the *Irish Times* for a 5-star hotel near Kilkenny. She thought a luxury night away might reignite some passion and add some excitement to their normal routine but when she rang him from work to tell him about it he didn't seem keen at all.

"*Hmm* ... Kilkenny? This Thursday?" He sounded so disinterested.

"Well, it's near Kilkenny but we wouldn't be going into the town," she explained. "It's the Lyrath Estate Hotel, and this is a bargain price for a 5-star hotel so if we're going I'd need to book now before it gets sold out. We have a teacher training day here so I have a day off school. The date is perfect for me."

"*Eh* ... can I think about it?"

"What's there to think about?" Paula said, getting annoyed now.

"Well, you've just sprung this on me ..."

"Oh god, Kevin, can we not be spontaneous for once!"

"Well, yes, we can – it's just ..."

"Forget it!"

"No, let me have a look and we can decide when you get home."

"No, forget it. I just thought it would be fun, you know, spontaneous ... romantic even."

"Yes ... well ... can we talk about it later?"

"No, forget it, go back to your work."

She hung up on him and sighed heavily. *For fuck sake, could he not just have said yes! Or ... was the thought of going with me just not that inviting to him?* Did he stop to think how that made her feel? Was it too much to expect him to want to spend time with his wife? Would he prefer to spend that time with a woman who shared his passion? Or maybe he was trying to hint at something she wasn't picking up on – that maybe he didn't enjoy her company anymore?

She knew she wasn't happy in herself. Maybe it had started with the menopause, maybe it started when the kids moved out. Even though she joked about how much free time she would have, not having to cook and clean for them, when they left she had felt a little lost.

Then came the pandemic. Despite doing home workouts with Joe Wicks on YouTube the pandemic pounds crept up. And on top of that, like many of her friends, she started the pandemic with brown hair and came out of it with grey! With the hairdressers closed it was either become your own hairdresser or go au natural. Although she didn't miss the ritual of getting her roots done every three weeks, the world had a way of viewing grey-haired women as old and invisible. This only fuelled her frustration.

Had she become impossible to live with? Was it her fault Kevin had lost interest in her?

Paula brushed these thoughts aside. She didn't have any of the answers yet. For better or for worse, she hoped this trip would help her find out what she wanted from her life. And, as for her and Kevin, with what she had uncovered just before leaving for this trip, she wasn't sure if there would be a relationship to revive.

It was getting brighter outside so she got out of bed and got down on the floor to do some stretching exercises. Her calves were a little sore after Day One so she wanted to give them a good stretch before heading off today.

What an interesting night it had been last night, she thought as she stretched into a downward dog yoga position. It was incredible how a trip like this fast-forwarded relationships. She would never learn as much about people so quickly if she was walking with a group of strangers back home. The collective experience of people coming here, looking for something, all walking on the one path in the one direction, seemed to make people open up quicker.

Packing up her bag, she deliberated whether to join Carlos for coffee. She dressed and packed up her toiletries. Applying sunblock on her face, she leaned in closer to the mirror. Why would a handsome man like Carlos be interested in this old face, she wondered, rubbing the cream in. She then applied some eyeliner and a tinted lip balm – the only cosmetics she had brought with her.

"I like him and I like his company and I'm doing nothing wrong," she said to her reflection as she sprayed on some deodorant.

Sitting on the side of the bed, she put the Vaseline all over her feet again, followed by her walking socks and trainers.

There is nothing wrong with two grown adults enjoying each other's company, she said to herself as she zipped up her fleece. And it was clear now that Kevin enjoyed the company of his fellow female hikers, she thought grimly. Carlos made her feel good. She picked up her backpack and headed downstairs to the kitchen. The smell of coffee wafting up the stairs made her smile and, when she reached the bottom, Carlos was standing in the kitchen with his back to her. A warm feeling came over her.

I shouldn't be doing this, she thought, but when he turned around and smiled at her, she smiled back and found herself walking towards him.

Cathy made sure to pack her suitcase and set her alarm before going to bed, so when the alarm went off at 7 am she jumped out of bed.

No point in having a shower now when I'll be having one when I finish walking today, she reckoned. She took some painkillers for her bruised hip and rubbed some Vaseline gently over it to save it from chafing against her trousers. She also applied some arnica to her neck as it seemed to be working on fading the bruises there. Then she pulled on her hiking trousers and a light high-neck top, making sure her neck was covered. Father Eduardo mentioned that there was a long walk before the first breakfast café so some of his group would have breakfast before heading out. But if they didn't see her on the road, she was free to join them for prayers in the Church of Santiago in Ligonde. He explained that he had contacted the caretaker in advance who agreed to be there to open the church.

She checked the Ninja app she had downloaded and decided to walk by herself to a place called Gonzar that had a big café and was about eight kilometres away. This, she reckoned, would take her just under two hours. She could eat there and then walk nine more kilometres to Ligonde and meet Father Eduardo and the Spanish group for prayers at noon. Gonzar to Ligonde would definitely take two hours so, allowing 30 minutes for breakfast, this meant she had to leave Portomarin at 7.30. She checked her watch. It was 7.15.

I'll leave on time today, she thought, smiling to herself.

She felt great. Yes, she was on her own but she had met the most wonderful people without trying and she hadn't annoyed anyone yet or made a nuisance of herself. Paula and Rachel had actually asked her to dinner. They wanted me there, she thought, smiling. And Father Eduardo was so kind to include me too. He was probably only speaking to me to practise his English but I don't care, because the prayer group was so comforting. I feel safe with them.

And he told me about the church today after Mass last night so maybe they do want to see me again. I'm not going to overthink it, she decided. People used to like me, I know they did. Maybe these people could like me too even for a little while.

She picked up her suitcase and closed the door behind her.

CHAPTER 12

Cathy felt great as she walked down the main street of Portomarin. The restaurants and cafés that were buzzing with hikers the previous night were closed now and the town was silent except for the footsteps of Camino walkers.

She stopped to take in the view of the river and the sun rising from behind the trees. At 7.30 there was already a steady stream of walkers ahead of her, like ants walking around the bend, over the bridge and then heading into the forest. Inhaling the fresh morning air, she smiled. How lucky am I that I get to do this?

The path through the forest was quite steep today so she wanted to take her time to enjoy the scenery and appreciate the nature around her. Yesterday she was a bit stressed at rising late and nearly missing bag collection and then she met Father Eduardo so she didn't take the time to be on her own with her thoughts. In some ways, she was afraid of those thoughts.

Taking out her phone she took a selfie with the valley behind her and the river below. She sent it to Sophie.

Have a lovely day. Mum x

Sophie replied immediately

You look great, Mum! Keep going. Love you. S x

Cathy looked at the photo again. She did look happy. She was only away three days but she could see that the familiar strained look that usually looked back at her from the mirror was missing from this photo.

Putting her phone away, she marched on again with a pep in her step. She had rung Sophie every night since she left and Sophie was so happy for her, proud even. She always worried that Sophie saw her as weak. Weak against Ted and his strict restrictions on their lives. Weak for not leaving him.

She had tried to make Sophie's childhood a happy one and, to the outside world, it was. She played sport and went to other kids' birthday parties, although Ted always insisted that Cathy stay with her which was at times very awkward as other mums, delighted with the break, usually dropped their kids off and left immediately.

He was so overprotective. He regularly told them that he loved them so much he wanted them to spend all their time as a family together, just the three of them. "We don't need anyone else," he would say. But that meant that Cathy had to miss out on social or community events in the area and, for Sophie, very few playdates. At the time she did believe that he loved them and that there was no bad feeling behind it. But over time it didn't feel like love, it felt like control.

It wasn't always bad. Sleepovers were a no-no but Cathy managed to get him to agree to Sophie having a sleepover with her in her mum's house. Cathy loved it when they went there. The two of them would squeeze into Cathy's old single bed in her childhood bedroom that hadn't changed since she moved out. She wanted Sophie to experience a house with no stress, free from tension.

When Ted was happy, everyone was happy, but when he was moody his mood brought everyone down. It wasn't so noticeable in the early days but any outside stress brought on a dark mood. It worsened when he was promoted to supervisor and then area manager. He was not a people person and social situations made him anxious so neither role suited him. The stress of having to deal with employees spilled over at home, resulting in him ranting about the people at work and it could go on all evening. If Cathy attempted to change the subject he accused her of not being supportive or not understanding how stressful things were for him.

In the early days, she tried to get him to go to the doctor, to get something to help with his stress levels, but he completely refused, saying there was nothing wrong with him and that if everyone else did what they were supposed to do then he would be fine.

Her biggest regret was not leaving him years ago. When he turned his back on Sophie because of who she was, that's when she should have packed up and left. Why didn't she? She had asked herself that question so many times over the years. Partly it the embarrassment of having to go back to live with her parents. It was also the shame of a failed marriage. But mostly it was finance. The bottom line was that she didn't have enough money to rent or buy somewhere else. She didn't know how much they had in joint accounts because Ted had all the passwords and account details. She could have got advice back then, but she didn't.

Instead, she and Sophie lived in a house with a man who hardly spoke to them, and who blamed Cathy for ruining their daughter. Sophie couldn't wait to move out of the house so it was no surprise when she chose a college course as far away as possible at University College Cork. She had flourished since moving there and found people who understood her. She cut and coloured her hair and had the space away from her suffocating father to figure out who she was and how to express that.

He wasn't opposed to Sophie leaving; in fact, he was very happy with her moving away. But Cathy believed that this was mostly because he wouldn't have to witness the "shame" as he called it, of seeing his daughter with another woman. He paid her college fees and even set up an expense account so that she would be okay for money. He was more relaxed in himself when Sophie left although Cathy was bereft. She missed her so much and realised that she had relied on Sophie as a distraction from how bad her marriage was. The thought of staying with Ted in that house for the rest of her life was unbearable. So, once Sophie was settled in college, she planned on telling Ted that she was leaving too. She just had to figure out the right way to do it.

Cathy marched on up the incline, feeling lighter than she had in a long time. She loved being out in the open air, and her only job was to put one foot in front of another and walk.

"*Buen Camino!*" she said to fellow walkers who passed her.

She was taking her time today, to enjoy every moment. Her thoughts were interrupted by her phone ringing. When she saw it was Ted's sister-in-law Patsy calling, she let it go to Voicemail and then waited to listen back.

Cathy, I tried calling but there was no answer. We still don't have a time for Ted's month's mind next Friday? I rang the church but the clerk knew nothing. Can you ring me back please?

Oh my god! Cathy felt the blood drain out of her. Her chest tightened. *How did I forget?*

Ted would be four weeks dead on Friday. The shock hit her like a punch in the stomach. She felt panicked and her breath quickened. Walking to a nearby rock, she sat down to steady her breath. The "month's mind" Mass was a tradition. It was to remember the person who passed, one month after they had died. It wasn't a big service like the funeral but the family of the deceased and some friends usually attended a particular Mass where the priest announced to the congregation that the Mass was in honour of said person.

Before she left, she had hesitated about telling Ted's family that she was going on the Camino but decided that in the long run it would be easier to tell them than come up with a lie about her absence. She didn't tell them she was going on her own though. Oh no, that would be too odd to them. So she said she was going with a church group from Dublin and that Father John had secured her a last-minute place. She threw in something about visiting all the churches on the route and, true to form, they asked nothing else about it.

But still, it was her job to organise the month's mind and she had completely forgotten.

"*How, how, how could I have forgotten this!*" she cried, feeling awful about it.

She took a deep breath of fresh mountain air to steady herself. I need to ring Father John, she thought. She quickly rang his number but it went to voicemail. So she sent him a WhatsApp.

Hi John, Cathy here. I forgot about Ted's month's mind and Patsy Kinsella is texting me. Is it too late to organise something? I feel so bad. How could I have forgotten?

She would have to wait for his reply. But that was only half the problem. She knew Patsy would expect Sophie and some of her family there. She needed to message Sophie in case Patsy tried to contact her.

Sophie, I forgot about your father's month's mind. Patsy texted me for the details. Father John will probably organise something but I won't be there obviously and I don't want her to pressure

you into going. I'm just messaging you in case she contacts you. Mum x

An answer came at once: **Thanks for the heads-up, Mum. I won't answer her if she calls. I'll just say I'm sick. I don't care what she thinks.**

Cathy let out a sigh of relief. Sophie could be abrupt but that's how she wanted her to be – a strong independent woman – so that she would never take any shit from anyone or be a total pushover like her mother.

She answered: **Grand. Well, be nice about it but be firm. Love you. Talk later. x**

Then her phone vibrated in her hand. It was a WhatsApp from Father John.

Tell them Friday 10 o'clock Mass.

She answered: **Thank you so much. I'm so upset here.**

He answered: **Don't be upset, Cathy, I'll take care of it. I don't want you to worry about a thing. I'm sorry I can't ring you but I'm getting ready for Mass here. Thinking of you out there walking The Way. Buen Camino!**

Her heart swelled. Once again John had her back. He was the only true friend she had.

Thank you so much! she wrote.

She added a heart emoji to her reply but then deleted it before pressing send.

She then texted Patsy back: **The month's mind is on Friday at 10 o'clock Mass. Sorry, I forgot to pass the information on, the coverage isn't great here. Sophie is not feeling well so she is staying in Cork. Sorry to miss it too. Cathy**

After she sent it she turned her phone off. She didn't want to see or hear any more about it. Putting her phone away, she realised her heart was pounding.

That bloody woman, she thought, wiping a tear away. I was so happy a minute ago and then just one message from her can make me feel like this. Have I done something wrong coming away so soon? Should I have stayed and waited for the month's mind? Oh, I don't know. What am I doing here? Maybe this was a mistake, maybe I should just leave. Who do I think I am, coming away thinking I could do this like a normal person?

She put her head in her hands as the tears came.

CHAPTER 13

Cathy didn't know how long she had been sitting there on the rock. Other walkers passed by. Some wished her a *Buen Camino*, some said nothing. It wasn't unusual to see people shed a tear on the Camino path. Some were mourning a loved one or family member, some were experiencing revelations about their lives, perhaps finding answers to long-held questions.

She felt stuck, she didn't know what to do. This has been a mistake, she decided. Taking the stone from home out of her pocket, she held it in her hand. I had hoped to find a place on this Camino where I could leave this stone behind me as a symbol of all the guilt and inadequate feelings I've had over the years. I just wanted to leave all my emotional baggage behind me but now … it looks like I'm always going to carry it with me. Maybe I shouldn't have come so soon. So much has happened in just four weeks. She sighed, thinking back to that fateful event that changed everything.

She had been sitting in work at the reception desk of Birchgate Nursing home when Ted's brother Mark called.

"Hello?"

She put the switchboard of Birchgate Nursing Home on hold as she answered her mobile. She usually kept her phone on the reception desk when she was working, in case Sophie rang for a quick chat between her lectures.

"Hey, Cathy, it's Mark."

"Oh hi, Mark, how are you?"

Her brother-in-law was always chipper, unlike Ted.

"Grand, yeah. Listen, do you know where Ted is?"

"In work, I presume."

"No, I've just been there – the receptionist said he didn't come in today. He was supposed to come and look at a car with me on his lunch break. I tried ringing him but it's ringing out. Is he out sick or something?"

"No. Well, he wasn't feeling great last night but maybe he just forgot. Did you ask them to page him?"

"The young one in reception tried but no answer. She was looking for him too because he has a meeting this afternoon."

"That's very strange. Unless he decided to visit a company this morning and didn't tell anyone. That sometimes happens. I was up and out before him this morning so I didn't speak to him. I'll try his phone now."

"You needn't bother, it's just ringing out. Look, you're working. I'll drive by the house and see if his car is there."

"Yeah, okay. I'll keep trying his phone anyway. Maybe he thought he was meeting you at the house? Or maybe he went home for his charger. He lets that bloody phone run down to the last bar."

"Yeah, that's probably it. Don't worry, I'll text you from there."

"Grand. There's a spare key under the plant pot at the front door if you need it."

"Okay. Thanks."

Cathy ended the call and looked around. The reception area was empty. It was lunchtime for the residents so things would be quiet for a while until visiting time.

Her hand trembled as she placed her mobile phone down on her desk and she pushed it away from her, as if it were the bearer of bad news. Touching the Miraculous Medal with its image of Mary that hung around her neck, she nervously ran it back and forth on its chain. Then she took her shoulder-length, lank brown hair out of its ponytail scrunchie and tied it back up again. This was a nervous habit she'd developed when she needed to do something with her hands.

She closed her eyes and took a deep breath as a feeling of dread ran through her. *Don't be ridiculous, everything is fine, everything is fine.*

RING!

The sound of the switchboard seemed amplified, making her jump.

Pull yourself together.

Taking another breath, she answered.

"Birchgate Nursing Home, how can I help you?"

Cathy spoke to the caller and transferred his call before taking another, all the time keeping an eye on her mobile. The clock on the wall said it was 1.15. It was time for her lunch, but she couldn't move from her chair.

At last her phone lit up. She let it ring for two rings.

"Mark! Did you find him?"

"Cathy, there's been an accident ... at the house. Ted's had a fall. I called the ambulance immediately and we're on the way to Mullingar General. Get a taxi, will you? Meet us there?"

"Wait! What happened?"

"I don't know ... eh ... look, they're taking us to A&E. I'll wait at the door for you."

"Is he okay? Mark, you're scaring me. *Is he okay?*"

"I don't know ... just get here."

Cathy hung up, grabbed her bag, and ran from the reception desk to the canteen beside the main door to see who was there.

One of the porters was sitting in the canteen, just about to have lunch.

"*Derek! Derek!*"

"Jesus, Cathy, are you okay?"

"No! I need to get to the hospital fast. Something's happened to Ted."

Derek stood up, grabbed his jacket from the back of his chair and gently took her arm.

"Come on, we'll be there in a jiffy," he said, leading her out to the car park.

"I'm scared," Cathy said almost in a whisper as she sat in the passenger seat.

"It'll be grand. He's in good hands," Derek said as they pulled out of the car park and sped down the country road.

He weaved in and out of the lunchtime traffic, ignoring the beeping horns of other drivers.

In no time they were at the Accident and Emergency Department.

Mark was standing there, sucking the last dregs out of his cigarette. He nodded to Derek as the car stopped.

"*Is he okay?*" Cathy said, stepping out of the car.

"I'll park the car," said Derek.

"Mark?" Cathy's heart was thumping.

"I don't know," he said, looking straight ahead. "Come on inside."

"Oh Jesus, you're making me nervous!"

Mark held her arm with his right hand and put his left arm at her back. "They told me to take you to the family room when you got here."

The noise of the hospital reception area faded as they headed down a long corridor. They didn't speak. The only sound was the squeaking of Mark's trainers on the freshly polished floor. The strong smell of disinfectant stung Cathy's nose.

The door of the family room was open and a nurse was there waiting for them.

"Hello, Cathy, I'm Ann." She turned to Mark. "Have you said anything?"

He shook his head as he led Cathy over to a two-seater couch and sat down beside her. The small room had a couch, three plastic chairs and a noticeboard with brochures for organ donations and charity organisations stuck haphazardly over each other, fighting for space.

"What's going on?" Cathy asked, looking from the nurse to Mark.

"When I got to the house," Mark began, "his car was there so I rang the bell but there was no answer. I took the key and let myself in, and … Ted was lying at the bottom of the stairs."

"*Oh god!*" Cathy gasped as her hand flew to her chest.

"He had a gash on his head and there was blood …" Mark trailed off, the memory of what greeted him so fresh in his mind.

"There were pictures knocked off the wall," the nurse said, "consistent with a fall. The Garda specialist will confirm, but it looks like that's what happened."

"So where is he now?"

"Cathy, he didn't make it." Mark started to shake as his tears fell. "I'm so sorry," he said as he put his arm around her, pulling her to him.

"*Wait – no!*" Cathy said, pushing him away. "There must be a mistake," she said, looking desperately at the nurse.

"I'm so sorry, Cathy," the nurse said, taking a seat on her other side. "It looks like a terrible accident. He hit his head against a hall table and I'm afraid that impact, and the bleeding, well ... I'm so sorry."

Cathy bent forward, clutching her stomach. She thought she was going to be sick but instead, when she opened her mouth, she let out a deep sound alien to her.

What followed then was a bit of a blur until the nurse brought her a glass of water and she gulped it down.

Then she heard Mark saying: "I tried my best, Cathy, I swear." He pulled a handful of tissues from the box beside him and blew his nose. "When I opened the door, he was just lying there at the bottom of the stairs. His eyes were closed, and he was unconscious but I thought he was still alive – I mean I didn't know ..." He ran his hands through his hair. "I rang 999 and they got there so fast. I just kept talking to him. I told him everything would be okay." Mark shook his head.

"I just can't believe this," Cathy said in a whisper.

"Falling in the home is a very common cause of head injuries," the nurse said, rubbing Cathy's arm. "It may have been the fall or the bleeding. I'm very sorry."

"I think I'm in shock."

"Of course you are," said the nurse, nodding. "I'm just going to let the doctor know you're here, and he will come in and talk to you."

As the nurse stood up, the door opened and a member of the catering staff came in, pushing a trolley with a pot of tea, two cups on saucers, and a selection of biscuits on a plate with a doily on it.

She left without saying a word or making eye contact with anyone.

"Do you take milk?" the nurse asked as she poured out two cups of tea.

Cathy just nodded.

The nurse moved a small coffee table in front of Mark and Cathy and placed the tea they never asked for and the plate of biscuits down in front of them.

"I'll be right back," she said as she left the room.

Mark was still sobbing, and Cathy passed him the box of tissues that were left on the couch beside her.

Cathy looked at the plate of biscuits, realising she was starving. She would have loved a custard crème but somehow it didn't seem appropriate to eat one even though the nurse had put them there. Instead, she picked up her teacup and took a sip. It tasted strange, metallic in her mouth, so she put it back on the table.

"I can't believe it," she repeated, leaning forward to ease the knot in her stomach. She put her head in her hands. "What am I supposed to do now?"

Mark straightened up and put an arm around her. "We'll all be here for you, Cathy, for you and Sophie."

"Oh Jesus, Sophie!" Cathy said suddenly, sitting up. "How am I going to tell Sophie?"

She took out her phone and brought up Sophie's number and then hesitated.

"I don't want to ring her in case she's working."

"Is she still in Cork?"

"Yes, she got a job in Eason's for the summer. I'll text her to see if she's working today and then I'll ring my cousin Maggie and get her to go around to her, so she won't be on her own when I tell her."

"Was she not living with your cousin?"

"Yes, during term time, but she got a flat last week with friends who are staying in Cork for the summer too. Maggie helped her move so she knows exactly where she is."

"I'm surprised Ted wasn't down there checking the place out," Mark said with a smile. "He was always a little overprotective, shall we say?"

Overprotective is putting it mildly, thought Cathy but she was surprised Mark even said that. Did everyone else notice and say nothing? "What do mean by ..."

Before she could ask him the door opened and a Garda walked in, her hat under her arm.

"Garda Byrne." Mark stood up and shook her hand. "This is my sister-in-law Cathy Kinsella."

"I'm so sorry for your trouble."

Cathy stood up, shook her outstretched hand and looked at Mark in confusion.

"Sorry, I was about to tell you. The Guards arrived after the paramedics. Garda Byrne is dealing with the ... situation."

"Please, please sit down," the garda said, pulling up a plastic chair for herself.

Mark and Cathy sat back down on the couch.

"It's just procedure, Mrs Kinsella," Garda Byrne explained. "When a call comes into the emergency services the ambulance gets the information from the caller." She nodded in Mark's direction. "We attend a lot of emergencies with the ambulance service and, depending on the case, we conduct our own report."

"I see."

"Do you have someone to stay with tonight?"

"*Em* ... I ..."

"It's best not to return to your house tonight. I will liaise with the doctors and the paramedics and complete my report and . . ." she looked at Mark, "you might want someone to ... *eh* ... return things to the way they were."

"Of course," Mark said, nodding at her.

"Oh god ..." Cathy moaned.

"There are specialty companies that deal with this sort of thing so I'll give you their number and I'll ring you when we're finished there," the garda said to Mark.

"I'll get it sorted," Mark assured Cathy. "I won't let you or Sophie back in there until everything is fixed."

They both knew what he was talking about without spelling it out.

"Your brother-in-law gave us a key and there will be a garda there tonight," Garda Byrne said. "It's just procedure."

Cathy nodded. She imagined all the twitching curtains on their terraced road. Ted had planted high hedging around their garden as he was obsessed with the idea that people were looking into their garden or house. His paranoia was completely unfounded but like all his other paranoias there was no talking to him. Having a squad car parked outside their house would bring all the nosey neighbours out now. He would hate that.

CHAPTER 14

While the Garda was there, a young doctor came in to offer his condolences and confirmed that Ted had died from the blow to his head wound. And that was that. There was very little left to say.

"Can I see him?" Cathy asked.

"Yes, of course," the doctor said. "Let me advise the chief nurse and they will come and take you down. Once again I'm very sorry for your loss."

"Thank you, Doctor."

Cathy felt sorry for him. He looked so young to be delivering news like this.

"Okay, let me organise that," he said, turning to leave.

"I'll come with you," Garda Byrne said as she stood up. "After you've seen your husband, I can give you both a lift if you need it?"

"I think Derek, a work colleague of mine, is still around," Cathy said. "He brought me here."

"And my wife Patsy is on her way," Mark said, "so we're grand, thanks, Garda. I'll let Derek go home, Cathy."

Cathy winced. She had never liked Patsy but now she had to be grateful to her for taking her in for a few nights.

"Okay, Mrs Kinsella, if I can take your number, I will call you when we're finished at your house and I will forward you," she turned to Mark "the number of the company that can get things back to the way they were."

Nobody was saying it, but Cathy imagined the bloodstains that must be on the dark-green carpet that she hated, on the old dark wood hall table that was too big and heavy for the space, and maybe on the felt wallpaper that was there for twenty years and Ted was too tight to replace. It was so old that it had faded spots from the sunlight coming in from the small glass strip at the top of the hall door. She hated it. She hated all of it.

After she gave the guard her number an older nurse arrived, introduced herself and took them down to a room at the end of the corridor.

A priest was sitting outside the door, and he stood up as they approached.

"Mrs Kinsella, I'm Father Desmond and I am so sorry for your loss," he said, putting his hand out to Cathy, "and to you also," he said to Mark. "I believe you are the deceased's brother."

"Yes. I'm Mark Kinsella."

"I'm the chaplain here. Would you like me to come in with you?"

"Yes, I would like that." Cathy took a deep breath.

Father Desmond nodded to the nurse, she opened the door and they stepped through.

The nurse stood close to Cathy as she looked around the room, taking in a candle lighting on a bedside locker, then the bed, and then Ted.

Her head spun a little and she had to steady herself before moving forward. There he was. He looked like he was sleeping except for the bandage at the back of his head where he must have hit it.

"*Oh god!*" Mark began to cry again.

Cathy looked at Ted again but didn't feel anything

"Would you like me to say a prayer?" said the chaplain.

"Yes, Father," whispered Cathy and the priest started a decade of the rosary. There was a smell of incense in the room that gave her comfort. Cathy had been a volunteer in her local church for nearly twenty years, not because she was particularly devout, but because it was the only place that Ted approved of her going outside the house without him.

When the decade of the Rosary was done, they thanked the priest and left.

Patsy had arrived and was waiting for them outside the door. Cathy almost laughed when she saw her. Patsy looked comical standing there in her leggings with her apron still on and her UGG slippers. Her round face was red from rushing and strands of her wiry brown short hair were dusted in flour.

"*Oh my god!*" she wailed, pulling Mark and Cathy into a hug.

Cathy wanted to recoil from her, but her grip was strong. Ever the dramatic one, her tears streaked down her blotchy red face. Cathy stood there until the ordeal was over.

"And what about poor Sophie?" asked Patsy.

"She doesn't know yet," Cathy said.

"*What!*"

"Patsy, we haven't had a minute," Mark said.

"I'm going to ring Maggie now ... can you ... give me a minute?" Cathy said, taking out her mobile and sitting down on a plastic chair in the corridor.

"*Em* ... I don't think you should be on your own. I'll stay with you," protested Patsy, nosey as ever.

"Come on," Mark said, leading Patsy away. "We'll give you space. We'll wait for you in the family room."

Oh God give me patience with that woman, thought Cathy as she dialled Maggie's number.

"Maggie?"

"Cathy, you just caught us! Sophie is here – will I put her on?"

"Listen – before you do, I have some terrible news."

"What's happened?"

"I'm glad Sophie is there with you because I need you to look after her."

"What's going on?"

"Ted has had an accident. Somehow, he fell down the stairs and hit his head badly, and ... the blow to the head killed him. He's dead, Maggie."

"*What? Oh, Jesus Mary, and Joseph! I don't believe it, I mean ...*"

"I know. Is Sophie near you?"

"No, she's upstairs packing up the last of her stuff. I'll call her now. Oh Jesus, Cathy, I'm so sorry!"

"I know."

Cathy heard Maggie call Sophie, then Sophie running down the stairs.

"Mum?"

"Hi, love."

"What's wrong?"

"Love, it's your dad."

"Oh. What's he done now?" she sighed, disinterested.

"Nothing. It's nothing like that. He had an accident, at home. He fell down the stairs. And he banged his head and he's ... he's dead, love."

Silence.

"Sophie?"

"But ... how ..." she asked, sounding upset and confused.

"It looks like he hit his head on the hall table. Uncle Mark found him. He was supposed to be meeting him over a car deal or something and your dad never showed up. So when he went round to ours he found him."

"Were you in work?"

"Yes, love. I went straight from there to the hospital."

"Oh my God! Where are you now?"

"Still here. I've just seen him."

"And he's definitely dead?"

"Yes. I've been here with Mark and Patsy has just arrived. I'm staying with them tonight. Listen, love, I'm going to ask Maggie to drive you up. Can you leave today?"

"Yes, of course. Do I have to stay with Patsy too?"

"Yes. It's just till they ... get the house back to the way it was. Sophie? Are you okay?"

"I'll put Maggie back on."

"Hello?"

"Is she okay?"

"Yes, I think she might be in shock."

"Maggie, can you drive her here today?"

"Of course, I'll ring Brian now and get him to come home from work. I'm so sorry, Cathy. I know Ted and I didn't get on, but this is just terrible."

"Yeah," sighed Cathy.

"Look, I'll sort Sophie out here and I'll ring you when we're half an hour away."

"Thanks, I'm sure you can stay in Patsy's too or, if she's full, I'll sort out a B&B nearby."

"Look, we'll sort all that out later. You get on with the arrangements and I'll take care of Sophie. Goodbye, love, and I'm so sorry."

Cathy sat looking at her phone. *Arrangements.* Ted had spoken of his wishes and had written them down in a special file, one of the many 'special files' he kept in an old briefcase. He wanted to be buried in the local graveyard and wanted Cathy to be buried there too. "*Together forever,*" he had said. Not a chance, thought Cathy, I'd rather be thrown in the river. And I won't be tending his grave either. I've spent enough of my life following his rules.

He's gone now.

Looking up she saw a small crucifix on the wall opposite her. Picking up her bag, she walked over to it. Looking around, she saw the corridor was empty, so she moved her mouth closer to it.

"*Thank you, God,*" she whispered. "*I'm free now. Thank you, thank you, thank you!*"

Putting on a sad face, she turned and walked towards the lift where Mark and Patsy were waiting.

CHAPTER 15

That had been only four weeks ago and now, sitting on a rock at the top of a steep hill, Cathy wondered if she had made the right decision to come out here at all.

She stood up, put the stone back in her pocket, and turned to take the path back to Portomarin.

"Excuse me?"

Cathy turned to see a woman with a very large backpack on her back. It had a Japanese flag emblem on it.

"I am sorry to disturb you. But could you take a photo of me, please?"

"Yes, of course." Cathy wiped any remaining tears from her face and, taking a deep breath, put on a smile for the stranger.

She took the smartphone from the woman.

"If you turn this way I can get the valley in," she suggested.

She took the photo. "*Buen Camino!*" she said as she handed the phone back.

"Thank you so much. *Em* ... do you know where the nearest café is for breakfast?" the young woman asked.

"Yes, I do. It's in Gonzar but that's about five or six kilometres from here."

"Oh, I see. I thought that I had missed a yellow arrow."

There was no one else around and the Japanese woman was also walking solo.

I could do with some breakfast, thought Cathy. Maybe I'll walk to Gonzar and get a taxi back from there to Portomarin.

"It's this way." Cathy pointed up ahead. "I'm hoping to get some breakfast there too."

They smiled at each other and started walking at a relaxed pace side by side.

"That is a very big backpack to be carrying all day."

"Yes, I made a mistake, I think. I should have left half my belongings in Santiago in a locker or something."

"You can get your baggage sent on to your next address, you know?"

"Ah yes, but so far I have stayed in albergues. I don't book in advance. I just find one when I arrive in each town so I cannot give a forwarding address. But my bag feels heavy today so maybe I will book somewhere in advance tonight for tomorrow's walk and then send my bag, even for a break of one day."

Cathy nodded in agreement.

"It is hard," continued the stranger, "but I think lots of things are hard and you have to keep going."

"*Hmm*. I don't know. I'm thinking I might go home."

"Why?" asked the young woman turning to Cathy, surprised.

"I just feel all wrong today. I don't know if this is my time to be here."

The Japanese woman nodded and they walked for a few minutes in silence.

"Where are you from?"

"Ireland. Sorry, I'm Cathy, and you?"

"Miyuki and I am from Japan."

"That is a long way to come for the Camino."

"It is part of my trip to Europe. I left Japan one month ago and flew to Finland."

"Do you have friends there?"

"No. I read a book that was set in Finland and decided to go there," Miyuki said, smiling.

"That's amazing!" Cathy tried to guess Miyuki's age. She could have been twenty-eight or thirty-eight. It was hard to judge on the Camino as everyone dressed in hiking clothes and most wore a hat while walking, covering their hair and shading their face from the sun.

"After Finland, I flew to Milan to meet a friend there from the Philippines and we went to Venice and Rome together. And then I flew here."

"So are you taking a long holiday?"

"No. In Japan, we get only five days' holidays from work so I left my job."

"Really?" said Cathy, surprised.

"Yes. I was fed up with my job – every day the same. None of my friends wanted to go travelling so I didn't go anywhere for years. Then I just decided that I have to go or I will regret not doing it, so I left my job and made a plan."

"*Wow*, that's very brave! What did your family and friends think?"

"They thought it was a crazy idea and they were worried about me going on my own but I had to go. I couldn't stay any longer."

"I understand that feeling," Cathy said, looking down at the path as she walked.

For the next fifteen minutes, the two walked side by side, mostly in silence, enjoying the meadows that stretched out on either side of this part of the trail.

"My husband died four weeks ago," Cathy said, breaking the silence.

This was the first time Cathy had said those words.

Miyuki nodded. "I am sorry. Is that why you are here?"

"Yes. I needed to go somewhere to think about my life now. But I think maybe I left home too soon and that some people might think badly of me for doing so."

"But you needed to leave for you."

"Yes ... yes, I did."

"Then it was the right thing to do," Miyuki said, looking straight ahead.

She's right, thought Cathy as they walked on, comfortable in each other's company.

Miyuki didn't ask any questions. She didn't inquire about how he died or how old he was, which was a relief. Cathy had spent a lot of time reliving that day and she didn't want to do it again.

Cathy started to feel a little lighter and soon the big café at Gonzar came into sight.

"Oh, I am happy to see that!" Cathy said. "I'm so hungry."

"Me too."

There was a big queue but the café, which was also an albergue, had a big picture board outside so people could decide what they wanted before they reached the counter.

The smell of bacon and chorizo wafted down the queue, making Cathy's mouth water.

"What are you going to have?" Miyuki asked, looking unsure.

"I think the bacon, eggs, and bread with some coffee," Cathy answered.

"Me too," said Miyuki, nodding.

"Why don't you find a table and set that bag down and I'll order for us?"

"Oh, thank you so much," Miyuki said and went off to get a table for both of them.

Look at me, thought Cathy. Two days ago I didn't know what to order for myself and now I'm ordering for myself and a new friend.

She felt a shift. How incredible is this, she thought as she shuffled along in the queue. Miyuki is exactly the person I needed to meet at that exact time. Maybe I can do this. I need this space. And, anyway, where would I stay if I went home? I don't want to return to my own house, it's too depressing. No, I need to stay here until I figure out my next move.

Cathy looked around to see where Miyuki was sitting and waved to her. As she did, she noticed large, stenciled writing on the wall in English above the table she had selected.

THE CAMINO PROVIDES, it said and Cathy smiled because it had done that this morning. It provided Miyuki just when she was about to give up.

CHAPTER 16

PALAS DE REI

Rachel's legs were burning and her left knee was particularly sore as she limped into the town of Palas de Rei. Whenever she pushed herself in the gym on the peloton stationary bike it was always her left knee that became painful. She put it down to an old basketball injury in secondary school. A push from an opposing player resulted in her twisting her knee and missing the rest of the basketball season. It rarely bothered her, but the extra kilometres today, along with skipping the breakfast stop in Gonzar and not taking a rest had taken a toll on her legs. She did stop twice at small cafés on the route but her goal was to get to the pension as early as possible. But the ground was uneven for the last five kilometres which put extra pressure on her already tender knee.

A lone Galician bagpiper was playing at the edge of the forest as she approached the town. It was a beautiful sound that carried through the trees. It lifted her heart and her spirit as she walked the last kilometre.

The town was very quiet and very hilly so Rachel was relieved when she finally found her pension using Google Maps. Arriving at Pension

Santirso, she enquired from the host and was relieved to find that Simon and Bernie were not booked into the same accommodation. The host informed her that her room was in the attic of the four-storey building so Rachel was relieved to see that the pension had a lift. She didn't think she could manage the stairs on her shaky legs.

Happy to see that her bag had arrived, she dragged it into the lift and went up to the top floor. Without unpacking it, she went straight to the bathroom for a long hot shower, hoping this would ease her burning legs. Wrapped in a towel, she flopped onto the bed. Taking out her phone she saw that she had three texts from Charley asking how she was getting on. I'd better ring her, Rachel thought, she will not believe what's happening here.

Charley was the only true friend she had and when her world was turned upside down by Craig, she was the only person she could confide in.

The days following Craig's betrayal Rachel had spent indoors in her pyjamas. When she got sick of her own company she threw on her gym gear and went for a run down to Sandymount Strand and back. She wasn't a runner and usually preferred the treadmill in the gym to exercising outside but she wanted to avoid any chance of bumping into Craig and hoped the crisp sea air would clear her head somehow.

When she texted him saying that she would not be attending his rearranged meeting with the bank, he was furious. He bombarded her with phone calls and texts and called to her house twice. She didn't answer the door or engage with him but she was feeling exhausted by it all and she hated to admit it but she missed him too.

She hadn't spoken to anyone about what had happened but she needed to now. His constant messages were making her jumpy. She was also second-guessing her decision to finish their relationship. It would be so much easier to take him back. She needed to talk to someone about it and there was only one person who knew her and would understand what she was going through and that person was Charley.

Charley and Rachel grew up together in a housing estate just outside Cork City. They attended the same schools and also went to University College Cork together. Charley settled in Cork and ran a gorgeous Bed and Breakfast in the city centre where she lived with her husband Seán and young children.

As Charley was busy in Cork and Rachel in Dublin, they didn't see each other often but if Charley could get away to Dublin for a break, Rachel always rearranged her plans to have her stay with her. They usually hung out in their jammies in Rachel's house, drinking vodka and eating snacks, like they were college students again. She was the one person Rachel could let her guard down with and totally be herself with.

When she picked up the phone and rang her, sobbing down the phone, Charley rearranged her day and was on the road within an hour. Rachel knew that she had to get the message through to Craig once and for all. So, knowing Charley was on her way and would be staying for a few days, she messaged Craig and arranged to meet him at the Sandymount Hotel around the corner.

By the afternoon, when Rachel opened the door to see Charley standing there, things were done and dusted.

"I love your flower display," Charley said jokingly, looking at the bouquets from Craig withering outside the front door.

Rachel smiled, hugged her friend, and sobbed again.

"This calls for vodka," Charley said, stepping into the house and marching down Rachel's hallway to the kitchen. She plonked her holdall down on the kitchen table, opened it and took out a bottle of vodka, two litres of Diet Coke, and multipacks of crisps and tortilla chips.

"Did you bring any clothes at all?" said Rachel, laughing.

"No, just my PJ's, and this lot. Right, get the glasses and some ice from that fancy fridge of yours."

Sitting at Rachel's kitchen table, the whole story came out.

"Ah Jesus Christ, what the fuck!" Charley sat back in shock. "What a bad asshole he is!"

"I know. I just feel so stupid that I didn't see these signs beforehand. I mean I knew he considered himself a big shot and I knew he had a big ego but that's what made him good at his job. He was like a dog with a bone, never giving up until he got what he wanted. I knew he could be tough in negotiations but I loved him and he said he loved me. I thought we were so suited to each other in business and in the bedroom. He made me feel like I was the only woman in the world for him. Well, obviously I wasn't ... I wasn't enough for him."

"It's not you! You are enough. You are too good for that wanker!" said Charley, shaking her head.

"I just can't believe he would do such a thing." Rachel rested her head in her hands. "He did admit it straight away and says it will never happen again but how do I believe that? If I hadn't have gone to his apartment I would never have known. I've been so stupid hoping that he was the one I could plan a future with."

"You are not stupid, girl," Charley said, reaching across and squeezing her friend's arm. "Think of it as a lucky escape. You came so close to signing yourself up to him in business and moving him in here. I know you're devastated now but you will be so thankful this happened now and not down the line when you would be legally tied to the prick."

Charley called a spade a spade and she was right too.

"You never liked him, did you?"

"Not really. Too handsome for my liking. Slick Dick, I used to call him."

Rachel laughed. "I never knew that!"

"Well, I was hardly going to call him that to his face, now was I? So tell me what happened when you met him today," Charley said, topping up both their glasses.

"I texted him and told him I wanted to meet him at the Sandymount Hotel. He was there when I arrived. He looked so good, I just wanted to fall into his arms and forget it ever happened but I had to steady myself and stand firm. He stood up and immediately tried to hug me. And I said in a very calm and low voice '*Don't touch me*'. Well, his face dropped and then he looked at the case and said, 'Going somewhere?' smiling like it was something funny. So I said, 'No, this is all your stuff and I want it out of my house'. We were still standing in the lobby at this stage. So he softened his face and turned on the charm, saying how he'd made a mistake and that I was the best thing to happen to him and …" Rachel hesitated.

"What?"

"I could see that he was hurting and I do believe that he wants me back. He looked drained as if he hadn't slept and he said he was sorry again but I don't know if he is sorry for cheating on me or just sorry he got caught and messed everything up. Is he upset about losing me or upset about losing the business? That's the problem. I can't tell which it is and I don't know if I can believe a word he says. It was so hard standing there in front of him. Part of me nearly gave in. If I pretended it didn't happen the business would be back on track but I couldn't do it. I would never have a moment's peace, wondering what he was up to, always on the lookout for signs. But I can't just turn off my feelings either and that's what hurts the most because I know the ball is my court and I'm not picking it up even if it breaks my heart. So I had to stick to my guns."

"Jesus! How did he take it?"

"He wasn't happy. He's so used to winning. He wanted to go somewhere quieter to talk about it but I deliberately picked that hotel lobby because it's always busy with people coming and going and I was afraid he might convince me to change my mind."

"So how did it end?"

"He asked if I needed more time and I said no, my decision was final. Everything between us was over and I needed him to stop contacting me. He looked devastated. He's left his apartment and is sleeping in his friend Roger's place. He asked me to think about it over the weekend and call him anytime day or night. And then I just walked away."

"*Good for you, girl!*" Charley said, pumping her fist in the air.

"My legs were shaking and I'm still afraid that he'll come to try to get me to change my mind."

"He wouldn't, would he? After today?"

"I don't know. My nerves are shot. Every time I hear a car pull up I think it's him. That's why I need to get away. I need space to think everything through."

Charley sighed. "Well, you'll certainly get plenty of space on the Camino, girl."

"Oh god, how did I get here?" Rachel said, taking a sip of her drink. "And how did I let another man blindside me again?"

"Simon never cheated on you but I know what you mean. He's back in Ireland now by the way, divorced, single, and looking after his mammy."

Rachel looked at Charley, exasperated. "Seriously? You're bringing him up now?"

"Oh, I'm sorry. You're right, let's not talk about men at all."

"Thank you. You're supposed to get drunk with me and let me wallow in the mess I've made of my life."

"Yes, boss!" Charley smiled as she topped up Rachel's glass again.

Just then the doorbell rang.

"Are you expecting anyone?"

"No. Oh my god, it must be him! I don't fucking believe it!" Rachel put her head in her hands

"You sit there and let me handle this," Charley said, standing and straightening herself up before walking down the hall.

Rachel got up from the table and stood behind the kitchen door, leaving a tiny gap so she could see and hear everything.

Charley answered the door and Craig's face went from smiling to confused.

"Hello, can I help you?" Charley said, looking him straight in the eye.

"Ah yes," he said, composing himself, "I'm here to see Rachel."

"She's not here."

"I need to speak to her."

"She's not here. She's gone away and I'm minding her house for her."

"I ... I just saw her today."

"Yes, I know. I know *everything*," Charley said, while giving him a filthy look.

"Look, I need to speak to her – when will she be back?"

"I don't think that is any of your business."

"I beg your pardon?" he said, looking annoyed and flustered. "I'm her business partner and it is precisely our business that I want to talk about."

"I believe she made it quite clear that she was done with you, Slick Dick!"

"Excuse me?"

Rachel had to put her hand over her mouth to stop herself from laughing.

Charley leaned towards him. "Listen up, you!" she said in her strongest Cork accent. "I believe she told you that she is done with you, Craigy boy, and yet here you are. So the question is, Craig, why are you still here at her door?"

"Listen here, I don't know who you are but –"

"Well, we've met twice actually but you're too ignorant to remember."

"*Who do you think you are?*" he said through gritted teeth.

"You are not welcome here. If you call here again I will call the Guards. And if you still don't get the message, I have five fine big brothers at home who will call over to your friend Roger's house and help you understand!"

"What? How do you –?"

"Oh yeah, I know everything, Craig. It's over. So back off and give her some space and don't come here again unless you're invited because I'll be here from now on. Now, get back in your fancy car and *FUCK OFF, YOU LANGER!*" She yelled the last bit so the neighbours walking by could hear.

Craig almost fell backward in shock.

Charley relished his expression for a few seconds before slamming the door in his face.

"Oh my god, I can't ... I can't believe you did that!" Rachel's jaw was hanging open as Charley walked back down the hall.

"Actually, I can't believe I did that myself. Look, my hands are shaking!" She held out her hands.

"You were amazing!" Rachel said, throwing her arms around her.

"Well, that's fixed him now. He won't be calling here again," Charley said, sitting back down at the table. "So top up my drink there and tell me about this big walk you're doing."

Rachel smiled as she remembered. Charley was like her knight in shining armour, rushing in to protect her when she needed her most, and now she needed her again.

Propping herself up on the bed with some pillows she leaned back against the headboard and rang her friend.

"Hello from the top of a mountain somewhere in Spain!" Rachel said as soon as Charley answered the phone.

"*Aw*, I'm delighted you rang. How are you getting on?"

"Well, this is my third day here and my second day walking and right now I'm lying on my bed dreading when I have to move again because the backs of my legs are burning."

"Ah, you poor pet! I hope you haven't overdone it and walked too fast. Take your time, you know how competitive you are. Are you stretching? Are you putting the Vaseline on your feet?"

"Yes, all of that, but honestly if I never walk again it will be the least of my problems here."

"What do you mean?"

"Brace yourself. Simon is here."

"*What! Simon Molloy?*"

"The very man. I arrived at my pension yesterday after my first day walking – completely sweaty, with no make-up on, and the first person I see is Bernie Molloy sitting there. That was the first shock. Then I turned around, and there he was, standing in front of me: Simon Molloy."

"I ... that's *fucking crazy!*"

"You're telling me. I swear to god, between this and the daily emails from Craig, I am going to crack up."

"No, you won't! I hope you are not replying to that Craig fella?"

"No, I'm not. I can't even think about him now Simon is bloody well here. And poor Bernie. I always liked her and I haven't seen her in years, but she doesn't look well at all."

"She was going through treatment during the lockdown. That's when Simon came home but my mum said she saw her recently and she looks very frail."

"She does. So I don't want to be rude by trying to avoid her but I just can't handle all these emotions right now. And your mum had no idea they were doing the Camino?"

"No."

"What a crazy coincidence!"

"How did he look?"

"He ... he looked great. That's the problem. I hate myself for saying this but all the old feelings came back. And I'm not imagining this but ... there was definitely some chemistry, feelings ... don't know, something between us."

"*Wow!* Well ... would it be the worst thing in the world if ..."

"Ah, Jesus, Charley! I came here to get my head straight after one asshole ruined my life only to run into another! This is the last thing I need."

"Well, at least Simon is an asshole who's good to his mother."

Rachel laughed. "Oh, I wish you were here. I ended up pouring my heart out to two strangers last night. I only met them two days ago and now they know the whole history between me and Simon."

"It's not like you to make friends – what's happened to you?" joked Charlie.

"*Ha, ha*, very funny. There was a mix-up on the first night and I had to share a room with them and they turned out to be very nice. I needed someone to bounce things off."

"Are Simon and Bernie on the same trip? Do you have to see them every day?"

"No. They are doing the same route but Bernie can't walk that much, so they walk a bit and taxi a bit and sometimes they stay two nights in places. In fact, the reason my legs are burning is that I walked like crazy to get here early to check if they were booked in here tonight but they're not."

"But what could you do about that?"

"I was going to stay somewhere else."

"*Aw*, Rachel, that's nuts. Why don't you let the Universe take care of it, or the Camino? Maybe this was meant to be."

"Charley, don't. It's not funny."

"I'm not being funny but what are the chances of bumping into Simon Molloy anywhere in the world, never mind up a mountain on the Camino? Surely it must mean something?"

"Have you been drinking? I rang for some sympathy and maybe a way out of this, not ... more drama in my life!"

"I'm just saying if you want to move on from Craig and you still feel something for Simon and you think he does too, well, you're both single ... so ... would it be the worst thing in the world if –"

"*Yes! Yes, it would*. I can't even think about that. And it's not that easy to forget Craig. I did love him, you know, and we had a life planned together."

"Okay, okay, I'm sorry. So what are you going to do?"

"I'm going to get up early tomorrow and walk fast like today and keep one step ahead of him if I can. I need to put both men out of my mind and think only of myself."

"Okay, well ... I do love you and I hate to see you hurting, so do whatever you need to."

"Yeah," sighed Rachel.

"Ring me tomorrow, okay, or any time."

"Thanks, I will. Bye."

Rachel hung up and stared at the ceiling. How could she clear her head and make plans for a life without Craig when she still missed his arms around her? And when she wasn't missing him she was thinking about Simon, how good he looked, and how much she wanted to reach out and push his long side fringe out of his eyes?

CHAPTER 17

PALAS DE REI

Cathy called into a supermarket when she arrived in Palas de Rei. She was so happy with how her walk went today but was exhausted and decided to eat in her room rather than go out to dinner tonight. After walking with people all day, she fancied a night in by herself. She messaged Rachel and Paula to let them know and Rachel replied immediately to say that she would be having an early night too and would be skipping dinner.

Pension Santirso was a tall four-storey building at the edge of the town. After Cathy checked in, she picked up her suitcase and the very kind host showed her to her room. It had a double and a single bed and was so quiet. Cathy was delighted with it. She unpacked her bag, put her supermarket shopping out on a desk in the corner, and then took a very long shower.

Taking some Ibuprofen and paracetamol for her aching legs and hips, she lay back on the double bed and sighed. Despite her sore legs and burning feet, she felt really happy. What a day it had been! Walking with

Miyuki today had been the greatest gift. She came along just when I needed her, she marvelled.

After breakfast with her in Gonzar, Cathy told Miyuki about her plans to meet the Spanish prayer group at twelve in Ligonde.

"*Hmm* ... I do not believe in God or religion but I do love churches," said Miyuki.

"Oh, then please come. The group is so nice. I only met them yesterday but they made me feel so welcome and less ... afraid."

"Sure I will come with you. Like you, I am travelling alone and most times it is nice but it is also nice to meet people. We can be so different and from very different parts of the world and yet we can also be so alike."

Cathy nodded in agreement and, after they ate, they got their stamp for their pilgrim passport and started walking again.

About half an hour before Ligonde, Cathy checked her watch.

"We have made great time – we are actually a little early. Will we stop for a coffee?"

"Oh yes, please."

Up ahead there was a cluster of buildings. Some were whitewashed with wrought-iron balconies, others in original brick. Narrow pergolas attached to the buildings provided support for grape vines that twisted themselves around the wooden frames. Window boxes of red geraniums lined the narrow street, throwing out their scent as they passed. Up ahead one of the buildings had a sign for coffee and 'SELLO' meaning stamp.

"If we stop here we can get our second stamp," Cathy said excitedly. This would fulfil the daily two-stamp requirement in their pilgrim passport, getting it done before midday.

The café had a lovely garden space with plenty of seating for weary walkers. Big wooden pergolas with mature vines growing on them provided shade from the sun. They chose a table in the shade and then went inside to order. The café countertop had a giant tortilla on a cake stand, the biggest Cathy had ever seen, and beside that a cake with a Saint James' Cross on it and a sign that read *Tarte de Santiago*.

"I think I need cake," Miyuki said with a smile.

"Me too. *Dos tarte de Santiago y dos café.*"

Cathy used her school Spanish to order and was delighted when the café owner understood what she was saying. She felt her confidence growing with every new encounter on this Camino.

They carried their tarte and café outside and sat in the sun, enjoying the delicious almond and lemon-flavoured cake, common everywhere along the Camino. The crumbly pastry base and light almond filling melted in the mouth while giving a much-needed sugar boost.

"*Miyuki!*" A tall man in his fifties came over to shake Miyuki's hand.

"Dan, this is Cathy," Miyuki said, turning to introduce her. "And, Cathy, this is Dan who I met on the road yesterday. How are you today, Dan?"

"I am okay," he sighed. "Still putting one foot in front of the other."

His accent was American – East Coast, Cathy guessed.

"Dan has been walking for four weeks now," Miyuki explained to Cathy.

"I so admire you – that's a long time walking," said Cathy.

"Well, some things take a long time to work out," he said, looking away. "I'd better get moving. Nice to meet you, Cathy, and lovely to see you again, Miyuki."

He bowed to Miyuki, Japanese style, and she bowed back where she sat before he headed off.

"It is very sad," Miyuki said. "Dan lost his wife six months ago. They were supposed to do this trip together. He is heartbroken and he is carrying her ashes."

Cathy gasped. "Just like *The Way*," she said, looking after him as he headed out of town.

"Yes, the movie. He said that yesterday but I did not know what he meant. I didn't see it."

"I have seen it about ten times. It's about the Camino. The main actor comes here because his son gets lost in bad weather and dies going over the Pyrenees. He then takes his ashes and finishes the journey for him, leaving some of his ashes along the way."

"Ah, that makes sense now!" Miyuki nodded.

Looking around, Cathy reckoned there were about twenty walkers sitting enjoying a drink in the sunshine. How many of them were carrying heartache like Dan? she wondered. How many were grieving? Maybe they came here because people would understand and not ask questions. You can bare your soul to people here because you know that you'll probably never see them again. There is a liberation in that. So many stories but also so many listeners.

Cathy looked away. What must it be like to love someone so much that you carry their ashes with you? There was no way she would have brought Ted's ashes with her. Carrying them would feel like he was still watching her every move. I would sooner flush them down the toilet, to make sure he was gone for good, she thought, as she turned back to finish her tarte.

After their break, they walked on to Ligonde. Arriving at the church, Cathy introduced Miyuki to the Spanish group.

Miyuki stayed for a few minutes and then decided to walk ahead.

"I will see you on the road. You walk faster than me so you might catch up with me and maybe we will get to Palais de Rei together," Miyuki said, smiling.

"Thank you for today," Cathy said as she hugged her Camino friend, not knowing if she would see her again. But this is the way of the Camino, she thought as she went to celebrate Mass with her Spanish friends and be thankful for Miyuki.

She didn't catch up with Miyuki but walked the rest of the way with Father Eduardo's group. After her confidence wobble that morning she didn't want to be alone today but she knew that sooner or later she would need to take some time to walk alone in order to figure things out and find a new way forward in her life.

CHAPTER 18

PALAS DE REI

Lying on her bed in the pension, Cathy took out her phone. Clicking into her banking app, she opened her account. She loved looking at her balance and counting the zeroes. She never had a smartphone before, just a basic Nokia one but Sophie made her buy one after Ted died so they could keep in contact through WhatsApp and Instagram. Sophie uploaded all the apps she needed and taught her how to use them. One of those apps was the banking app and the money from their joint account had been transferred to her account the day before she left for this trip.

She had no idea Ted had so much money in his account. Having been on a tight budget for their whole married life, with no updating of the house, no foreign holidays and no new car, she nearly fell over when the bank manager transferred the amount that was sitting in their joint account to her personal one.

She thought the only account they had together was for the mortgage. She knew Ted had a savings account and when she asked about getting the house painted or going on holiday he always said they needed to budget for the future and they could do those things later. But later never came. And all that time Ted had a direct debit going into this other joint account with both their names on it. They must have opened it together with the mortgage account when they first married but Cathy had no recollection of it.

She couldn't believe that just under two hundred thousand euros had been sitting there in both their names. She could have taken money out at any time if only she had known about it.

Ted was so tight. She had to give him a receipt for everything she spent which he then filed away in boxes. She had very little money of her own to spend even though she worked full-time, as her salary went into their joint account.

Ted transferred one hundred euros into her account every week for the food shop. He took care of everything else. This was a system he set up after Sophie was born.

Cathy had been so tired in the weeks following Sophie's birth, later realising that she had also suffered from post-natal depression. She had thought the 'baby blues' were normal and her mother reinforced this idea by telling her she'd get over it, but when the district nurse visited to weigh Sophie and check up on both of them, she suggested that Cathy speak to GP about it.

But her mother disagreed with the district nurse and insisted it was normal to feel this way and that it would pass. Cathy was too tired to make her own way to the doctor's office so she never did get it checked out. The loneliness didn't help her mood either. As Ted took the car to work each day, she relied on her mother's visits to stop her going insane. Being the youngest in the family by fifteen years and having elderly parents meant she had very little support from her family when Sophie came along.

There were other mums in the estate but Ted didn't want people 'knowing their business', as he called it. He never spoke to the neighbours and dissuaded her from making friends.

"People talk and twist things," he used to say and, then, when she queried this he would say that he just wanted to keep their family in a private bubble just for them.

He didn't like her mother calling too often either so she didn't always tell him when she had been. She knew that wasn't normal behaviour but she also didn't have the energy to quarrel with him over it.

It was around this time that Ted suggested her wages go into a joint account while she was on maternity leave so that she didn't have to worry about money and, as she was adjusting to motherhood, it seemed like a good idea at the time.

"I will take care of everything," he'd said.

She had heard that line from him so many times. At first, it was a relief. He took care of all the bills and the mortgage, and all she had to do was get the weekly shopping done and cook the meals.

As Sophie got older and needed more things, she asked to have access to the bank accounts, but Ted would say there was no need.

"All you have to do is ask," he'd say. "Have I ever refused you anything?"

Whenever she asked, he did write a cheque straight away or bring home whatever cash she needed but that was not the same as Cathy having access to their accounts and he knew it.

She had no idea how many accounts Ted had or how much was in them. So, when it came to the funeral, this was a problem. Cathy was afraid it would look bad if she went running to the bank just days after her husband had died to see how much he had in his accounts and she didn't know how long it would take to process his will.

But she did know someone who could help her with that.

The morning after Ted died, while she was staying with Patsy and Mark, the funeral conversation came up. Patsy actually brought it up.

"I know it's hard, Cathy, but we need to organise the funeral, you know. Maybe we could visit your friend the priest?"

"Yes, of course. The only problem is that Ted dealt with the money in our house and, to be honest, I have no idea how much is in our accounts. I think they are all in Ted's name. I know he has a will in the house and he definitely had life insurance. He kept all the important documents in an old briefcase – that's in the house. And I don't know how long these things take to process. So, I may need yourself and Mark to cover the funeral costs until I get access to the accounts."

Patsy and Mark looked at each other in dismay.

"*Em* ... I'm sure we can ... come up with ..." Mark started.

"What Mark is saying," Patsy said, interrupting him, "is that I'm sure we can help you sort everything out with the bank and the solicitor too."

Cathy knew well how tight Patsy was and that she would never agree to pay for her brother-in-law's funeral.

"I was going to ring the bank myself but I was afraid of how it would look with Ted only recently passed ..." Cathy said, pulling out a tissue from her sleeve to blow her nose.

"You don't worry about any of that now," Patsy said, coming around to Cathy and putting a hand on her shoulder to comfort her. "Mark will ring for you."

"B-but I don't think they will g-give me that information," stuttered Mark.

"Just ring your pal, Larry MacMahon – he'll sort this out," Patsy said, nodding at the door and signalling for Mark to make the call immediately.

Mark, given his orders, left the kitchen to make his call and came back a few minutes later.

"Larry says we need a solicitor to sort it. I gave you Philip Nolan's number, Cathy, didn't I?"

"The solicitor? Yes, you did. Is it too soon to ring him? Would it look bad?"

"Not at all," Patsy said, sitting down in front of her. "Listen now, what goes on in a solicitor's office is confidential but we could ask him to come here if that suits you."

Cathy nodded.

"Mark, ring Philip," she said over her shoulder, not even looking at him.

Cathy marvelled at how Patsy could just tell Mark what to do and he'd do it. She could never have done that with Ted.

"So now, love, try to remember where Ted kept that old briefcase with the will and everything else in it."

"Oh, I know – it's in the bottom drawer of the bureau in our bedroom but there's a combination lock on it."

Patsy nodded to Mark.

"Okay, leave that to me," said Mark, putting his jacket on. "I'll go up to the house and get that. Larry did say that there is a joint account so he can transfer funds from that to your account or give you the details but we need to go into his office to sign forms. He said we would need a death certificate and a marriage certificate to sort everything else out. A doctor at the hospital would have had to sign off on the death cert so I can ring the hospital or I could ring Garda Byrne who was dealing with the case. She probably knows all about this kind of thing."

"Would you? I'd be very grateful," Cathy said, twisting her handkerchief, "and our marriage certificate is in that briefcase too."

"Great. Sure, we have everything we need so," Patsy said, all businesslike. "Mark will go to the house and take the briefcase to the solicitor and we can go to the bank. After that, we can talk to your priest friend and make the arrangements. Now, time for a cup of tea, love!"

Patsy stood up, rubbing her hands together, obviously relieved to have got out of parting with any money.

"Thank you, you've been marvellous, Patsy," Cathy said, smiling.

Patsy was full of energy now. There was no way she was going to let one penny of her money be spent on Ted's funeral.

Just as I expected – her meanness around money is working in my favour, thought Cathy. She'll get Mark working on the paperwork and she'll get those bank accounts sorted out for me and I can just sit back and let them do it.

CHAPTER 19

Paula looked at her watch as she walked through a small village. A farmer passed her herding cattle up the road and she smiled and waved as he passed, although the smell from the cows was almost overpowering.

She was following the yellow arrows on the walls of the bare-bricked farm buildings. Maybe an hour more to go, she guessed. Today felt longer or maybe the excitement and first day nerves of yesterday made the time go quicker. Either way, she felt tired and the little toe on her right foot was throbbing, indicating that a blister might be on its way.

She could hear the chatter of conversation up ahead. Turning a corner, she saw a small blackboard with "*Café e Sello*" written on it and when she looked in through what looked like a farm gate, she saw a very pretty garden café. White plastic tables and chairs had been placed around the garden and window boxes and flowerpots provided a mix of colour and wonderful scents. Although it made sense to plod on and just get the bloody walk done, she craved a cold drink. The water she had been carrying was warm now and not cutting her thirst at all.

Queuing up inside the small café, she ordered a Coca-Cola Lite and then carried it out to a shaded seat in the corner of the garden. Putting down her poles, she pulled over a chair opposite to her and lifted each leg to rest on it.

That's better, she thought, taking a sip of her ice-cold drink and closing her eyes for a minute. When she opened them again a woman was standing in front of her, smiling.

"Hi there, I didn't want to disturb you but my pole is under your seat."

"Oh, I'm sorry! Let me get it for you." Paula leaned down and picked it up. "I was just taking a breather."

"Thank you," the woman said, taking the pole.

"You're Irish too?"

"Yes, I'm Sheila. I'm from Kildare."

"I'm Paula, from Dublin"

"How are the feet holding up?"

"Well, they're very tired at the moment but, sure, not long to go. The thought of a shower and my bed will get me going again in a minute."

"That's a good motivator alright. See you on the road." Sheila waved as she headed off.

People are just so nice, thought Paula. So many women here seem to be travelling solo and most are over fifty. I wonder if that's the same all year round? I must ask Carlos. Carlos ... is it wrong that I look forward to talking to him?

This would never happen at home but here she'd had chats with so many different men and women on the Camino. It's such a natural thing to do when you are walking along and someone says *"Buen Camino"* and you say *"Buen Camino"* back and then they might carry on walking or they might ask where you are from and you strike up a conversation and that's it. It's two people sharing a common journey. And then you might, or might not, see them again.

But she knew it was different with Carlos. She was drawn to him. For years that side of life, the sexual side, for her and Kevin had ... well, it wasn't dead but it wasn't on fire either. Completely natural, of course. They were both older, used to each other, together thirty-five years, so you don't expect sparks. Or at least that's what she thought up to a week ago. Before that she thought they were both happy enough with how things were between them.

She sighed heavily, wondering again if her moodiness and frustrations about hitting sixty had led Kevin to tire of her.

The disastrous birthday party nearly tipped her over the edge. She cringed when she remembered what happened.

"Happy Birthday to you! Happy birthday to you!"

Paula had smiled as Kevin carried out the huge birthday cake. He was singing and smiling. Everyone was. Jessica and Michael walked on either side of their dad. She loved them to bits. Jessica was smiling but looked anxious as usual. Michael was swaying a bit, tipsy as usual.

Paula looked around. The smiling faces of lifelong friends and work colleagues all looking in her direction, clapping and singing along, made her feel so self-conscious. Feeling very insecure about her new grey pixie haircut, she nervously pushed a strand of hair behind her ear as everyone took out their phones to take pictures. Most of her friends were in their sixties now and some were retired or were planning it. Where did the time go, she wondered as she smiled anxiously at them now.

They used to have so much fun together, at rock concerts, festivals and camping holidays when the kids were small. Now all the talk was about pensions, taking up bridge and playing golf.

She felt lightheaded.

The *Happy 60th Birthday* banner reflected the coloured lights of the rugby-club hall. The buffet had looked nice, but she couldn't touch any of it.

What is wrong with me?

She felt hot, her mouth felt so dry. She tried to smile but her face felt numb. She never wanted this party. It was Kevin's idea. She knew she should feel grateful. Everyone seemed to be enjoying themselves. But she wasn't. She hated being the centre of attention like this, she liked to socialise in smaller groups, unlike Kevin who loved being in the middle of everything.

Even tonight he had spent the whole night talking and buying pints for everyone as if it was his party. It was exactly the kind of party he loved. She just felt detached from it all.

What's wrong with me?

They were still singing. She could see their lips move but it sounded muffled. Looking around at friends and family who loved her, she felt panicked. Was it turning sixty? She looked at her friends. Was this it? What was there to look forward to? Bridge? Golf? Retirement villages in Spain?

Her breath quickened. She knew she was lucky and that she should feel grateful but right now she felt panicked.

She tried to smile again. They were still singing. Her breathing quickened. Her skin felt clammy. She felt claustrophobic. Her clothes felt tight as if they were strangling her. *Happy Birthday, dear Paula, Happy Birthday to you!* As her family and friends approached, a single tear ran down her face. She felt her chest tighten.

She looked at her family, grown-up kids leading their own lives now and her friends winding down their lives.

I want something different in my life ... I need something different...

Trying to catch her breath, she gasped for air and then passed out.

———— ❈ ————

She woke up in the back of an ambulance. It had to be the stress of the party, a party she didn't want. And poor Kevin had been so worried. The doctor said it was an anxiety attack and sent her home with a mindfulness and meditation brochure and signed her off work for a week.

Why couldn't I just go with the flow? she had said to herself, embarrassed at having brought all this on herself by overthinking everything.

She took a few days off work and promised herself that she would practise mindfulness and gratefulness and try to be happy with her lot. And that approach seemed to be working until she got a WhatsApp message that triggered her anger and frustration again.

She was standing in a queue at her local supermarket, staring into space, when her phone buzzed in her hand. It was a WhatsApp from Aileen.

New Group – Paula's 60th at the Villa!

Oh no! Paula could feel her frustration rising.

"Next!"

I said I was going away and for her *not* to organise anything.

"Next!"

"Oh, I'm sorry," Paula hadn't heard the cashier calling her. She pushed her sandwich, apple, and bottle of juice down the belt.

"That'll be seven euro eighty-five, please," the cashier said in a bored voice.

"Thank you," Paula said, rooting around in her purse for change.

The man behind her sighed heavily.

"Oh here, I'll tap," she said, pulling out her bank card, feeling flustered.

"Take your time," the cashier said, smiling at Paula before glaring at the impatient man behind.

"Thank you. I'm just frustrated today," she said, tapping.

"Aren't we all?" the cashier said as she handed her the receipt. "Next!"

Paula walked to her car and started to angry-eat her sandwich.

Bloody Aileen, I told her it didn't suit. I told her I was going away with Jill.

"*For God's sake!*" she shouted before taking a deep breath in, holding it for a count of six, and letting it out slowly. She had been practising breathing techniques from different relaxation apps the hospital had recommended since the incident at the party.

Why am I getting so angry about this? she wondered, shaking her head. It's a very generous gesture.

If that cashier knew why I was annoyed she'd think I was an ungrateful cow. But I won't be forced into a jolly party in Spain just because everyone else wants it.

Finishing her lunch without even tasting it, she drove back to school and went straight to Jill's office.

"*Come in!*" Jill called out when Paula knocked. "Oh, it's you," she said, looking up. "I didn't see you at lunchtime. Did you go out?"

"Yes, I forgot my bloody lunch."

"Go easy on yourself. It's not even a week since the party and your fabulous exit!"

"*Ha ha*, very funny." She sat down opposite Jill.

"Honestly, I nearly laughed when you passed out because I didn't know if it was a brilliant stunt or not."

"I'm not that good an actress."

"But, seriously, how are you feeling?"

"I'm fine. They checked everything at the hospital, so all good."

"Well, if you need some more time off just ask, okay?"

"Thanks, I'm fine honestly, but I'm actually here about the Camino. Is your offer still open?"

"Yes, of course," Jill said, leaning back in her chair, looking very surprised. "What's changed your mind?"

"I've been thinking about it and I need to get away and sort my head out without anyone near me, well, except you, obviously."

"Oh, as I told you, I am perfectly capable of ignoring you for hours on end, believe me. I go for the quiet too. Did you have a look at the email I sent you with the itinerary from *Follow the Camino*?"

"Yes and no. Yes, I opened it and Kevin read it, but it looks perfect to me."

"Are you sure? You should read it, it has kilometres and gradients ..."

"I don't need to. I'm one hundred percent sure this is what I need."

"Great! Well, I'll ring the company now and get you booked. It's not an organised tour with a group of other people. The company books the flights, accommodation and baggage transfers. You get breakfast along the way and the accommodation is in small pensions and some small hotels. These towns are small so it's nothing fancy. Are you okay with that?"

"Yes, that sounds perfect."

"I can see if they have a single room but at this late stage we might be sharing."

"I'm fine with that if you are?"

"Great, consider it done. I'll get them to email you the flight details and costs. This is great news. I really think you will get something out of it."

"Thanks, Jill, you're a lifesaver," Paula said, getting up.

"Make sure you read the emails when they come in. It's a bit more than just a walk, you know," Jill said as Paula was leaving.

"I will, I will, I will!" Paula laughed as she left and closed the door behind her.

I'm actually doing this, she thought, feeling relief flood over her. I'm going on an adventure.

Paula had been so excited to get home to tell Kevin she was definitely going on the Camino and he couldn't have been more supportive.

His car was in the driveway as he was working from home today.

"*I'm home!*" Paula called out as she put the key in her front door.

"*In here!*"

Being semi-retired meant that he worked two half days from home and one full day in the office. This was his choice. He liked to go into in the office one day a week to keep up to speed on everything and stay in touch with the staff.

Paula threw her car keys into a bowl they kept near the front door on what they called the telephone table although it was many years since a telephone sat there.

Kicking off her shoes, she slid her feet into the flip-flops that she kept under the telephone table and headed down the hall to the kitchen.

"Fancy a cuppa?" she asked Kevin who was sitting at the kitchen table, engrossed in something on his laptop.

"Yes, please."

"There's no biscuits, mind – I've haven't done the shopping yet."

Filling the kettle, Paula hummed an Abba song she'd just heard on the car radio.

"You're in good form?" Kevin said, turning around in his seat to face her.

"Well ... I have news," she said, switching on the kettle and turning to face him.

"Go on," he said with a nod.

"The travel agent got back to Jill and they have a place for me on her Camino trip so it's done, I'm booked."

"That's great news!" Kevin's face lit up. "I wasn't sure if you would go ahead with it, but I'm delighted you have." He got up and came over to kiss her on her cheek. Leaning back, he grinned at her. "This wouldn't have anything to do with a certain WhatsApp group that was set up today, would it?"

"No!" she said playfully, slapping his arm as she untangled herself to make the tea.

"Really?"

"Okay, yes, maybe just a little. To be honest, I was furious when I saw that bloody WhatsApp group and, yes, I know I'm an ungrateful cow, but I said I'd get back to her and she clearly couldn't wait and had to go about organising something."

"She means well."

"I know but I find it suffocating at the moment."

Taking the teabags out of the mugs, Paula carried them to the kitchen table. "Can you grab the milk, please? Anyway, I'm very excited now that my trip is booked," she said, sitting down at the table.

"I can have a look at the route if you like?"

Paula felt her chest tighten. "I know this is your thing love, but can I figure this out by myself?"

"Oh, okay," said Kevin, looking disappointed.

"It's just that Jill has everything under control, and we are walking part of the Camino Frances. The French route starts in the Pyrenees but we are doing the last 100 kilometres which start in Spain in a town called Sarria and by all accounts is less of a hike and more like a big walk."

"Oh, I think you'll find that –"

Paula reached out and put her hand on his arm. "Please."

"Okay. Well, I have some exciting news too," Kevin said, taking a sip from his tea. "Now, nothing is booked, and if this doesn't suit you then …"

"What is it?"

"Tony rang me about an hour ago – in fact, I'd just got off the phone with him when you came home."

Kevin and Tony were best friends. They grew up on the same street and were in the same class all their school days. During this time they also joined the Scouts, where their love of the outdoors grew. They were Scout leaders for years and still helped out on big days at the Scout hall. Tony was his hiking buddy and, for as long as Paula knew Kevin, the two of them would head off on hikes about twice a month, sometimes for a day but usually overnight. Once a year they did a big hike in Europe for a week or ten days. Now that Kevin was semi-retired, and Tony had been divorced for years with grown-up children, they both had more time and had been talking about taking a longer trip.

"So you know he's been looking for a big hiking trip? Well, he found one that suits his time off work but it's soon, very soon."

"Okay," nodded Paula.

"It's South America. Peru, Bolivia and Chile."

"The dream! How long have you guys been talking about going to South America?"

"Yes, I know but it's a three-week trip and it's leaving at the end of next week – that's why the price is good. They had some cancellations."

"Go! You have to go!" Paula said, leaning in and putting her hand on his shoulder.

"Are you sure? I told him I couldn't confirm anything until I spoke to you."

"Go, love, this is your dream."

"But, you know, after the party ... and you said you haven't been yourself ..."

"That was because I felt like something was missing in my life. Maybe it's because the kids are gone now but I think what's missing is adventure. There is no adventure in my life. So this is so exciting, me doing my thing and you doing your thing. This is the opposite of dull!"

"But it's three weeks. It's longer than any of my other trips."

"Do it! We should be having more adventures at our age not less."

Kevin turned in his chair and wrapped his arms around her. "I do love you and I want to have more adventures but I'd like to do them with you," he said, looking into her eyes.

"I do too. Why don't we use this break to put our thinking caps on and come up with some ideas? The kids are gone – we could do anything!"

"That's true but are you sure about me going away for so long?"

"Yes, most definitely," she said, giving him a peck on the lips. "Now, go ring Tony and tell him you're going. What are the dates?"

"Next Friday! I think."

"A week before I go. That works out great. I'll leave a week after you so we'll get home around the same date."

"Is yours seven days?"

"Yes, but I might add on some days at the end because Santiago is supposed to be beautiful. Or I might have so many blisters I'd be happy to get home. I don't know yet but that's what I love about it."

"Look at us, both off travelling the world," Kevin said, smiling.

"I know! It's exciting, isn't it? This is exactly what I need."

"What about Aileen's WhatsApp group?"

"Oh, I'll take great pleasure announcing that we are both heading off travelling and for them to work away without us."

"You never know, you might fancy lying by a pool after the Camino – it's not a simple walk, you know."

"I'll be fine. Don't get me wrong, I love the idea of lying by a pool but not with a big Happy 60th Birthday balloon beside me!" she said, laughing.

Paula hugged her mug and smiled as Kevin picked up the phone to ring Tony like an excited schoolboy.

Now, sitting in a café up the side of a mountain in Spain, she couldn't help but be a little suspicious of how supportive he had been. Is this what he wanted? For them to start going their separate ways? She would never have believed it a week ago but that was before she saw the message on his phone, the message that threw their whole future into doubt.

CHAPTER 20

The night before he left on his trip they were both in the kitchen. Kevin had lined up his travel documents on the kitchen table, double-checking he had everything ready.

"*Hmm*, passport, tickets, itinerary, insurance, maps ..."

"Maps? Do you still use those?" Paula asked as she sat down at the table, carrying a mug of tea.

"Yes. I much prefer a map and, besides, they can be vital when you are out of phone coverage. So don't worry if you haven't heard from me for a day or two. You know what it's like in those places."

"Rather you than me. I'd be lost without Wi-Fi. Honestly, I'm as bad as the kids in the school!"

Kevin laughed. "I can't believe I left my good charger behind me in Kerry though. I'm going to have to buy a new one at the airport now. It was an expensive one too," he said, scratching his head. "Oh, and while I was getting these maps out I found a book detailing all the Camino routes, let me get it for you."

"Sure. I suppose I should have some idea where I'm going." Paula smiled as she picked up her mug of tea. "And while you're doing that, can I check the party photos on your phone? I'm hoping we have one good family photo from my disastrous night."

"Yeah, sure," he said, handing it to her. "The password is still the same – your birthday."

"Which is so you don't forget it!"

"As if!" he said mockingly as he headed into his office.

Just as Paula typed in the code, his phone vibrated and a text popped up. It was from someone named Noreen Kerry Guide in his contacts.

I'm so sorry about Saturday night, Kevin. I crossed a line ...

She could only see the first line but it was enough to make her lightheaded. Her finger hovered over the text for a second before she pressed it to reveal the full message.

I'm so sorry about Saturday night, Kevin. I crossed a line. I hope this doesn't change things between us. Noreen

Kevin and Tony had been hiking in Kerry on Saturday. It was one of their favourite places to hike. Quickly she opened his camera app, scrolling to the previous Saturday.

She could feel her heart thumping in her chest.

"Here it is!" Kevin arrived back into the kitchen with a travel guide in his hand. "It's an old copy but sure that route hasn't changed."

He stopped and stared at her.

"What? What's wrong?" he asked.

"Who is Noreen?"

"Noreen?"

Paula turned the phone screen around to face him. "This text came in while I was holding your phone."

"Oh, right." Kevin read the message over her shoulder and winced. He pulled out a chair and sat down slowly. "*Em,* well ... Noreen is a hiking guide in Kerry. We've known her for years from going down there and, *em* ..." He shifted uncomfortably in his chair.

"What does this text mean?"

Kevin let out a big sigh. "Look, this is awkward, but I've known Noreen for years. She leads groups on hikes up Carrauntoohil, Torc, and other hikes. She's a lovely person and, of course, mad about hiking like me."

Paula felt nauseous.

"The whole hiking crowd down there get on very well and me and Tony would often meet her for a bite to eat or a pint after a hike. And ... this is embarrassing but I think she has a bit of a thing for me."

"A thing for you?" Paula sat back, eyebrows raised, trying to take in what she was hearing.

"Now it's not what you're thinking. I had no idea. Tony used to slag me over it but I swear I never saw it. Sure she's at least twenty years younger than me."

"Oh great!" sighed Paula. "And Tony knows about this and slags you about it?"

"I want you to know that nothing serious happened, okay?" he said, looking pleadingly at her.

"Well, something happened for her to send this text." Paula tried to keep her voice calm. "So what's going on?"

"About four months ago ..."

"Four months ago!"

"Yes. I walked her home from the pub because she'd had a few drinks. Tony was staying in the pub for the music. Anyway, when we got to her door ... she kissed me. I pulled back immediately. She was tipsy and I thought nothing of it."

"So why the text now?"

"Well, I've been to Kerry a few times since then and things were fine – I saw her and it wasn't awkward or anything."

"Oh god ... I feel a 'but' coming..."

"I just want you to know that –"

"She said she crossed a line!" Paula interrupted him, holding the phone up to him again.

Kevin ran his hand nervously through his hair.

"Last weekend there was a gang of us in the bar in The Hikers' Inn," he began. "My phone was charging in the dorm so I went up to get it. The door was open and when I turned around Noreen was there. She walked up to me and kissed me. Now I'm telling you all this because nothing else happened."

"Did you kiss her back?"

Paula looked at him and knew the answer. She could read him like a book.

"Oh god, Kevin!"

"I'm sorry, I just responded for a second. I was stupid," he said, shaking his head, "flattered maybe ... but it went no further. I told her I wasn't interested. She ... we kissed again and then I asked her to leave."

"And?"

"She went back down to the bar and I waited a bit before I went down."

"Does Tony know?"

"Yes. He saw her go after me when I left the bar and he tried to ring me but my phone was on charge, of course. I swear to you I have no interest in her. I always considered her a hiking friend, nothing more."

Paula looked into his eyes. She believed his story but questions flew around her head. Was that really all they did? Did he enjoy it? Did he put his hands on her body? Was he aroused by it? How long did they kiss for?

"Look, this is a one-way street here. You can see by her text she knows she has crossed a line," he said, pointing to the phone.

"It doesn't change the fact that you kissed somebody else alone in a hotel bedroom! And, if it's completely innocent, why didn't you come home and tell me? You could have come in and said –a funny thing happened to me in Kerry!"

"I pushed it out of my mind. You've been so stressed lately and I didn't want to give you something else to worry about."

"*Well, you have now!* And you're saying that you both just went back down the bar and continued drinking as if nothing had happened?"

"Yes. I didn't stay long. We were driving home on Sunday morning so I went to bed early. Look I'm sorry you saw that text. But it was nothing, I swear, and I have no interest in it being anything."

"I don't know what to think," Paula said, turning away. "I just see you in my head with a younger, fitter woman in your arms." *Kissing her the way I want to be kissed.*

"Oh don't, honey."

A car beeped loudly outside, breaking the tension in the kitchen.

"*Aw*, feck it, that's Dave. He's taking a loan of my golf clubs while I'm away," Kevin said, standing up.

"Go out to him then."

Kevin hesitated.

"Unless there's anything else you want to get off your chest?" she said.

Kevin held her gaze. "No. Nothing. Here, pass me the phone and I'll get those party pictures up for you after he goes," he said, putting his hand out.

Something in his eyes made Paula hold onto his phone and press the camera icon.

"Paula ..."

"What? You've nothing to hide, right?"

Kevin looked down at the table. He was moving nervously from one foot to another. It didn't take long for Paula to find the photo Kevin didn't want her to see. Kevin smiling into the camera with his arm around a younger, fit-looking female. It was a selfie and their heads were touching and their faces were glowing.

"Is this fucking Noreen?"

"Yes, but it's just a selfie, that's why we're sitting like that," he said, pointing at the phone.

The car horn beeped again.

"Oh for fuck sake! I better go out to Dave."

Kevin went out to the front door and she heard him chatting to Dave and opening the garage door. She scrolled through his camera. Kevin and Noreen heading off with a group. Kevin and Noreen at the top of some bloody mountain. Kevin and Noreen holding up pints. She felt sick.

Pushing the phone away, she stood up, picked her mug up and emptied the contents down the sink.

She heard Kevin shout goodbye to Dave as she washed out her mug.

"I'm sorry about all this," he said as he came back into the kitchen.

"I'm going to bed." Paula placed her mug on the draining board and wiped her hands with a tea towel.

"Can we not talk about this now? I'm heading away tomorrow."

"Is Noreen going?"

"No! Of course not. It's not like that! It was just one stupid kiss and you can see from her message that she knew it was wrong."

"Fine," Paula said, turning away from him while she folded the tea towel. She wasn't fine but he was leaving tomorrow and she wouldn't see him for three weeks. "I believe you," she said, turning back to him, "but your lovey-dovey photos don't help."

"They're just photos."

"And how would you feel if the situation was reversed and it was me with photos on my phone of a man I had kissed?"

"I know, I know," he said shaking his head, "I've let you down. I'm sorry."

"Why did you keep going back to Kerry if you knew she had a thing for you?"

"It ... it's a great place to hike."

Paula sighed loudly. *Feckin' hiking.*

"Don't leave things like this, love," he said, placing a hand gently on her arm. "Look at me. We're not going to see each other for three weeks."

"Okay," Paula sighed turning to face him, "but this is not over."

"I'm going to delete those photos."

"And block her number?"

Kevin nodded. "Consider it done. Can I have a hug?"

Paula stepped in for a hug. "Hopefully the women of South America can keep their hands off you."

A look of relief came over Kevin's face. "Very funny. I will miss you, you know? And I want you to enjoy every minute of your trip."

Paula didn't answer him.

"I'm leaving at three-thirty for the airport so I'll sleep in the spare room."

"Okay."

"I do love you," he said, placing his hands on her shoulders, "and I'm sorry about this Kerry nonsense."

"We'll deal with that when we get back. Now is not the time."

"Love you," he said, kissing her gently on the lips before returning to the table to organise his documents.

Paula poured herself a glass of water. She glanced over at Kevin as he sorted through his maps. She felt disgusted with him but now was not the time to deal with it. Climbing the stairs to her bedroom, she felt a weight of sadness with each step she took. There was no point in arguing over it now just before he left on his trip. He said it was nothing and that he had told her everything but they looked very cosy in those photos. And if he had nothing to hide why did she feel so uneasy?

Paula pottered around the house the next day, feeling miserable.

I should be getting excited about my trip but how can I?

She busied herself by giving the house a good clean but cleaning the kitchen cupboards, washing the windows, and filling a bag of winter clothes for the local charity shop did not get rid of the niggling feeling she had over this 'Noreen' situation.

Why would she even have a thing for Kevin, she wondered. Tony was divorced, kept himself fit, and didn't have a receding hairline. He was an attractive man and he was available. Why Kevin? All this time I've been looking for excitement in my life and bloody Kevin is snogging someone twenty years younger than him!

"*I'm so angry!*" she shouted as she threw the hoover back under the stairs.

Walking into the kitchen, she switched on the kettle and took down a mug from her sparkling clean cupboard. This would be her fourth mug of tea today and it was only eleven o'clock in the morning. Opening a new packet of fig rolls, she sat at the kitchen table eating one after another.

This is going to drive me mad, she thought. Am I overreacting or is there something else going on here? She ran over their conversation again in her mind. Something didn't sit right. Just as the kettle reached the boil she got it. *The dorm!*

Kevin said his phone was charging in the dorm. But he never stayed in a dorm. He and Tony always got single rooms due to Tony's snoring. There is no way Kevin would stay in a dorm by choice, she realised, and if there was no other option he would have moaned about it all week.

Taking her phone from her back pocket, she googled The Hikers' Inn. She paused with her finger over the phone number.

Do you really want to do this? she asked herself. She reached for another fig roll and slowly ate around the sides as she thought about the answer. Finishing the rest of it, she wiped the crumbs away from her lips and pressed call.

"Hello, The Hikers' Inn," a cheery young man's voice answered the phone.

"Hi there, my name is Paula Byrne. My husband thinks he may have left his international charger behind in your dorm on Saturday night and I'm wondering if anyone found them? His name is Kevin Byrne."

"Oh, right. I didn't hear anything myself but let me check the system here."

Her mouth dried up as she heard his fingers type in the background.

"Here ye are now, Mrs Byrne. You guys were in the double room – Room 401?"

Paula opened her mouth to speak but couldn't get the words out.

"Hello?"

"Yes, sorry, the double room. I thought he said he charged his phone in the dorm for some reason and that he might have left it there."

"No, definitely not the dorm. I can check with the manager but it says here he booked a double room for the two of you, no breakfast. If you hold on there I can ask …"

Paula hung up. She'd heard all she needed to hear. Standing up, she ran to the kitchen sink and threw up the three fig rolls she just ate.

She had deliberated whether to ring Kevin straight away to confront him but he was somewhere over the Atlantic ocean at this stage. She also decided that she needed to see him in person and judge his reaction face to face.

"*A double room for the two of ye*," that's what the young fella had said. The news had been a shock and was now making her question everything. Had he had any other flings while he was away? She never asked him much about his trips because she was so used to him going on them and, if she was honest, she didn't have much interest in them. She still found the news hard to believe, especially with Tony around. Surely Tony wasn't in on this, was he?

She couldn't believe this was happening to her. She had never been tempted to cheat on Kevin, never. It wasn't something she could ever imagine herself doing. At least that's what she thought last week but … with these revelations about Kevin nothing was certain in her life anymore.

And Carlos, well, what was that about? Did she want another man to make her feel … excited? Wanted? Aroused? She didn't know. Was she just flattered that a handsome, sexy man wanted to make her coffee and seemed to enjoy her company, although they said very little? Was it the image of her husband with his arm around a woman twenty years his junior making her imagine a connection with Carlos that wasn't really there?

Her head was wrecked, thinking about it. She had thought that that side of her, the sexual side, was slowly closing up shop – but maybe not.

Maybe it just needed a new exciting person to open it up again. But then what?

After all, she wasn't looking for a new man, she didn't want a new man. When she said she wanted more adventure in her life, it didn't involve an affair or sex with a bus driver in Spain, for god's sake! No, that was not what she was looking for and it wouldn't solve any long-term problems. But maybe that is what Kevin is looking for. She couldn't know for sure until she saw him and right now she didn't want to know.

I came here to find out what will make me happy. I need to find those answers and focus on me first before I deal with him and his hiking fling when we both get home, she thought as she picked up her bag.

Carefully she lifted her legs off the seat and stood up to get going on the last hour to Palas de Rei.

Her phone buzzed just as she picked it up. It was another picture from Kevin.

Local Village. Love U. Have a great day. X

"He can feck off with his 'love you'!" she said to herself before picking up her poles and marching on.

CHAPTER 21

When Paula arrived in Palas de Rei she was ready for her bed. The host checked her in and showed her to her room on the ground floor. She was delighted not to have to walk up any stairs as she had just climbed a flight of steps looking for this place. Just as she went to plug her phone into her charger, she saw a message from Rachel and Cathy in their WhatsApp Camino group. Neither was going out to dinner tonight.

Aw, that's a pity, she thought. She sent a thumbs-up emoji and put the phone down.

Maybe I should have messaged them earlier with the restaurant recommendation. PASTA was the name of a restaurant that another pilgrim had told her about. An Irishwoman and her husband ran it and the reviews were excellent.

Well, feck that, I'm going anyway, she decided. She had been looking forward to a comforting bowl of pasta ever since the pilgrim told her about it.

She checked her watch. A quick shower and change and then I'll go eat. It was only four o'clock but the backs of her legs hurt so much and her little toe was swollen now, so she wanted to get back early and rest her legs for as long as possible.

If I even sit on that bed, she thought looking at it, I'll never move again. After her shower, she pulled out a pair of leggings and a clean T-shirt from her backpack and slipped into her sandals to give her feet a break from her trainers. Grabbing her bag, she headed out to look for the restaurant.

Palas de Rei was unfortunately a hilly town with lots of steps and ramps which didn't help her aches and pains, but she found the restaurant easily enough.

"Table for one, please," she said as she entered.

"Ah, another Irish traveller," smiled the owner. "I'm Bridget."

Her friendly host introduced herself and her English husband who was behind the counter cooking.

"The tables are upstairs."

Paula groaned when she saw the stairs but was thankful for the banister to help get her to the top. I feel one hundred years old, she thought as she made full use of the banister to pull herself up the staircase.

The small restaurant had about eight tables for two. Most seemed to be occupied by tired walkers.

After taking a table and viewing the menu, Paula was eager to order.

"I'll have the Chicken Alfredo and a glass of Alberino, please."

"Coming up! How did you get on today?"

"Today was hard. That's why I'm eating early. Hopefully, I'll sleep off the soreness. Where are you from?"

"Northern Ireland. My husband is English and we've been here for five years now."

"You must meet so many different people coming through."

"Yes, that's what I like about it here. Being a Camino town we have a steady stream of people for most of the year, from all over the world. December and January are the quietest months but you still get a few walkers even in wintertime."

"I see you have a mug of tea on the menu," smiled Paula.

"It's Barry's tea. We get so many Irish and English who love a proper mug of tea," she said, laughing. "I'll be back with your wine."

What a lovely woman, thought Paula. Imagine just picking up your life and moving to this small Spanish town in the mountains to set up a business. They were both in their fifties as far as she could tell, younger than her anyway and here they were with this lovely restaurant in the mountains.

Bridget brought the wine and went to serve other customers. Taking a sip of the cold Alberino, she took out her phone to send some WhatsApp messages. Picking a few landscape pictures from today she sent them to Jill, Kevin and the kids on the family WhatsApp group, with the message:

Lovely route. Legs burning. Early night for me. P x

She and Kevin had been putting some pictures up every night just to keep the kids in the loop. Jessica, being a worrier, always replied immediately but Michael who was so laid back might send a thumbs-up emoji hours later or not at all.

She then messaged Jill.

Hi there, how's your mum?

She answered immediately: **Hello!! Great to hear from you. I'm sitting with her now. Nothing they can do for her fractured hip except painkillers and rest. They are moving her to the Orthopaedic Hospital in Clontarf so at least she will be nearer home. How are you getting on? Your pictures look great.**

Paula answered: **I'm still standing despite no training and no research! I'm just following the signs and the crowds. I've met lovely people but no big revelation for me yet. Today was hard. I'm shattered and the backs of my legs ache. I don't know how I'll manage 30km tomorrow.**

I remember that feeling, Jill replied. **Day one is exciting but day two is a little longer and your legs are still adjusting so go easy on yourself and take as many breaks as you need. Some people race ahead to the next destination but listen to your body and rest when you want. And it can be very emotional, especially when you are tired. If something comes up for you, just let it happen.**

Paula answered: **The only thing coming up for me is a blister on my little toe! But you are right about the emotions. I'm three days here and I don't know what I want. If anything I am more confused.**

Jill said: **Just let it happen. Don't try to force solutions. The only thing you have to do is put one foot in front of the other.**

Yes, miss! Paula replied.

Jill said: **And don't forget to STRETCH! Look at those YouTube videos on stretching that I sent you and keep doing them before you start and when you finish. And try putting your legs up against the wall for fifteen minutes too, it definitely helps. Enjoy the journey! X**

Paula's pasta arrived and smelled divine. I feel a bit better now, she thought, twirling the pasta on her fork. Jill is right, I was hardly going to be enlightened in just three days.

She hadn't said a word to Jill about Kevin. In one way it would have been good to get her opinion as she was so level-headed but Paula knew she had to get her own head around it first. Her whole future as she saw it only a week ago could be changed completely after she confronted him when they got home.

Carlos came into her mind again. If Jill was on this trip with me, would I be getting up early and having coffee with him?

She put down her fork and took a sip of her wine. The answer was no, probably not. And if it was entirely innocent, why didn't I tell her about it?

Paula sighed. Jill's right, stop overthinking things. Just get up each day and walk, that's all I have to do.

Just then her phone buzzed with a text message from Jill.

Good news! I just checked the distance for tomorrow. As Palas de Rei to Arzua is thirty kilometres, if you need to, you can stop after 15 kilometres in Melide and get a taxi from there to Arzua. You will still be eligible for the Compostella Certificate because Sarria is 115 kilometres from Santiago, giving you kilometres to spare. You can do this!

Paula smiled, feeling relieved.

You have made my day! Thank you.

Opening her Camino Ninja App, she double-checked the distances. Yes, I can do that. I can definitely walk fifteen kilometres. Feeling much better about the task tomorrow, she forwarded Jill's message to Rachel and Cathy. They had to be as sore as she was today, so they might want to do this too, she thought as she pressed send.

Just as she finished her pasta, a familiar figure waved and came over to her. It was Sheila, the woman she'd met at the café earlier. She was with a friend who went downstairs to pay the bill.

"Hello there! I'm sorry I had my back to you so I didn't see you come in. You could have joined us."

"Oh, that's fine," replied Paula.

"Delicious food, isn't it?"

"Yes, and just what I needed. I was feeling sorry for myself and now I feel nourished."

"Well, if you have any space left, we've just had the homemade lemon cheesecake and it was superb. Bridget makes it herself."

"Isn't it amazing that you can find yourself in a small town up a mountain in Spain and still run into an Irish person," said Paula. smiling.

"Yes," said Sheila, "we're everywhere! Well, enjoy your meal and I might see you on the road tomorrow."

"Yes, I'll look out for you."

"*Buen Camino*," Sheila said and headed downstairs.

People are so nice, thought Paula, and even if you only have a short conversation on the walk, it feels like seeing an old friend when you bump into them again. No other holiday is like that. Maybe that's another reason why people like to do this.

"Everything okay?" Bridget appeared and picked up the empty pasta bowl.

"Yes, delicious, thank you. I have been told that I have to try your cheesecake, so can I order that and have a mug of tea with it, please?"

"Yes, of course," Bridget said with a smile as she cleared the dish away.

Just then Paula's phone buzzed again. She didn't recognise the number but then she saw the message

Paula, this is Carlos. You are staying at a family hotel so no coffee tomorrow. Buen Camino for tomorrow. Carlos

It's probably just as well, she thought but she couldn't help feeling disappointed. She did fancy him – he was a good-looking man. It's ridiculous – a woman my age feeling flirty with a man like him! Would I be like this if I didn't know what Kevin has been up to? I don't know. I don't know what I'm doing at all. Maybe I'm just tired and emotional.

She ordered another glass of Alberino while she waited for her cheesecake and mug of tea to arrive. And thinking of Carlos, she saved his number in her phone.

CHAPTER 22

PALAS DE REI-ARZUA

Rachel woke in a sweat, her legs tangled in her sheets.

"*Jesus!*"

She'd had a crazy dream where Craig was chasing her. Everywhere she turned he blocked her way. And then a door opened and Simon was there calling her. If she went through the door she would be safe from Craig but would have to go with Simon. In the dream, she fell to the ground, clutching her head. It felt like it was going to explode and that's when she woke up.

She sat up in bed and put her head in her hands.

I can't keep running, she said to herself. I don't want to live abroad again but, if I go back to Dublin, Craig will be there and we're bound to cross paths as we will be mixing in the same business circles and, if I go home to Cork, Simon will be there.

It was still dark outside. She had left the blind up to let the morning light in but it was only 5 am. Pulling back the duvet, she sat on the side of the bed. Sunrise was at 6.50 which meant it would start getting light at 6.15.

Well, I'm awake now so I'll go at dawn. The quiet might help clear my head, she reckoned. I need to put both men out of my head and think about what I want to do from here. The easiest thing would be to return home, go back to work for Helen in Troy & O'Doherty and forget about setting up a practice in Dublin. I don't have the energy to start looking for and trusting a new business partner male or female now, so that idea is definitely on hold. Equally, the thought of going back to work long hours for someone else did not appeal. But my bills won't pay themselves, she sighed, so I'll have to think of something fast.

"Right! Shower and then pack!" she said, pushing herself up from the bed. "*Ouch!*" Standing up her left knee hurt and wobbled under her. "Okay, I need to watch this today." She massaged the sore spot.

What I wouldn't give for a massage today, she thought as she limped to the shower.

As the hot water ran over her she remembered the trip she and Craig took to Marrakesh. He had booked a 5-star hotel with its own spa hammam and the massages were out of this world. Every day of their 4-day trip they spent at least an hour in the hammam having traditional spa and steam room treatments before heading out in the evening to the exotic main square of Marrakesh, Jemaa el-Fnaa. She closed her eyes, remembering the scent of the spice market, the bright lantern stalls and the call to prayer in the background.

Their huge suite came with a jacuzzi on a private terrace with a view of the Atlas Mountains in the distance. They made love on the beautiful canopy bed every morning and evening as the white linen curtains moved gently in the jasmine-scented breeze that cooled their hot bodies.

Rachel felt her chest ache as the tears started to fall. Oh god, it was fantastic. But did the glamour and excitement of his lifestyle distract me from how we really were as a couple, she wondered. Grabbing the shampoo, she squirted it on and scrubbed her hair vigorously, trying to scrub thoughts of Craig from her mind.

Stepping out of the shower, she wrapped one big towel around her body and, bending over, twisted her long red hair like a rope, squeezing the heavy wet out of it. Heading out early, the morning air would be chilly so she wanted to dry her hair as much as she could. Squeezing the ends now with a towel, she twisted it around her head.

Feeling a little better, she made plans for the day ahead. Maybe I will need walking poles after all, she thought.

She had scoffed when she saw the people at the airport with their walking poles but she had already seen how useful they were, especially for navigating the steep declines and uneven ground in the forests.

Picking up her phone, she checked her Camino Ninja App. Nothing would be open in Palas de Rei this early so she needed to find the nearest big town on the route. She needed a shop that sold walking poles and a pharmacy for more painkillers and possibly a knee support. Every big town along the Camino catered for pilgrims' needs so she just had to make it to the next one.

"Damn it, it looks like Melide is the next big town and that's fifteen kilometres away," she sighed.

Taking out her small first-aid bag, she emptied it on the bed. She had nothing with her to support her knee. She could feel a blister coming up on the side of her big toe so she applied a Compeed plaster to that and put more blister plasters in her small backpack to take with her. Then she counted out her paracetamol and Ibuprofen. She had two of each left.

Opening her bottle of water, she swallowed the four tablets. Hopefully, that would get her to Melide.

The thought crossed her mind that she could go back to bed and just wait until everyone left and then order a taxi. Nobody would care. But something inside her wanted to push on. She was too stubborn to give in yet. After twenty-four kilometres yesterday, sixteen should be a doddle, she convinced herself. If I leave here at six thirty I'll get to Melide by ten and then I can get a taxi to Arzua.

Cathy had set the alarm on her phone for 6 am. When it went off, she took her time getting ready, doing some leg stretches before getting dressed.

She had slept so well. She was sleeping deeper and longer since Ted died and definitely feeling the better for it.

How many years have I slept lightly, she wondered, keeping an ear out to hear him moving around the house downstairs, tensing every muscle in my body upon hearing his footsteps on the stairs? She shuddered at the thought of it.

Leaning into the mirror she lifted her hair back from her neck. The bruising was almost gone. She had made sure to zip her light fleece jacket right up to the top when she was out in case anyone noticed the now yellow marks. One mark on the left side of her throat made her sick to the stomach. To an onlooker it was a yellow line but to Cathy it was the mark Ted's thumb left when he tried to strangle the life out of her. She had a wardrobe full of polo-neck tops at home to cover up these types of marks. Gently rubbing arnica cream over the marks, she looked at herself in the mirror.

"Today will be a good day," she said to her reflection.

Yesterday's shock about forgetting the month's mind had been erased, firstly by meeting Miyuki at the right time and then walking in prayer in the afternoon with Father Eduardo and his group. Again Marta in the group took time to walk and talk to her. She felt that Marta could sense that she had been through a lot and seemed to know when she needed a pick-me-up.

But today she wanted to walk alone as much as she could. There were a lot of decisions to be made when she got home and she had to figure out what exactly her next move should be and how she was going to execute it.

How she wished she could sit in her mother's kitchen beside the Aga and talk things out with her, like she used to do as a child. But her mother didn't recognise her now and her dad was frail and lost without his wife.

Cathy and her dad had tried everything they could to keep her mum at home for as long as they could, but her worsening dementia made this impossible and a farm was not the safest place for someone vulnerable who liked to go wandering in the night.

Her brothers lived too far away to be any help and none of them had any interest in taking over the farm. After her mother went into the local nursing home, her dad lost interest in the farm too, so he leased out the land and used his time to visit the nursing home every day.

Cathy visited as often as she could too but it was hard watching the deterioration of her mother and soon she was completely non-verbal. Seeing her mum sitting in the nursing home, staring out the window, frightened Cathy. But it also made her wake up to her own situation and, now that Sophie had left, she decided that she wasn't prepared to live that way anymore.

She didn't want to burden Sophie with her problems. Ted had made Sophie miserable enough. So she confided in Father John. He was the only person she could trust to listen to her and never judge. She just needed a plan and then she needed to figure out how she was going to tell Ted she was leaving him. That was the difficult part, the dangerous part. She lay awake at night, trying to think of the safest way to get out of her situation.

And then Ted had his accident.

Packing up her backpack, she looked out the window. The moon was still up in one direction but the sky was lightening up in the other. She would never walk in the dark at home but here she wasn't afraid. I never need to be afraid ever again, she thought as she picked up her bag and left.

Paula woke with a cracking headache. She'd had a terrible night's sleep, tossing and turning, waking every few hours. She didn't know if it was the three glasses of Alberino she'd had with her dinner or her uneasy thoughts that caused it. She had walked home slowly from the restaurant as her legs were so sore and then took Jill's advice and typed '**exercises for sore legs**' into YouTube and followed a few different trainers as they demonstrated stretches. In the end, she decided to go with the legs up the wall as it required the least amount of effort.

Lying on the bed with her legs leaning up against the wall she thought about the route ahead. Thanks to Jill, she was going to walk sixteen kilometres to Melide and get a taxi to Arzua which was their next stopover. Taking out her phone, she put a message in the Camino group.

Morning, girls. Just to let you know, I will be walking to Melide and getting a taxi to Arzua. My legs and hips are too sore to walk the whole way. See you there! Buen Camino!

Rachel replied immediately.

I'm doing that today too, Paula, because my knee is acting up. See you in Arzua.

No reply from Cathy.

Paula put her phone away.

It is so nice meeting new people every day but today I need to walk alone, she decided.

She rubbed anti-inflammatory gel all over her legs and put a fresh Compeed plaster on her swollen, red baby toe. After getting dressed, she packed away her toiletries, took her bag down to reception and then headed out into the street.

Two walkers were just ahead of her so she followed them down the town, down more steep steps, past the town's fountain and a statue of a Santiago Peregrino – Saint James as a pilgrim. Once she reached that, she could see the Camino signs for herself.

I have sixteen kilometres to ask myself questions and try to figure out the answers, she thought as she crossed the main road out of Palas de Rei and followed the signs into the woods. Her mood was lower than the last two days and her legs were sore and stiff. The ground was damp so she had to walk head down to watch her step on the uneven forest floor. At the start, the trail passed by the back gardens of people's houses as it rose through the forest. Nearly every house had a polytunnel and vegetables growing in their gardens. Pausing to take a photo of an open polytunnel bursting with wildflowers, she inhaled the peppery onion scent of leeks and wild garlic growing nearby. The birdsong over her head made her smile and, knowing she only had sixteen kilometres to go, she slowed her pace and decided to take time to appreciate the forests and countryside on her journey today.

CHAPTER 23

Rachel marched ahead on the route, trying to ignore the pain in her knee. She had come across two Frenchwomen on her walks the previous days. They were memorable because they were identical twins. She guessed their age to be about sixty-five. They wore matching clothes and both wore their grey hair in ponytails sticking out the back of their baseball caps. They didn't seem to speak to anyone but murmured prayers in French. Rachel remembered that their pace was similar to hers so she walked a couple of metres behind them. The gentle rhythm of the three pairs of feet walking helped Rachel switch off and just follow their lead.

Just as they arrived at a farming hamlet almost four kilometres in, Rachel had to stop. The stabbing pain in the side of her knee was worsening. A café sign on one of the old stone buildings caught her eye and, having skipped dinner the night before, she was starving. Limping over, she was relieved to see they were open early.

The owner, standing behind the bar, was cutting big slices of a giant tortilla that was displayed on the counter on a cake stand.

"*Buenos Dias!*"

"*Buenos Dias, one tortilla y orange y espresso, por favor.*"

Her Spanish was poor but he nodded and smiled.

"Four euros, please."

She had just paid when she heard her name being called.

"*Rachel!*"

Turning around she saw Bernie at a table, waving at her, and beside her sat Simon who raised his hand and nodded.

Damn it! If I had seen them in here, I wouldn't have ordered, she sighed.

"Please sit and we will bring it to you," the barman said as a queue formed behind her.

She had no choice but to join Bernie and Simon.

"Hi there, great to see you," she said, smiling, and bent down to kiss Bernie on the cheek while ignoring Simon.

"How are you, love? Did I see you limping?" Bernie asked.

"Yes, I'm afraid so. My left knee is giving me trouble."

"It looks swollen alright," Simon said.

She ignored him and continued to direct the conversation to Bernie. "I think I overdid it on day one and I may have walked too fast yesterday."

"It's not a race, love. You can get injured or get some nasty blisters if you go too fast. Have you put anything on it?"

"Not really. I took paracetamol and Ibuprofen this morning. But when I get to Melide I'll go to a pharmacy and get a support and some walking poles."

"*Tortilla?*" The barman arrived with her food and put it down in front of her.

"*Gracias.*" She noticed that Bernie and Simon had finished their food and hoped they would move on soon.

"*Senor, podemos tener una toalla con un poco de hielo?*" Simon said to the barman.

"*Si, senor,*" he replied.

"You speak Spanish?" Rachel asked Simon.

"Not a lot." He shrugged. "But when I researched this trip, people mentioned that not much English is spoken in these small villages so I learned the basics online."

The barman returned with a tea towel full of ice and gave it to Simon.

"Now put this on your knee," Simon said.

"I'm fine, I don't need you to ..."

"Just do it, Rachel – that knee is very swollen and it will help."

"Put your leg up here," said Bernie, pointing to the seat beside her.

Rachel sighed. She didn't need looking after but she had to admit that the ice was a great idea and would definitely help her knee.

"Thank you. I do appreciate it," she said, looking at Simon this time. Her stomach flipped. He looked so good.

She put her leg up on the seat beside Bernie as she was told and Simon came around and bent down on one knee beside her. Very gently he placed the ice pack on her knee. She nearly jumped when she felt the touch of his hand on the back of her knee. It was like an electric shock shooting through her.

Looking up at her with his green eyes, he said, "Try to balance the ice on your knee against this chair while you eat."

She just nodded. She had to drag her eyes away from his. They were hypnotising. When he stood up and passed behind her chair she could smell his cologne. It was lemon-scented and she imagined him spraying it on his tanned hairless chest. Oh God, she thought, starting to sweat.

"So how are you getting on?" she asked Bernie, changing the subject from her knee while beginning to eat her tortilla.

"I was very tired yesterday but I feel better today. We're walking to Melide and then getting a taxi to Arzua."

"Me too." The words were out before she could stop them.

"Oh, maybe we can share a taxi if you like?" Bernie said with a big smile, looking from Rachel to Simon.

"Well ... I ..."

"We might hold Rachel back with our pace, Mum," Simon said, picking up his cup and finishing off his coffee.

"Of course. But you need to walk slowly today too, Rachel, until you get support for that knee. Maybe we can text you when we get there? Do you have Simon's number?"

Rachel gulped her orange juice so as not to answer that question.

"Mum," Simon said with a sigh.

"I'm only trying to help," Bernie said, holding her hands up in defence. "Actually, I might have something to help." She picked up her backpack. Unzipping the front pocket, she took out a bottle of tablets. "These are very strong anti-inflammatories but one should be fine," she said, twisting the top and shaking one out into her hand.

"Mum, you can't give people your prescribed medication!" Simon protested.

"Can you spare it?" Rachel asked. She needed to get to Melide before they did as she certainly was not sharing a taxi with Simon Molloy.

"I can, love," Bernie replied so Rachel took the tablet and threw it back with a gulp of her orange juice.

Simon shook his head at his mother.

"Thank you, Bernie," Rachel said. "Hopefully, that will do the trick."

Having finished her tortilla and juice, she drank her coffee quickly, eager to get back walking. She could feel Simon's eyes on her the whole time.

"Okay, thank you both," she said, lifting the ice-pack towel from her leg. "I'm going to go ahead and take my time like you said."

"Yes, do that," said Bernie.

"Thank you for organising the ice, it does feel better," Rachel said to Simon.

"Maybe we'll see you later?" he said with a half-smile, tilting his head and looking right into her eyes.

"Who knows?" She shrugged, wondering what he meant by that.

Standing, she picked up her small backpack and put it on her back.

"*Buen Camino*," she said to Bernie and headed out to join the path again.

She'd only walked a few steps when she heard Simon call her name.

"Take these," he said, catching up with her, his walking poles in his hand.

"No, I can't, I'll ... get some later."

"Seriously. I don't need them and they'll take the pressure off that knee."

"Simon ..." She paused. "This is all too weird for me. I'm out here trying to work through something big that happened at home and seeing you here has thrown me."

"I don't want to upset you or add to anything you have going on but ..." Simon hesitated and shifted uncomfortably before looking back at her. "Look, just take the poles, will you? They're adjustable and they will help." He thrust them at her.

"But ...?"

"Mind yourself," he said and then walked back to the café.

Rachel stood for a second, watching him walk away. But what? He said but ... What was he going to say?

CHAPTER 24

Cathy arrived in Melide in great form. It felt strange walking through this big town in her hiking gear with dust up the back of her leggings as people went about their normal business, shopping, going to the bank, and pushing babies in buggies. As she left the forest and walked over a bridge approaching Melide, a Spanish guitarist was sitting on the steps of an old church. He played so beautifully that she had to move on to prevent the tears from coming. She felt very fragile, her emotions still so raw that the kindest of gestures or a simple piece of music could have the tears flowing.

She had thought a lot about Father John today. So many times she thought 'John would love this' as she walked through a quiet forest or stopped to watch horses playing in a field. He was such a good friend to her and never far from her thoughts.

As the buildings got bigger so did the elaborate painted murals on the walls. One particular one of the Pope in a beekeeping suit made her smile as she headed into the big town.

Along the main street old men sitting outside cafés wished her a "*Buen Camino*" as they played chess and drank espresso. The noise of the traffic seemed strange too, having walked most of the day through forests and through sleepy terracotta-roofed mountain hamlets.

Passing an outdoor adventure shop, she stopped to go inside for a look.

Ten minutes later, she left with exactly what she'd been looking for: a proper hiking backpack. The suitcase that she brought with her, which Carlos collected every day, was going in the bin. She hated it. It was the suitcase that she and Ted used on their honeymoon to Venice and their annual holidays to Kerry. When she looked at it, she remembered what an excited optimistic bride she had been, packing for her honeymoon and also how quickly she became a weary nervous spouse packing for holidays where she dreaded having extra time with Ted. It was so old-fashioned looking and represented another time in her life, a time she wanted to leave behind and never think about again. This new purchase represented a new and adventures time for her. She promised herself that she would travel with this new backpack and felt so much lighter leaving the shop with it.

I have been starved of adventure in my life but that stops now, she thought, heading for the main square.

Paula was sitting on a bench in the main square of Melide, drinking from her water bottle, when she saw Cathy approach.

"Hello there!" called Cathy, waving.

"Well, you look like a proper Camino walker! Did you just buy that?"

"Yes," said Cathy, sitting down and putting the bag down in front of her. "I didn't have time to buy one before I left and I bloody hate that old suitcase – so when I saw an outdoor shop up the road there, I just bought it."

"Good for you. So do you plan on travelling more?"

"Yes, well, I don't have any definite plans but I want to. I always wanted to travel more but my husband –"

"Sorry, is that Rachel?" Paula interrupted

"Oh gosh, I think it is."

They both squinted to see Rachel limping badly towards them. Cathy rushed over to her, putting an arm around her waist to support her, taking her poles from her.

"Lean on me," she said.

Paula arrived and took her other side. "Jesus, Rachel, what have you done to yourself?"

"I'm so happy to see you guys," she said as she eased herself onto the bench.

"Why didn't you message us?"

"My phone ran out of power and I just wanted to get here."

"That knee looks very swollen," Cathy said. "I think you need to see someone."

"Yeah, another pilgrim told me that the pharmacy at the square here is very good and they'll check it out for me. These poles saved me, to be honest," she said, holding them up, "and you'll never guess who gave them to me?"

"Who?" asked Paula.

"Simon," Rachel said, rolling her eyes.

"Oh-kay …" Paula looked at Cathy and back to Rachel. "How did that happen?"

"I bumped into him and Bernie at breakfast and in fairness he got some ice for my knee and gave me his poles – so I can't even be angry at him now."

"Well, let's get you up and over to the pharmacy and get this looked at."

The two friends supported Rachel and carried her bag and her poles to the pharmacy where a lovely pharmacist, who had seen all types of injuries from walkers before, knelt down beside Rachel to examine her knee.

"It's very swollen. Did you twist it at any stage?"

"I injured it years ago playing basketball and anytime I overdo it in the gym it flares up again."

"I see this all the time. On the Camino, any old injury can get inflamed again," the pharmacist said. "Try to slow your pace or shorten your walking day. On the Camino, there are different terrains and your knee is doing so much more work than if you were walking on the flat at home."

Rachel nodded. In her hurry to avoid meeting Simon, she had now caused an injury that could slow her down considerably.

"So what can I do now?"

The pharmacist took a leaflet in English, from the shelf. "R-I-C-E."

"Rice?"

"Yes. This is what is recommended for any inflammation like this. *Rest, Ice, Compression, Elevation.* You are on your way to Santiago, yes? I will give you a support stocking for your knee and an ice-holder. You can ask any café to fill the holder with ice. Place it on your knee and do this every time you stop. I see you have walking poles?"

"Yes, but I borrowed these. I'm going to get my own."

"Good, they will help. I will also give you painkillers and anti-inflammatory tablets but for the best results you must rest it for at least twenty-four hours. If you continue to walk to the next town tomorrow it will not heal itself."

Rachel shook her head. "Well, that's just great," she sighed. "Thank you for your help. I'll take everything you recommend."

The pharmacist went off to get her medication.

"I'm sorry this has happened to you, Rachel," Cathy said, "but maybe with a bit of rest …"

"I don't know. This trip has been a bit of a disaster, to be honest. I came here to have head space to figure things out and then Simon shows up to mess with my head and my feelings. And then when I try to get ahead to avoid him, this happens. I think my time here is done."

"Well, let's get you into a taxi and to our next pension," suggested Paula when the pharmacist returned with Rachel's items. "It looks like a lovely place. I had a look at their website and it has a big kitchen where we can all hang out. How about I go to the supermarket when we arrive and pick up things for lunch? We can sit and eat and see if we can come up with a plan. How does that sound?"

"That sounds great, and thanks, guys," Rachel said as she looked at these two women who were strangers three days ago and were now her lifesavers.

CHAPTER 25

ARZUA

The accommodation in Arzua didn't normally open check-in until one but when Paula rang to explain their situation, the owner immediately agreed to open early for them. Pension Luis was located just off the main square in Arzua. The whitewashed building with dark-green shutters had some table and chairs out the front on the pavement and beautiful white flowers growing from standalone pots and hanging baskets.

The owner, Nuria, very kindly gave Rachel a room on the ground floor so she wouldn't have to walk up the stairs. The women decided to have quick showers and change out of their hiking gear and then meet in the big kitchen area on the ground floor.

Paula went to a nearby supermarket recommended by the owner and returned with fresh bread rolls, a variety of sliced meats and cheeses, bottles of fizzy water, and a bottle of white wine.

After laying everything out on the table, she messaged the others.

"Oh thanks a million, Paula, this looks great," Rachel said as she came into the kitchen, leaning on a crutch that she'd bought in the pharmacy.

"No bother at all. Sit yourself down there and put that leg up," she said, moving a chair opposite Rachel.

Cathy came down the stairs and joined them. "This looks delicious. How does your knee feel?"

"It doesn't feel as bad when I'm walking on flat surfaces but any incline and it feels like being kicked in the knee."

The fresh crusty bread was cut up and everyone helped themselves to the toppings.

"This is a perfect lunch after today's walk," Cathy said, passing around the serrano ham.

"Hang on," Paula said, going to the fridge and taking out the bottle of white wine.

Grabbing three glasses from the cupboard, she returned to the table and opened the wine.

"It's not even lunchtime," Rachel laughed.

"I don't care, it's been an eventful day," Paula said, filling their glasses, "and it's so cheap here to buy a really good bottle of wine so it would be a crime not to."

"Is wine okay with your tablets?" Cathy asked Rachel.

"Yes, I'm only on painkillers, and at this stage I couldn't care less." Rachel took a sip of the cold Alberino. "Yes, this is definitely worth it," she said with a smile.

Cathy hadn't had a drink in years. Ted disapproved of her drinking but it didn't stop him. He often spent a Saturday night drinking cans of cheap lager in front of the television until he passed out there. On the rare occasions when she did have a drink, like at her brother's wedding, he accused her of becoming loud and embarrassing. *Drunk, lush, slut* being just some of the words he spat at her when they got home. She knew none of these things were true, just another way for Ted to make her feel small and self-conscious. It made him feel like he had control over what she did. She knew this at the time but arguing with Ted was pointless so it was easier for her not to drink at all and give him less reasons to belittle her.

But today was about Rachel and she needed to break the patterns of behaviour and rules that Ted had imposed on her. Feeling nervous but exhilarated, she held up her glass for Paula to fill it.

"*To Camino friends!*" she said, raising her glass, and the others joined her.

"*To Camino friends!*"

"Thanks, guys, I really appreciate this," Rachel said. "But what a disaster!"

"*Aw*, pet, I'm so sorry this happened to you," Paula said.

"It's my own fault for racing ahead and not listening to my body when this knee started to give me trouble. I'd better think about my next move carefully now."

"The pharmacist said you shouldn't walk on it for twenty-four hours so that rules out tomorrow."

"Yes, I reckon I have three choices. Either I leave here tomorrow and get a taxi to O Pedrouzo and hang around there until I can check in. But check-out here is ten and check in there is at two so that's a lot of time to fill. And it's a much smaller town than here so there may not be many places open. Or I pay for day use here and get a late taxi to O Pedrouzo, overnight there and carry on and see how much of the O Pedrouzo to Santiago route I can do. Or I call it quits and get a taxi straight to Santiago and stay there until it's time to go home."

"But if you take any of those options you won't get your Compostela," said Cathy.

"I honestly don't care about the certificate. I came away to hopefully walk and walk until I had sorted my life out, so it was never for the cert."

"I just mention it," Cathy said, "because if you stayed here an extra night you might be able to walk from here to O Pedrouzo with the crutch, taking your time, and then on to Santiago and still get your Compostella."

"She has a point," said Paula, "and I've been out around the town here and the main square is just a hundred metres away and it's gorgeous. Nuria says there will be music there tonight too as it's festival season so there will be lots going on and it's so pretty down there."

"That would mean staying one night instead of two in Santiago, though," said Rachel, trying to figure things out.

"It still gives us one night to celebrate in Santiago and the flight doesn't leave until eleven thirty the next night, so we'd have that whole day," Paula said.

"We? Girls, I wouldn't expect you to stay with me. Honestly, this is my problem. You two need to carry on with the route."

Paula and Cathy looked at each other.

"I'd love a day off, Rachel," said Paula. "If you're happy to stay here an extra night I'd love to stay here with you. My legs are burning and my hips are so stiff. Honestly, I could use a rest day."

"Me too! I would love to stop for one day and let the experience sink in," said Cathy.

"No, I couldn't possibly ask you to do that!"

"Seriously," said Paula, "I came out here to get some answers too and I think I'm too bloody tired at the end of the day for my brain to even begin to think about my future."

"But, Cathy, what about your prayer group? Don't you see them every day?"

"Yes, but I don't know their schedule and I need some time to sort things out myself too. At this rate, I'll arrive in Santiago with nothing but blisters and rosary beads."

Rachel burst out laughing at the image.

"I have walked and prayed," said Cathy, "but I could do with some time sitting quietly with my thoughts. I would love an extra day here."

"*Wow!*" Rachel's eyes started to fill up. "Thank you so much. I usually hate relying on people. I know I have this image of being tough and independent but I'm all over the place emotionally and now physically," she said, pointing to her knee, "and you guys don't even know me but you're willing to stay with me?"

"Isn't that the beauty of the Camino though?" said Cathy. "You meet people where they are at now in their lives, no past, no history, just where they are today and that's very freeing. I met a Japanese woman yesterday and told her things about my life that hardly anyone else knows and I might never see her again and that's fine. Actually ..." she hesitated, "she was the first person I told that my husband has just recently passed away."

"*What?*" Paula said.

Rachel looked shocked.

"Yes, I probably should have said something sooner but I'm still coming to terms with it."

"When did he die?" Paula asked, placing her hand on Cathy's arm.

"Four weeks ago."

"Oh Cathy, that's shocking, you poor thing!"

"It's okay. It was a shock and I'm still letting it sink in but ... it wasn't a good marriage and I was planning to leave him ... but even so ... I came here to get my head around it all and figure out what's next for me."

"Oh Cathy, I'm so sorry!" *I was so wrapped up in my own drama*, Rachel thought, *that I never noticed that she might be grieving.*

"We're here for you if you need to talk about it," Paula said, rubbing her arm.

"Thank you. I'm fine, honestly. I really don't want to talk about it. Our marriage was over but he was a huge part of my life and there was just the two of us living in the house so it's a big adjustment for me. I'm trying to figure out my life now on my own so I would love a day off here tomorrow to help process everything."

"Right so ... have we got a plan then?" Paula asked.

"Yes, I think we do," said Rachel, "but we just need to check that they can take us here."

"I'll ask Nuria," Paula said, getting up and walking to the reception desk.

Rachel leaned over and squeezed Cathy's hand. "I'm sorry for your loss, really I am."

Cathy nodded. She was glad she told them.

"Okay, guys, we have a decision to make," Paula said, returning with Nuria. "Other pilgrims are booked in tomorrow night but ... there is one solution."

"Oh god!" laughed Cathy.

"What?" said Rachel.

"It's a triple room," Paula said, laughing.

"Oh my god, that's hilarious," said Rachel, laughing. "This time I'll take it!"

"That's a yes, Nuria," Paula said.

Nuria nodded and went off to make the reservation, looking bemused – not knowing why everyone thought it was so funny.

"Well, let's drink to our new plans and to our stay in Arzua!"

"*Arzua!*"

They clinked glasses and had some more wine, still laughing at their triple-room arrangement. Before the lunch ended, the plan was put in place. Paula had emailed *Follow the Camino*, the company they all booked with and explained the situation. They replied immediately and rearranged the remainder of their trip. She then remembered that she had Carlos' number and messaged him.

"Right, this wine has made me very sleepy," said Cathy, standing up. "Let me know how much I owe you for lunch. I'm off for a rest."

"Me too," said Rachel, taking her leg down from the chair. "Thanks, Paula, that lunch was just the tonic I needed."

"Shall we meet later and go to the square for dinner? Say six?" asked Paula.

"That sounds great," Rachel said.

"Okay, you two go off. I'll tidy up here and see you in reception at six."

Paula felt relieved. So far this trip was not making things any clearer for her. And now Cathy's revelation had really thrown her. All this time she was grieving and they never knew. She shook her head. God love her, she thought as she tidied up.

I need to get my own thoughts in order before I go home or this trip will have been a complete waste, she thought as she poured out the last few drops of wine from the bottle and drank them off.

CHAPTER 26

The ladies met in the reception area of the pension at six and then headed out to the main square at the end of their street. Tall trees surrounded the square, providing welcome shade for diners at nearby cafés seated outdoors. The atmosphere was vibrant as pilgrims and locals enjoyed the evening sun. Families with small children stood talking with friends while their children played around them and babies were rocked in buggies.

"Oh, this is so nice," Cathy said. "Let's look for a table."

"*Rachel!*"

Rachel looked to the left to see Bernie waving at her.

"I'd better go over."

"Sure, we'll all go," said Paula.

"Oh, my dear, your knee," Bernie said, standing up to hug Rachel. "Sit down here."

"We were just going to get a table over there …" Rachel began.

"We've loads of room here," Bernie said and she was right. There were two empty tables beside her while the rest of the square was quite full.

"Sure, why not?" Rachel conceded, not wanting to move around much on her injured knee, so she pulled out a seat and sat down.

The others took her lead and pushed the two tables together.

"Simon has gone to get menus," Bernie told them.

Rachel didn't bother to protest. She was done trying to avoid Simon Molloy. It was pointless.

"Here he is," Bernie said, smiling.

Rachel looked around and there he was, walking through the square with the sun behind him. He had a waitress with him who looked like she was hanging on his every word. He is still a very attractive man, thought Rachel, she couldn't deny it.

His face lit up when he locked eyes with hers.

"Hey, great to see you all! How's the knee?" he said, pulling up a chair between Rachel and Bernie.

"Why don't we order some drinks and we can tell you all about it," Paula suggested.

The waitress took their order and left the food menu.

Just as Rachel was about to speak, a brass band arrived from a side street and started playing while marching around the square. Everybody stopped what they were doing and began clapping along. Young Spanish children followed the band around the square in a celebration of some kind.

"Our pension owner, Nuria, said there was a festival on," Paula said.

"Nuria? Are you staying in Pension Louis?"

Paula nodded.

"So are we! How lovely! It must be full of Irish people!"

"How long are you staying?" Paula asked, knowing that Rachel wanted to know the answer.

"Two nights," answered Bernie.

"Oh, so are we," said Cathy. "We've all decided to take a day off walking tomorrow and just relax. Rachel needs to rest her knee and I, for one, could do with a day off – it's all going by so fast."

"That's true. It's lovely that we are all staying in the same place," said Bernie, delighted with the company.

Although it must have been awkward for Rachel, Paula thought, it was lovely to see Bernie's face so happy and animated.

Rachel was clapping along, watching the band pass, when she felt Simon looking at her. She turned to look at him while everyone else was watching the band.

He still has feelings for me, she thought. Her stomach flipped and her breath quickened as she realised she had strong feelings for him too.

I'm in trouble, she thought, big trouble.

The group ended up having a great night. The restaurant specialised in paella so they all ordered different types and had a few bottles of wine to accompany it. The square was lively all evening with people coming and going.

Paula went to say hello to two women she had chatted with on the road that day.

Then Marta came over to chat with Cathy and, after she introduced her to everyone, Cathy explained that she was taking a day off and wouldn't see them tomorrow. Marta gave Cathy her phone number and told her to message her when she was one hour away from the Cathedral de Santiago and that she would meet her there to welcome her.

"Isn't that such a nice thing for her to do?" said Bernie when she had left.

"Yes, I was so blessed to meet them on my first day. They welcomed me into their group and I have met them every day since. Father Eduardo isn't here tonight but he is so lovely. They also taught me so much about the Camino that I didn't know. For example, did you know that the pilgrim passport that we use today was actually a document given out by bishops over a thousand years ago, to pilgrims in other countries starting their journey? They carried it with them to get free lodgings and food along the route and then had it stamped to prove they had done the journey. Isn't it incredible that we are walking some of that same path and that we do something similar today?"

"That is incredible," replied Bernie. "I knew pilgrims had to return to their countries with the Compostela as proof but I didn't know about the history of the pilgrim passport. Then again, when you are walking, you really feel like you are walking in the footsteps of generations of pilgrims before you because the route hasn't changed since the ninth century. It really is a privilege."

"Marta says they are going to seven o' clock Mass here in the morning before they set off so I'm going to join them."

"Oh, that sounds lovely!" Bernie said. "Could I go to that?"

"Of course, the church is just around the corner here," Cathy said, pointing over her shoulder.

"Oh good, I should be able to get there myself."

"Come with me. We could leave at a quarter to seven and I can introduce you to Father Eduardo. He is a young priest but so wise for his age. And afterward, if you like, we could go for breakfast."

"Oh, I'd love that and it would give Simon a break from being with his mother 24/7."

"So you are staying here an extra night then?" Simon asked Rachel.

As he leaned forward to top up her wine glass, she got butterflies in her stomach. "Yes, doctor's orders as such."

"And the crutch?"

"Unbelievably, you can buy a crutch in a pharmacy here and it's a huge help but if I walk tomorrow I could do more long-term damage, so I need to rest it."

"Well, I'm here tomorrow too if you would like to do something?"

"Paula and Cathy are staying with me, their choice by the way, so I think I'll be fine, thanks."

"Well, if it's okay with you," Simon said, lowering his voice and leaning towards her, "I would love to take you out to dinner?"

Rachel sighed. "I don't know what I'm doing, Simon."

"Okay, sure let me know tomorrow or whenever."

"I don't mean about tomorrow night – I mean with my life. Everything has been turned upside down and I'm not sure that going to dinner with you would help that."

"I see," he said, looking disappointed. "No problem."

Paula had just returned to the table when she saw Carlos approaching. Her heart beat faster as she watched him walk through the square, sunglasses on, wearing jeans and a tight T-shirt. He waved and smiled when he saw her. He really is a handsome man, she thought.

"Ah, this is where you all are," he said.

"Carlos, this is Bernie and her son Simon, also from Ireland. Carlos is our wonderful driver," Paula said as he shook hands with everyone.

"Please sit with us," Simon said, pulling out a seat for him.

"*Gracias*," he said, sitting down. "I came to see how you are, Rachel."

"You are very kind. It's my knee, an old injury. I'm afraid I brought this on myself by walking too fast and not taking enough breaks. Lesson learned!"

"Does this mess you around, Carlos?" Paula asked him. "Us staying an extra night here?"

"No, it is okay for me as it is the same amount of days overall and the company has put me in a nice place here in Arzua so I also have a day off tomorrow."

"Oh, that's great," Cathy said.

"That is why I looked for you. As I have tomorrow off I was wondering if the group might like to take a trip to a lake tomorrow, in the morning before it gets too hot?"

Paula answered first. "That sounds great. Count me in."

"Bernie and I are going to Mass and then breakfast," said Cathy.

"And that is probably enough activity for me." Bernie said. "I need a few siestas in my day … but thank you."

"I need to rest this knee and I'm looking forward to having a lie-in for a change, so I'll opt out as well," Rachel answered.

"I'm going to pass too, but thank you," said Simon.

"So just you and me, Paula," Carlos said, smiling.

"Well, if you're sure?" Paula felt a hot flush run through her.

"Yes," he said, leaning his head towards her. "Of course."

He held her gaze and Paula felt butterflies again. She looked around to see if anyone noticed but Cathy was talking to Bernie and Simon was looking at Rachel. So she looked back and Carlos was still looking at her.

"Mañana," he said, getting up from his chair. "Eight o'clock okay?"

"Yes," Paula croaked, her throat suddenly very dry.

What on earth am I doing, she asked herself, as she watched him walk away.

CHAPTER 27

The next morning Rachel was woken by the sound of the front door closing. Her room was right beside it. She checked her watch. That must be Cathy and Bernie, she thought, heading out to Mass.

They had offered to come back to take her to breakfast but Rachel preferred to spend some time alone today so she told them to go on without her.

Lying in bed, looking at the ceiling, she ran through the events of the last few days. She had tried running away from Simon and avoiding crossing paths with him but the Universe stepped in in a big way and stopped her from running anymore. And it threw them together by having them stay in the same accommodation again for two nights. Surely this was more than a coincidence?

Sitting in the square last night in the evening sun, she felt happy. When Paula told a funny story and everyone cracked up laughing, she looked around the table. These strangers had become her friends. And Bernie knew her from when she was a teenager so she could be herself with her. It was so good to see Bernie laughing and at one stage when she looked at Simon, he was looking at his mum so lovingly with tears in his eyes. It really moved her. This trip had to be hard for him and he was looking after Bernie so well. She didn't know the extent of Bernie's illness but it was clear that Simon was stepping up to the plate and putting her needs before his.

Would Craig have done that for anyone, she wondered. It was his ambition and drive that she first found attractive about him but he was sometimes cold and lacked empathy about people he saw as weaker than him. He also believed he was right in every argument and this led to heated rows between them. She knew she was hot-headed but it infuriated her when he refused to accept any other side of an argument. Rachel gave as much as she got in those rows and sometimes they wouldn't speak for a few days until they had both cooled down and then had amazing sex to make up.

But she had loved him and she had seen a softer sometimes vulnerable side of him over their two years that he would never let anyone else see. When she fell ill in work and was rushed to hospital with abdominal pains, that resulted in her gallbladder being removed, he cancelled all his work meetings to stay at her bedside before and after her surgery. He also took time off work to help her for a few days when she returned home.

There probably were signs there of his true colours if she searched hard enough but maybe she hadn't wanted to see them. She had unopened texts from him on her phone. She knew he was sorry and that he wanted them to go back to how they were. She never thought he would cheat on her and her biggest fear now was, if she couldn't trust him after being with him for two years, how could she trust anyone else? Simon had already broken her heart and she didn't see that coming either. Am I just a complete mug, she wondered as she pulled the duvet up and went back for a snooze.

Cathy introduced Bernie to Father Eduardo and the prayer group. Marta gave them both a big hug.

"It is so nice to meet you," Father Eduardo said as he took Bernie's hand and held it in both of his. "We have enjoyed having Cathy with us and we hope to see you both again in Santiago."

"I have Cathy's number now," Marta added, "so I said we could meet her in the square when she arrives."

"We will also be attending a Pilgrims' Mass," said Father Eduardo. "There are four a day but only one in English which is at ten-thirty – the rest are in Spanish."

"And what about confession, Father?" asked Bernie.

"Confession is held twice a day, in the morning between ten and twelve and after the last Mass, I think, at seven-thirty."

"Do you have to go to an English-speaking priest or can you go to any?" asked Cathy.

"There will be English-speaking priests there, even if it is not their first language. They put a sign outside to say what language they speak."

"*Hmm*, that is definitely something I want to do, thank you," said Bernie.

"Me too," said Cathy but she wasn't sure if an English-speaking priest would be ready for what she had to tell him. But then if he didn't hear your sins or understand you, how could he wipe them away? She didn't want a conversation – she just wanted absolution.

Paula's alarm went off at seven. She sat straight up in bed. What am I doing? Am I mad? No, she berated herself, it's just a visit to a lake. Cop yourself on, woman!

Carlos had said he would be here at eight but he never said anything about breakfast. She checked her phone. She had one WhatsApp message from him.

Are you okay to walk for one hour at the lake and then have breakfast?

He had sent it 30 minutes ago.

Yes, that sounds lovely.

That gave her one hour to have a shower, get dressed and have a coffee. The kitchen in Pension Louis had the basics for a cup of coffee, she noticed yesterday, so that should help wake her up.

So just me and Carlos this morning, she thought. At least he asked everyone if they wanted to go to the lake not just me, so it looks innocent. Hang on, it *is* innocent. He has never given any indication that their chats were anything other than innocent. But then again she did feel some chemistry between them ... or maybe she was imagining it. Maybe it was easier to live in a dream world than sit down and figure out what she really wanted. Was Carlos just a form of procrastination, a distraction from thinking about her life at home?

"*Oh, shut up with these thoughts!*" she shouted to herself as she got out of bed and hopped into the shower.

CHAPTER 28

Carlos smiled as Paula opened the passenger door of his van and sat in beside him.

"*Buenos dias*," he said, smiling.

"*Buenos dias*," she replied.

God, he looks great, she thought, securing her belt and returning his smile.

They drove down the main street of Arzua and then out along the motorway for ten minutes before turning off the main road that brought them through a forested area.

"This is lovely."

"Wait until you see where we are going," Carlos said, looking straight ahead.

The van climbed a hill and when they got to the top Paula got her first glimpse of the water. A narrow road led down to the shore.

Carlos started beeping the horn.

"What are you doing?" Paula laughed as there was no one else around.

He was smiling to himself. When they reached the shore a man waved to him and it was then that Paula saw the barge.

"What is this?"

"It is a ferry to take us across the lake."

"You're joking?"

"No, just wait and see."

The drawbridge came down and Carlos drove the van straight on. They were the only vehicle on it. Once the drawbridge came up, the ferry slowly chugged across the lake. Carlos got out of the van and Paula followed his lead and joined him to look out at the lake.

"It's huge," Paula remarked as the full size of the lake came into sight.

"It is a reservoir. But the view is better from the other side. There you can see the full size."

Paula enjoyed the feeling of the breeze on her face. The sun was high in the sky and it looked like it would be another beautiful day.

Just before they reached the other side, Carlos motioned for her to get back in the van. Waving to the ferry operator, he drove off and parked a little bit away.

"Perfect," he said, getting out of the van. He then went to help Paula alight.

They walked past some men who were fishing off a short boardwalk and continued until they came to a grassy opening that gave a full view of the lake.

"This is beautiful," Paula said, throwing her arms in the air and taking in a deep breath of the fresh mountain air.

Carlos sat down on the grass and patted the space beside him for her to join him. For a few moments they just sat there looking out onto the lake, listening to the birds and watching for air bubbles and the occasional fish coming up for air.

"Thank you for bringing me here, it's so peaceful," she said. "Do you come here often?

"No, just once a year."

"So you don't visit when you are here every week or do you work other routes each week?"

Carlos shook his head. "No, just once. I only volunteer to drive once a year, in this week."

"Volunteer? Are all the drivers volunteers here?"

"No, no, just me. For the rest of the drivers, this is their full-time job. There are volunteers in the Camino centres, but I am the only volunteer driver that I know of."

"Oh, so I take it you're not from around here then?"

"Correct. I live in Madrid and ... can you keep a secret?" Carlos looked at her and smiled cheekily.

He tilted his head and Paula felt her stomach flip.

Oh what the hell is this, she thought, pulling her eyes away from his. I'm actually blushing.

"Of course," she replied, trying to pull herself together.

Carlos took a deep breath and looked off into the distance. "I am a policeman. That is my job in Madrid. But I don't want people to know that. I work in the centre of Madrid but every year I take one week to volunteer here."

Paula began to imagine how good he must look in a police uniform but she could see by the uncomfortable look on his face that there was more to the story.

"Well, that is very good of you."

A silence hung between them. A gentle breeze caused a ripple across the lake and the trees made a hush sound as they swayed.

Carlos pulled a handful of grass and started separating the blades.

"Everyone on the Camino has a story and I am no exception. My wife and I walked this route at this time three years ago," he said, turning to

Paula and then looking back again at the blades in his hand. "It was her wish to do it," he paused, "while she was still well."

He turned to Paula, and she could see in his eyes that this was a painful memory.

"Maria was diagnosed with breast cancer three years ago," he said.

"Oh my goodness, I'm so sorry to hear that."

"We thought we had lots of time. We thought that she would be one of the lucky ones. She was so positive. We made so many plans for afterward. She would say – after the cancer, we will go to Brazil – after the cancer, we will go skiing."

Carlos picked up a stone and flung it into the lake with anger at these painful memories.

Paula reached over and put her hand on his shoulder. "I'm so sorry, Carlos."

"For two years I have been coming here and listening to other people's stories, other people's grief. I never felt like speaking of my own story, but I wanted to tell you."

Paula nodded, keeping her hand on his shoulder.

"Maria was only forty-eight when she died. We were together for five years and married for three, but when she got the diagnosis we didn't even get one year. She was so fit and healthy too. She used to go for a run at six in the morning before work. She worked for a charity for children with disabilities. Oh, how she loved those kids, and they loved her too. We tried for kids, but it didn't happen for us. We thought we had time, Paula," he said shaking his head, "but it was not to be for us."

"I'm sorry you had to go through this."

"I was so angry. I had to stay strong for Maria, but I was angry at God, angry at the cancer, angry at the world. She could see that it was eating me up and she said, 'Let's walk the Camino'. I said no immediately because I thought it was a pilgrimage just for religious people and I was fighting with God. But Maria said it would be good for us to get away from everything and have space and time to think without distraction. So she picked this route, and we did it three years ago this very week."

"Is it not hard for you to return?"

"Yes and no. We met so many people who shared their stories and their reasons for walking the Camino – some also with cancer, and others grieving loved ones. I didn't want to talk about our reasons but Maria did. She was walking slowly by then and we took many breaks but the spirit of the people on the Camino lifted her. It brought a light to her face. I cannot describe it but being here, in nature, just walking day after day gave her peace."

He paused, staring out into the distance.

"I started the Camino angry but after three days I broke down. I cried for a day and a night. It was a terrible time and a beautiful time. We cried together. The pressure of being positive all the time was too much for both of us so we let it go. My anger wasn't serving me and it wasn't helping Maria so I just let it go too. Something changed out here on these roads."

"I don't know what to say – you have been through such an awful and painful time," said Paula, holding back the tears.

"Yes, but many people have also. After Maria passed and this week came around I decided that this is where I wanted to be. Maria and I, we experienced the worst time of our life here but we felt something here that helped us, supported us and that is why I came back just to be in the same places again."

Carlos turned to Paula and looked moved to see tears running down her face.

"Thank you for telling me all this, for sharing it," she said,

"I keep to myself out here. You are the first person I have told."

Carlos moved nearer to Paula, lifted her chin, and wiped away her tears.

"You do deserve to be happy again, Carlos, you know?"

Carlos smiled. "Maria will always be the big love of my life but, who knows, maybe someday in the future ... but not now, not yet."

"Well, it sounds like you were a wonderful husband and I hope you find happiness again, I really do."

"My heart is not ready but I will not close my mind to it completely. Thank you, Paula. For a long time it felt too painful to talk about Maria but today it didn't hurt as much anymore."

He picked up Paula's hand and kissed the back of it while keeping his eyes on hers.

"But now," he said, looking at his watch, "we must get back."

Carlos stood up and held his hands out to help Paula up. Standing up fast, she found herself leaning against him. He pulled her in for a hug. His firm chest and his strong arms holding her almost made her dizzy.

Pulling away, Carlos took her face in his hands. Her heart was beating out of her chest and her body flooded with desire for him. He looked into her eyes and moved his face closer. She closed her eyes. Waiting for his lips on hers. She wanted to kiss him so badly.

He tilted her head down and kissed her on her forehead.

"*Andiamo*, let's go," he said with a smile. "Time to eat."

He took her hand and they headed towards the bus.

Paula was unsure about what had just happened but was happy for him to take her hand.

I wanted to kiss him, she thought as the van pulled away. You silly woman, she said to herself. He is just a friend who confided something very personal. She berated herself harshly before pushing down the feelings of lust racing through her body.

CHAPTER 29

Rachel spent the morning sitting at the small desk in her room, writing in her journal. She had never journalled before, thinking it was too *woo-woo* for her. She was a fan of digital lists and planners on her phone or on her laptop but writing her feelings down on paper was never for her. She found it really awkward at first, staring at a blank page. With so much rage over Craig and confusion over Simon, she hoped that scribbling her feelings down would make her feel calmer and hopefully it might help her in finding a way forward from the mess her life was now.

She had a quick look at her emails on her phone. She wanted to keep abreast of things at work so she wouldn't be too much out of the loop when she returned. And she wanted to see if there were any more emails from Craig. He had been texting her and emailing her before she left, trying to get her to talk to him.

There were a few texts there that she hadn't opened but the emails were less frequent now. In one way she was happy to see that he was trying to win her back but in another way seeing the emails sitting there in her inbox just made her sad and a little heartbroken that her dream was over. So many times she wanted to say yes to one of his texts and agree to see him. So many times she wondered if she had reacted too harshly and wondered if they could work through this and find a solution, but she didn't feel strong enough to face him yet.

Then one email from her boss seemed to confirm that he had moved on with his life and she really didn't know how to feel about that.

You may be interested to know that your ex, Craig, has been seen at various meetings with Howster & Howster in London. According to my sources, he has been saying that Dublin is too small a market for him and that he is London-bound. Good news all round.

"London." Rachel let out a big breath. "Well, I guess that's that."

Bumping into Craig at the many legal conferences she had to attend in a year, had been something she had been dreading, so his being in London would be a great help. It just feels so final though, she thought. Craig being out of my life living in a different country should make me happy but it doesn't.

"So I guess that's back to work for me at Troy and O'Doherty," she said but saying it out loud didn't bring her any lift at all. Right now she didn't have any desire to go back to work. Having her own business had been her dream and she had almost achieved it. Now it felt like starting all over again, but the legal business was all she knew so she had no choice but to go back. What else could she do?

She wasn't going to think about that today. The news about Craig moving to London had pushed the whole situation along. If he was moving to London then things were well and truly over.

"This is what you wanted," she said to herself.

I need a break from this room, she decided. Grabbing her crutch and her wallet, she picked up her key and left the room.

"*Hola, Nuria!*" she called out to the receptionist.

"*Hola!*"

"Good morning." Simon's voice came from a corner in the communal area, where he was sitting with his laptop open in front of him.

"I didn't see you there," Rachel said, walking over to him. "Getting some work done?"

"Yes. Mum is still out with Cathy so I thought I'd catch up on some emails."

"I see."

Rachel turned to leave but then stopped. "I'm going out for a coffee. Do you want to join me?"

A smile crossed his face. "Absolutely, I could do with a break," he said, closing his laptop. "Let me just drop this back in my room."

"Sure. I'll meet you outside," Rachel said, making her way to the door.

Outside the sun was shining and the street was busy with local people going about their business. She googled some bakeries as she waited for Simon.

"So do you have anywhere in mind or will we just wander?" he asked when he joined her.

"I googled some bakeries and have the name of a place called Panderia Vazquez, five minutes away. It is a traditional Spanish bakery and I fancy something nice."

"Lead the way. How is the knee today?"

"It's a lot better than it was yesterday but I'm still not sure how far I will be able to walk tomorrow even with this crutch."

They reached the corner of the road and waited to cross at a pedestrian crossing.

"Here, take my arm," Simon said, holding out his arm while looking up and down the road for traffic.

Rachel hesitated but then linked his arm. It did make walking easier, using him for support on one side and the crutch on the other.

"Okay?"

"Yes, it helps actually." Rachel could feel the heat of his body against her arm, giving her butterflies again.

"We're here," he said, looking up at the bakery sign. He released his arm to open the door, letting her walk in ahead of him.

Inside the café felt like stepping back in time.

"I read that the décor hasn't changed since the seventies and it's very popular with the locals," Rachel said, looking around.

A glass counter held lots of delicious cakes, including Tarte de Santiago in different sizes. Behind the counter were shelves of freshly baked bread of all shapes. Further up there was a full bar.

A lone local man was sitting on a bar stool, talking to a waitress. There were plenty of tables and chairs in the big seating area. One table was occupied by two men playing chess, another by three older women discussing some topic animatedly.

"Do you know what you want?" Simon asked.

"Yes, I'd like a slice of Tarte de Santiago and a cappuccino."

"Why don't you get a table and I'll order?"

"Thanks."

Rachel picked a table against the wall and sat down.

Just then her phone buzzed. It was a WhatsApp from Charley.

How are you? Where are you? Why haven't you messaged me back?

Rachel had completely forgotten that Charley had messaged her while she was in the square last night and she had forgotten to get back to her.

She smiled and started typing.

Can't talk now having coffee and cake with Simon
WHAT???
Rachel laughed.
I'll ring you later.
OMG!!
Simon came and sat beside her. "Something funny?"

"Oh, I'm just replying to Charley. She still makes me laugh."

"She's funny all right. I met her a few weeks ago. Or rather I heard her first. She was in the supermarket and let's just say young Jack was giving her grief. I think he was throwing a tantrum over something."

"Oh god!"

"She still managed to wrangle him into a supermarket trolley while carrying on a full conversation."

"She has her hands full with him," said Rachel.

They both smiled and held each other's gaze for a moment before the waiter arrived with a tray and put the coffee and cakes down.

"Complimentary," he said as he put down a plate with two pieces of lemon cake on it.

"*Muchas gracias*," they both said at the same time.

"That's so nice," said Rachel.

"It is, yeah. It's happened to Mum and me a few times on this trip. The Galicians are so kind to pilgrims. I like this place," he said, looking around. "It's very authentic."

They continued chatting long after the coffee was finished, mostly about people they both knew from school and college. Some were still in Cork and others were scattered all over the world.

Simon's phone vibrated on the table. "Oh, that'll be Mum," he said, opening his phone. "Let me just take this."

She watched his expression soften as he answered.

"Hi, Mum . . . Yes, I'm nearby. Give me five minutes." He closed his phone. "I'm afraid I have to go. Mum is back and I want to make sure she gets all her meds before her rest."

"Sure, let's go back. I should do the same. I need to rest this leg as much as I can."

Standing up, he came around to her side of the table and handed her the crutch.

"Rachel, I just want to say that it has been amazing bumping into you out here. I know it was the last thing you wanted but I hope we can be friends now."

"Of course," sighed Rachel, but she was past wanting to be just friends now.

"So does that mean you will let me take you out to dinner tonight?"

Rachel stalled. "*Em* ..."

She enjoyed his company and, although he broke her heart all those years ago, she knew she had to let that anger go. He was nothing like Craig, she could see that now. And it seemed like Craig had moved on with his life. Maybe they could be friends? And maybe it couldn't do any harm to have dinner with him?

"I'd love that," Rachel answered honestly.

Simon held out his arm and she took it. She let him help her back to the pension even though her knee pain was the furthest thing from her mind now.

CHAPTER 30

Cathy was relaxing in her room when she got a WhatsApp message from Bernie, inviting her out to dinner. It seemed Simon and Rachel were going out to dinner together, which was a surprise.

I'd be delighted. Cathy replied. **Will we go early, say 6?**

Yes, that suits me as I need an early night before walking again tomorrow.

See you in reception at 6 so, thanks. C x

That's a turn-up for the books, thought Cathy. Rachel had done her best to avoid Simon but fate had put a stop to her gallop and now they were having dinner together. They looked so good together and it was clear last night that Rachel was no longer angry at him. In fact, they looked very cosy. Maybe there was something more there. But, then again, what did she know about relationships?

She had been in Rachel's position once. She had her heart broken and felt humiliated when she found out that her boyfriend at the time, Luke Kennedy, her first love, had cheated on her and everyone in the town knew but her. But instead of moving away as Rachel did, she stayed and ended up with the opposite of her normal type.

Ted was dull, conservative, and a Mass-goer but he was solid. She knew he would never cheat on her and at that time she could no longer trust her judgement of men, having got it so wrong with Luke. Little did she know she was jumping from the frying pan into the fire. It was a slow-burning fire though.

After they were married she believed she had found what she had been looking for, a stable relationship, a house in a nice area, and a protective man who was a home bird and rarely went out. He didn't drink much then, so he had no interest in sitting in pubs watching sport or anything else for that matter. He spent most of his free time helping out on his mother's farm. His mother was too tight to employ a farm worker so she made her sons do the work even though they had lives of their own.

Cathy complained about the amount of time he spent there but learned early on never to criticize his mother. When he told her that his mother would always be the number one woman in his life, she was taken aback.

"I'll always be there to help Mam out," he had said. "She comes first. What you need to do is come with me and make an effort like Patsy does."

Cathy could feel her teeth grinding. Patsy was a nosey interfering wagon and Mark, Ted's brother, was like a lapdog around her. Patsy and Ted's mum were the best of pals and spent their Saturday afternoons gossiping about the neighbours or criticising Cathy. She refused to go so Ted didn't speak to her for a whole weekend.

When Monday came around Ted acted as if nothing had happened. Cathy soon learned that this was his way of dealing with things. If she didn't agree with him, he sulked and blocked her out and then after a few days acted as if nothing had happened. If she mentioned any disagreement he would say, "I don't know what you're talking about, it was just a difference of opinion," making her second-guess herself. But normal people didn't stop talking to their partners for two days over a difference of opinion.

Cathy didn't know what normal couples did. Her old friends were living in England and her family lived on the other side of Mullingar and never visited her. When they gathered for family occasions Ted was the perfect gentleman, chatting to everyone, laughing and joking. He was the same at work, a top salesman.

But at home after work, he was moody and complained about the idiots he worked with. He didn't like socialising, said it drained him, so he avoided any kind of social gathering. But he didn't want her going out either, accusing her of wanting to spend more time with strangers than with her husband.

In the early days, if she had a social night arranged he would sulk and promise her a night in with a movie instead or that he would order in a special meal for her and, feeling guilty, she would cancel her plans. But when the night rolled around the movie or meal wouldn't happen. And when she asked him about it he'd say, "You picked me up wrong". Sometimes he completely denied that the conversation ever happened, making her think she was going mad or imagining things.

She knew within six months of marrying him that it had been a mistake. But it was a mistake of her own doing and she knew it. She had rushed into the relationship and ignored warnings from family that maybe he wasn't the one for her. Her mother told her to wait a while but she didn't listen. And they were all right and she did live to regret it.

It was when Ted was out at his mother's one Saturday afternoon that Father John called to the house. He was the new priest in the parish and was calling door to door to introduce himself. Ted didn't usually like people calling in but it had just started to rain so Cathy felt she had to ask him in and offer him a cup of tea. He was a young priest compared to what they'd had before. Most priests in the area were over seventy but Father John was only about ten years older than Cathy.

While she made him a cup of tea, they talked for a while. She could tell he was a kind soul and he talked excitedly about the things he wanted to set up in the parish. When he asked if she would like to volunteer to help, she said yes straight away.

She would never have been interested before but he was so enthusiastic. She had time on her hands and wanted to help him with some of his projects. She also knew that the old fuddy-duddies in the area wouldn't like change, especially from a young priest, and that things could get lonely for him. But most of all she knew that Ted, being a devout Catholic, wouldn't object to her leaving the house to help with church activities. So it was a win-win as far as she was concerned. She craved a social outlet where she could meet people without worrying about Ted's disapproval and this might just be the answer.

It turned out to be a lifesaver for her. She helped Father John organise Meals-on-Wheels for the elderly, set up a games hall for young teens once a week, and organised information nights for Baptism, First Communion, and Confirmation. She also became a minister of the Eucharist, just to have somewhere to go on a Sunday morning.

They became very good friends. She could laugh freely with him without feeling guilty and, although he never asked out straight and she never divulged, he knew she wasn't happy in her marriage. She was less than two years married when she knew she had to leave Ted or be miserable for the rest of her life.

She was trying to figure out a way to leave him when she discovered she was pregnant and that put an end to that.

Cathy showered and put on some fresh clothes. She loved her new rucksack. When she'd arrived at Pension Luis with her new purchase, she'd laid out all the clothes she'd brought in her suitcase and put them into piles of what was necessary and what was not. The not necessary pile went into the case. She planned on asking Nuria if there was a charity shop in town where she could donate the clothes and the suitcase.

It had felt good to shed some weight. She'd only kept two hiking outfits and two evening outfits. Everything else went.

Tonight she was wearing black leggings and a new colourful top she bought when out with Bernie earlier around town. Ted preferred her to wear plain clothes so she was trying hard to break that habit and buy colourful clothes that she liked. The red top she bought today was more like a fancy T-shirt. It had a round neck and short sleeves. Bernie suggested she try on a smaller size but she wasn't ready for that step yet. Ted preferred her to wear loose clothes, saying she would only be asking for unwanted male attention by wearing figure-hugging tops, so she always bought tops two sizes too big. It was going to take a while before she could feel comfortable in anything smaller. But the top went well with her dark hair which she was going to wear down tonight instead of her usual tied-back look. She had brought a small neck scarf with her to hide any bruising and it had some red in it to match her new top. Clutching her Miraculous Medal nervously, she ran it up and back along its chain as she looked in the mirror. The medal had been a present from Father John, a gift for all the help she gave him. She had it for years and touched it every time she was nervous as it soothed her. Of course she couldn't tell Ted she got it from Father John. She was going to tell him that it was her mother's if he asked, but he never did.

And it was Father John who gave her the gift of this Camino. She had called in to him a few days after Ted's funeral.

"Cathy!" Father John looked up from the parish newsletter he was reading when he saw her enter the church. He walked down the aisle towards her. Although he was ten years older than Cathy and the same age as Ted, his wavy hair, short beard and sense of humour made him seem younger. He also worked with the youth in the area and played basketball with them in the school and this kept him fit and active. And although he admitted to Cathy that he felt very lonely sometimes, he still got more joy out of life than Ted ever did.

"John!"

He hugged her and tears came to her eyes.

"There now," he said, rubbing her back. "I'm so sorry, Cathy. Come on, let's have a cup of tea."

The door at the side of the altar that was so familiar to her seemed foreign to her today. So many times she had helped other people through this door to sit with Father John and tell him their problems. And, at other times, they held meetings there to arrange happy occasions like Christenings and First Communions. Today it was he who was comforting her. Her faith was a comfort to her, and she believed it was the only thing that helped her put one foot in front of another some days.

Father John made a proper pot of tea, taking a box of Barry's tea bags from the press.

"The good tea bags, Father?" Cathy managed a smile when he brought the pot to the table.

"Oh, I think it's a good-tea-bags moment," he said, turning away to take out a biscuit tin from the press and the milk from a mini-fridge in the corner.

"Now," he said, sitting down and putting her milk in first and then his own, "how are you?"

"In shock, I think," Cathy said, turning her mug around and lifting it to her lips.

"Understandable. Ted was not an easy man to live with and dying so tragically like that ... in your own home ... it will take time to adjust no doubt."

Cathy nodded.

"But he is gone now, Cathy, so it's time for you to think about yourself," he said, leaning across and squeezing her free hand, "and decide what life you want to live, you and Sophie."

"Yes," nodded Cathy, looking into her mug.

Father John saw more than he ever said. He wasn't blind to her domestic situation. Over the years he had been a shoulder to cry on, on more than one occasion.

"How is Sophie taking the news?"

"She is remarkably fine. She was upset at the service, but having her girlfriend Becky there was a great support to her. She didn't stay long, eager to get back to Cork and her pals. I'd planned to go down and stay with Maggie for a few days just to keep an eye on her, but she has good friends and she has her own place with Becky now so she's very happy about that."

"Good. She'll be fine, you both will. And Ted's family?"

"They'll probably give me the cold shoulder because of the cremation. I don't care. I couldn't do right for wrong in their eyes when Ted was alive, so I won't miss their judgemental looks now. Mark was okay about it – but Patsy? You'd swear I had him burned at the stake the way she went on about it. I'll certainly be glad to get home to my own house despite ..."

"Ah yes, you've been back to see it. How was it? I told you I'd go with you."

"I know and thank you but I felt I needed to go by myself. It was strange. It still is strange. I had the clean-up company throw out the carpet and the big hall table that I hated so the hall looks different, but I don't want to stay there. I'm going to sell up once everything gets sorted."

"A fresh start. That's exactly what you need, Cathy, and what you deserve. Will selling the house cause problems for you – with the Kinsellas, I mean?"

"I'm sure they would prefer for me to keep the house as a shrine to Ted and live out my days mourning him but I won't be doing that."

Her whole married life Cathy had to deal with the Kinsella family's judgment of everything she did.

"They're a quare family," her dad had said before she married Ted. "They always have a puss on them and that mother of his is always moaning about something."

Cathy had laughed off her dad's concerns, but she knew they were an odd family. At the time, she could hardly believe that quiet calm Ted was from the same family. He was so different to them or so she had thought when she married him. But, then again, she was the youngest by fifteen years in her house and the only girl. Her three brothers were married and moved out by the time she hit her teens, leaving her living with much older parents than her friends.

"I have a lot to figure out," Cathy said, taking a sip of her tea. "Ted didn't give me access to his bank accounts, so I have no idea how I'm fixed yet. I could be flat broke. I'm waiting for the solicitor to get back to me about his will, so hopefully I'll find out soon. I just want to get away while all that is being sorted, as soon as I can actually."

"I can understand that. Do you think you'll stay living in Mullingar?"

"I don't want to. I like my job and my father is here, but I want to live somewhere completely different – maybe somewhere in Cork to be nearer Sophie. Ideally, if I could sell the house and get somewhere smaller for me, I'd be happy. I don't need much. I just want a quiet life now."

"And maybe travel a bit?"

"Oh god, yes. All the years I have dreamed about the places I wanted to visit but Ted ... well, you know, he wouldn't have it. No, it was Kerry or nothing. No offense to Kerry, but I never want to go there again!" She laughed. "Every year for twenty years is enough! Work has given me four weeks off, so I want to go somewhere to clear my head."

"You should! You are still a young woman with many choices and options ahead of you," he said with a wink.

"I'm fifty years of age, John!" She laughed. "Hardly a young one!"

"And you still haven't celebrated that birthday yet."

"Ah, it's months ago now. No, I need to look forward now not back."

"That's true and the world is your oyster as they say, so why not go out and see it?"

"But what will you do without me!" joked Cathy.

"I'll be happy knowing you're enjoying yourself," he said, holding her gaze.

"While you stay here saving the souls of Mullingar?"

"And surrounding area, I'll have you know!"

Cathy looked at him and smiled. "I'll miss not seeing you though."

"We will always be there for each other," he said, reaching over and squeezing her hand. "I really believe that. Even when we're old and grey."

Cathy smiled back at him, feeling their special connection run between them. He had been there for her so many times. And she had been a comfort to him. They had saved each other.

"And, sure, Sophie and I are always texting each other," he said, removing his hand.

"I think she messages you more than she does me!" Cathy said, laughing.

Father John had known Sophie since she was a baby. He baptised her and was there for her Holy Communion and her Confirmation. He helped her so much during those hard teen years, especially when Ted turned his back on her. And, although the Church did not approve of homosexuality, Father John supported Sophie in a way her own father wouldn't.

"So are you going to open that biscuit tin before my tea is gone?" she asked to lighten the mood.

Father John nodded and opened the tin.

Cathy gasped. "Where did all that come from?"

"Don't you worry. It's from my own personal account," he said, taking the rolled-up euro notes out and closing the lid again. He held the money out to her.

Cathy sat back in shock. "I can't take that," she said, almost in a whisper.

"Yes, you can, and you will," he said, opening her hand and closing it around the notes.

"John!"

"It's just sitting there in my account doing nothing. I want you to use it, to spend on whatever you want, a new start or a great trip for yourself. You deserve all the happiness in the world and, hopefully, this will go a little way to getting you there."

"I don't know what to say." Cathy sniffled as a tear rolled down her face and she tried to take in what this could mean for her. "I promise that I will pay you back when this whole business is sorted."

"No need. You have choices now, Cathy," he said, getting up and putting the tin away in the press and locking the door. "Why don't you go on the Camino now?"

"Oh, I don't know," she said, wiping the tear away with the sleeve of her cardigan.

"You have the time now – and how many times have you watched that movie *The Way*?"

"I've lost count," Cathy said, shaking her head.

"Well, you are free to make your own decisions now and that would be the perfect place to reassess and think about where you go from here."

Cathy stood up and put the money in her bag. She was free to make her own decisions now, but did she know how?

"Make good use of that money and message to let me know your plans," Father John said, standing up.

"I don't know what to say," she said, walking over to hug him. She laid her head on his chest, inhaling the smell of incense from his jumper. Then she pulled back and said, "You could come with me?"

Father John sighed, "Cathy, I ..."

"It's okay, forget I asked. I'll let you know what I'm going to do but, if it's okay with you, I'd prefer if the Kinsellas didn't know my business or my whereabouts for a bit."

"Oh, you leave the Kinsellas to me, girl!" He winked while keeping his arms around her. "I'm well able for them. Forget about them now. As you said, look forward, not back."

Cathy went home and pulled out an old suitcase from under the bed. It held travel brochures and cut-outs from magazines and newspapers of all the places she dreamed of visiting. The Camino was her favourite dream destination. She loved looking through the brochures and imagining planning her own trip. Could she really go now? By herself? Father John seemed to think so. She knew Sophie would be delighted for her too if she went. She opened a new page in her diary and took down the phone numbers of the companies organising trips there.

"Can I really do this?" she asked herself as she clutched the brochures to her chest.

She felt butterflies in her stomach and took it as a sign. "Father John thinks I can, so maybe I need to believe I can too."

CHAPTER 31

Looking in the mirror now, she could feel her confidence growing. Father John believed she could do anything now. She just had to believe it herself.

Taking a deep breath she smiled, took a selfie and sent it to Sophie. She was happy with how she looked and she had to start enjoying that feeling.

Looking great, Mum X was the reply she got back immediately.

Her heart felt full. She missed Sophie and she hoped that they could both move on with their lives now.

Cathy was so depressed when Sophie moved away. With her gone, Ted no longer hid his belittling behaviour towards her. She dreaded going home because she never knew which version of Ted would be waiting for her.

If he had a bad day at work he would insist that she sit and listen while he shouted and ranted. This could go on for hours. If he had a good day he was happy to ignore her. She knew the right thing to do was to leave and Father John had said he would help her in any way he could but Ted had destroyed her confidence so much that she found it hard to make even the smallest decisions for herself.

Cathy shuddered, thinking back to the situation she had been living in for so long.

Standing in front of the mirror, she looked closely at herself.

"*I will never be in that position again,*" she said to her reflection.

Picking up her small backpack, she went out to reception to meet Bernie.

"Oh you look lovely, sweetheart!" Bernie said when she saw her.

"Thank you, so do you."

Bernie had worn different-coloured turbans every night and they always matched the tops she was wearing. Tonight she wore a loose green top and a green camouflage turban.

"Simon was slagging my turban. He thinks it looks like something a US marine would wear," she said, laughing.

"Oh, that is funny!" Cathy offered her arm for Bernie to lean on. "Any preference for food?"

"I was thinking we could go back to the square again for more paella, if that's okay with you?"

"Of course."

Cathy opened the front door and they stepped outside.

Bernie stopped and turned her face to the sun, closing her eyes.

"This is so lovely. Don't you just love the feel of the evening sun on your face? Let's sit in the sun and start with a cold glass of wine, Cathy."

"Anything you say." Cathy smiled as they headed for the square.

The square was less busy tonight or maybe it was because they were out earlier, but they had their pick of tables and the waitress remembered them from the night before. They ordered paella again and a lovely cold bottle of Alberino.

"Now, tell me, Cathy, what made you come on the Camino?" Bernie asked after they finished their food.

"*Hmm*, well, my husband died four weeks ago."

"Oh my goodness, you poor thing!" Bernie said, looking shocked and leaning towards her. "I'm so sorry. I had no idea."

"That's okay. The thing is ..." Cathy said shifting uncomfortably, "it wasn't a good marriage."

"I see," Bernie said, nodding.

"In fact ..."

Before Cathy could go on, a loud crash erupted behind them as a waitress accidentally dropped two plates.

"*Aaah!*" Cathy cried out, her hands flying to protect either side of her head as she ducked down in her seat.

"Are you okay? Cathy?" Bernie asked, taken aback by Cathy's reaction.

But Cathy couldn't answer her.

"Are you okay, love?" Bernie stood up and put her arm around her shoulder.

Cathy sat up, her whole body shaking.

"Jesus, Cathy, you're as white as a sheet! And you're shaking. Are you okay, love?"

Cathy opened and closed her mouth but the words wouldn't come.

"Can I have a glass of water, please?" Bernie asked the concerned waitress who had come over to see what was wrong.

"*Shhh*, it's okay, pet, it's okay," Bernie said, moving her chair closer to sit right beside Cathy.

"I'm sorry," Cathy whispered as she looked at Bernie, tears in her eyes.

"There, there, you're okay," said Bernie as she rocked her gently. "But what happened to you, love?"

Cathy looked at her shaking hands. She was shocked by her own reaction to the smashed plates, transporting her right back to that Saturday afternoon in her kitchen. Taking a sip of the water the waitress brought, she steadied her breathing and told the story to Bernie.

She had been sick for a few days with the flu and had spent most of the day in bed, falling in and out of sleep. As usual on a Saturday, Ted was spending the day helping his mother on the family farm. He was a stickler for routine and when he returned from the farm he expected a dinner of lamb chops, mashed potatoes and carrots. It was his regular Saturday dinner.

As Cathy had no car and felt too weak to walk to the butcher's she dragged herself out of bed to see what she could cook for him instead. She found a packet of sausages in the fridge and cooked them as well as the mashed potatoes and carrots. She had no appetite herself and the smell of the food made her nauseous.

Standing in the kitchen, her whole body stiffened when she heard his key in the door. Placing his dinner on the kitchen table, she turned back to the sink to wash up the pots while he sat down.

"What's this?"

Taking a deep breath she turned around.

"If you mean the sausages, I was too sick to leave the house and that's the best I could do."

Ted stood up, his chair scraping on the lino.

"*I have been out working all day and I come back to this?*" he shouted, banging his fist on the table.

Cathy was furious. "*I am sick! I dragged myself out of bed to make food for you so either eat it or don't eat it, I don't care anymore!*"

She saw his anger rise. His face reddened and his knuckles whitened as he dug them into the table.

"*Don't you raise your voice to me!*" he roared as he picked up the plate of food and threw it at her. She turned her face to the wall just in time as the plate flew by her head. But it smashed against the tiled wall over the sink shattering into shards. A piece of enamel embedded itself into her right cheek, barely missing her eye. Her hand flew to her face and when she looked at it, it was covered in blood.

Turning around slowly she saw his red face, so full of fury, go white as the blood trickled down her face. For a second his eyes softened and he made to walk towards her but then he stopped and his face hardened again.

"*Look what you made me do!*" he hissed. "*Clean this mess up!*"

And with that, he picked up his jacket and left, slamming the front door behind him.

Cathy stumbled to the kitchen table and fell into a chair, sobbing and shaking. She sat there until she could catch her breath.

Then she took a small mirror from her handbag on the worktop and, wetting some kitchen roll under the tap, wiped away the blood until she could see the shard clearly and pulled it out.

She found a small plaster in the first-aid box to cover the wound. While she sat there, she thought of the bruise on her hip from him banging the fridge door into her deliberately, the cut on the back on her ankle when he drove the wheelie bin into the back of her legs claiming it slipped out of his hands, the marks on her neck that she kept covered up from the many times he pinned her to the wall, his big hand wrapped around her throat, to make her listen to him.

Since Sophie left the assaults had escalated. And while she wiped the mashed potatoes mixed with delf off the kitchen floor, she realised that this must end.

Cathy sighed and looked at Bernie. Her face looked shocked as she listened to her story.

"I knew then that if I didn't leave him he could kill me."

"Oh my god, you poor pet," said Bernie, still with an arm around Cathy's shoulders.

"I started making plans to leave him after that. But then ... he died ..."

"What happened to him?"

"It was an accident," Cathy said, looking at Bernie. "It happened at home. He ... fell down the stairs and hit his head on a stupid big hall table that his mother gave us. I always hated that table. He was in the house alone. His brother found him."

"I'm so sorry."

"The thing is ... I don't feel anything."

"Well, I think that's completely understandable given the circumstances, love."

"It's not that, it's ... I told him I was leaving him. That morning before I left for work I told him. We were upstairs and I told him and he started shouting at me so I just ran out of the house. He died that morning. And I keep thinking that maybe it was my fault. Maybe the shock made him lose his balance or ..."

"You can't think that, Cathy," Bernie said.

"But it could be true. If I had waited until the evening to tell him instead of the morning ... If I never said anything, hadn't told him I was leaving, would he still be alive today? But ... I had to leave him. It wasn't safe for me to stay there. I nearly drove myself mad asking myself these questions. The what if's ... and the guilt ... I hated being back in that house afterwards too so I had to get away."

"Oh, darling, you've had so much to deal with!"

Cathy nodded. "I needed to get away from everything and try to make sense of it."

"And what about your family or friends? Have they helped?"

"My daughter Sophie is in Cork, as you know, and I don't have many friends, to be honest. Ted hated me seeing my friends and I was too ashamed of the sham marriage I rushed into, so it was easier for me to distance myself from them so they couldn't see what a mess I'd made of my life. I reconnected with my cousin Maggie when she moved back from the UK five years ago and I think she had an idea that things weren't great. She's the one Sophie stayed with when she moved to Cork. The only other person I can call a real friend is John, Father John. He has been my closest friend actually. It was he who suggested I come here to clear my head and figure out what I want to do next because he knows I love the film *The Way*."

"And has it helped?"

"Yes, in so many ways. I'm so happy to have met all of you. It has given me confidence to know that I can meet people and not be an embarrassment. And I have met so many women on the Camino who are older than me, just doing their own thing, and that's really opened my eyes."

"Oh, Cathy you are so young!"

"I'm fifty."

"Exactly. You have so much more life to live. You can live anywhere and do anything. I'm sorry your husband has died but you were moving on anyway, Cathy, and it sounds like you had no choice but to leave the marriage. It's your turn now to live life on your terms."

"I'm terrified though. What if I make the wrong decisions? I have so little confidence and I doubt myself all the time and I have this guilt weighing so heavily on me. Every day here I walk and I pray. I pray for forgiveness."

"Cathy, the only person you need forgiveness from is yourself. Forgive yourself, love. What happened, happened. It was a terrible accident and I'm so sorry he lost his life, but you still have yours. Believe me, I know how precious that is."

Bernie had tears in her eyes now.

"Oh, I'm sorry, Bernie. I must sound so selfish."

"No, you do not. You have been through so much, Cathy, so much pain. But I want you to promise me that you will throw that guilt off your back and go out there and live your life, do you hear me? I'm sixty-eight. I've had a good life, a good husband, and beautiful children. When I lost Bill I had to keep going for the kids and now that I know my time is short I am so selfish. I want more time but I'm not going to get it. So please stop beating yourself up, forgive yourself, and go and live your life, Cathy. It's a gift, it truly is."

Cathy nodded through her tears. She put her arms around Bernie and hugged her.

"Thank you," she said.

Sitting back in her chair she felt a weight had shifted. Saying everything out loud really helped. Like the old suitcase that she was throwing out today, she was going to pack up her guilt and throw that away too. Bernie said it all: she had a life to live.

As she poured them both another glass of wine and sat back in the Galician sun, she made another decision. She was never staying a night in that house again. She was selling it and leaving. Leaving her job and leaving Mullingar. She wanted her new life to start as soon as she got home and this time she didn't care what anyone thought about that.

CHAPTER 32

Cathy had messaged Paula earlier to see if she wanted to join Bernie and her for dinner but she wanted to be alone. Feeling a little foolish after her encounter with Carlos that morning, she had gone for a long walk out of Arzua and had lunch by herself about five kilometres away. She was so frustrated and annoyed at herself. She was wasting time harbouring some holiday-romance ideas with Carlos instead of coming up with plans for the next part of her life. She didn't even know if Kevin wanted to be part of that future with her. It was one thing to live the Shirley Valentine experience with Carlos out here in Spain, but even Shirley Valentine ended up on her own in the end and Paula did not want that.

On her walk, she repeated the words: "Show me what I need to know" and "What is my lesson on this Camino?" She had met people on her walks who had clarity on issues they were dealing with and she wanted that clarity. It felt good to walk and think of nothing and see what might come up, but she was getting impatient.

Maybe I need to stop forcing the answers to come and stop getting frustrated when they don't. She had gone to the supermarket to buy a bottle of wine, some bread and serrano ham for an early dinner for herself. She was in no mood to talk to people so planned to drink the whole bottle of wine herself and have an early night.

"*Paula!*"

Paula turned when she heard someone call her name. It was sunny so she had to squint. Someone was waving at her from across the park.

When she walked towards the person waving at her she saw that it was Sheila, who she had met a few times on the trail. She was sitting outside a traditional taverna with a big fruity drink in front of her.

"Oh hi, Sheila, good to see you."

"You too. Will you join me?"

"Are you on your own?"

"Yes, pull up a chair there."

Paula hesitated, but she had hoped to bump into Sheila again so she pulled up a seat and sat down. "I thought you would have been in the next town by now?" she said, putting her shopping under the table in the shade.

"O Pedrouzo? No, I decided to take an extra night here."

"So did we. One of the women in our group injured her knee so we decided to stay an extra night here instead of two in Santiago. What about you?"

"I was here a few years ago doing the same Camino trail and I was sorry we didn't get to spend more time here in Arzua because it's a lovely place. Sometimes on the Camino it feels like you're rushing to the next place so I wanted to pace it more this time."

"I know what you mean."

"Here's the waiter now. Let me buy you a drink."

"What can I get for you?" the waiter asked Paula.

"Can I have …" Paula hesitated. "What are you drinking?" she asked Sheila.

"Sangria. It's gorgeous and I'm fooling myself into thinking it's one of my five a day because there's fruit in it!" Sheila laughed.

"I like your style," said Paula, smiling. "I'll have what she's having, please."

"Make it a jug then," Sheila said to the waiter. "When in Spain ..." she shrugged at Paula.

They chatted about the relaxed pace of living in this part of Spain until the waiter returned with a big jug of sangria. He poured Paula a glass and topped Sheila's up.

"*Cheers!*" Sheila raised her glass.

"*Cheers!* I need this today."

"Oh?"

"Don't mind me, I'm just having an off day."

"We all have off days on the Camino," said Sheila. "I think it's part of the process. One day I'm loving it and the next day I'm asking myself what the hell am I doing here when I can hardly walk up the stairs to my bed."

"Oh, I know that feeling – my legs were so sore in Palas de Rei that, honestly, I nearly gave up and got a taxi all the way here."

"How are they now?"

"Oh, they're fine, I'm just frustrated today. I came on this trip to get rid of my frustration and get some clarity about what I want to do but so far I have no answers."

Sheila nodded.

"Sorry," Paula said, "I don't want to ruin your afternoon with my self-pity."

"Hey, you're not, honestly. I'm all ears."

"It's just ... I was so frustrated and uneasy before I came out here and I was hoping all the walking would help get it out of my system but that hasn't happened yet."

"Do you know why you were frustrated?"

"Well, a few reasons but I turned sixty last month and a lot of my friends are either retired or counting down the day to retirement and it terrifies me. It makes me feel so old. While all my friends are winding down, I want more adventure in my life and I don't know what that will look like or where that will be. And it's hard because I love my friends but I can't talk to them about this. Then some other personal stuff came up too just before I left, so my head is all over the place."

"Well, there are some things we can't talk to our friends about," agreed Sheila. "But you can talk to me about those frustrations because I was exactly the same when I turned sixty."

"Really?"

"Yes, just two years ago. In my case, I came out of a dreadful relationship with a man who literally put me out of his house in the middle of a storm. As I was driving home, an electrical pole came down and my car was trapped between live wires. It was one of those times you call 999 and ask if you could record a few last words for your loved ones. And they agreed it was a good move which scared me more!"

"*Oh, my goodness!*" Paula gasped.

"Anyway, that was that and I decided I was done with relationships and would die single. Which was fine until I wondered what I would do until then. So, I googled, 'What should a sixty-year-old do with her time in retirement?'. And the answer that came up first was 'Travel and Volunteer. See the world and experience life'. So, basically, my search led me to an organization for people over fifty, who travel together in a group but with one very important difference. Each trip has a volunteering element in the middle of it, so you visit a new and exciting country and spend five to ten days volunteering during your trip. This way you are giving back to the country you are visiting."

"That sounds amazing."

"It changed my life, Paula. I had never done anything adventurous like that, but something kept pushing me towards it. So, after a lot of research and hesitation, I went on my first trip in 2018 to Thailand. And I was hooked. 2019 was India and it only got better. I had more trips planned: Uganda, Tahiti, Bali, and Vietnam. There are so many places to do this. But, of course, the Universe had other plans, and we all had our wings clipped until 2022."

"The pandemic."

"Yep."

"But once that was over I was ready to go again, my passion for travel still alive. I knew there had to be other women and men who would love to travel this way. So long story short: I set up a Facebook page and I couldn't believe the response."

"What did you call it?"

"EVA. It stands for Ethical Volunteering Adventures."

"I love it! So, are you a travel agent now?"

"No, not at all. I feature and promote tour operators that I either personally know, have travelled with, or come recommended and who are ethical and run approved volunteer projects. I don't arrange tours or travel, and I don't accept anything in return."

"That's ... incredible," said Paula, feeling very excited. "You basically built a community out of nothing."

"Yes, I did. I can't believe it myself sometimes, but I love, love, love seeing people over fifty, and some over seventy I might add, travelling to a place like Vietnam and building chicken coops for a local village and sitting down eating and drinking with the locals. It's a fantastic feeling."

"You are amazing, you really are."

"No, I'm not. Honestly, I was terrified the first time I went, but then I just said feck-off to fear and went for it. That's what I'm saying to you. We all need to think outside the box sometimes and make the change we want in our lives. I know I sound like Oprah but if I had let fear hold me back I don't know where I would be now. Certainly not up a mountain in Spain drinking sangria in the sun."

"I'm so delighted I met you today," said Paula.

"Ah, will you stop!"

"No, I mean it. I was feeling annoyed and sorry for myself and now I feel excited and invigorated. What you are doing sounds exactly what I'm looking for – adventure."

"Well, you'll have plenty of adventure on one of our trips. My advice? Don't let fear stop you. It stops so many people from doing something different."

"I'll drink to that!" Paula said, as she poured herself and Sheila another glass of sangria.

CHAPTER 33

"*You're what?*" Charley shouted down the phone.

"You heard me. I'm going to dinner with Simon. He asked, and I said yes."

"Well, you've changed your tune."

"I don't know what I'm doing, to be honest. Two days ago I was horrified he was here and did everything to avoid him but ..."

"But what?"

"Don't laugh but I feel like something – the Camino or the Universe – is pushing us together. I mean, what are the chances of him being here and then, when I tried to run away from him, I get injured and literally cannot run from him anymore."

"The Universe? Hello? Can you put me on to Rachel, please?"

"Very funny."

"What has happened to you out there? You don't believe in all that stuff. You're a hard-ass businesswoman who deals in facts. You have actually said that line to me before."

"I know, I know but ... this seems too much of a coincidence."

"I agree, but are you saying that you're not angry with him anymore?"

"It's just dinner, Charley, I'm not running down the aisle or anything. But ... there is definite chemistry there. I have butterflies in my stomach when I see him, and I just want to reach out and touch him when he sits near me."

"Oh, Jesus, girl, you've got it bad!"

"Do you think I'm mad going to dinner with him?"

"No, not at all."

"I'm just more open to sitting down and seeing what he has to say for himself, that's all. And I got some news today from my boss – it looks like Craig is moving to a company in London. Apparently Dublin is too small for him, so I guess he's moved on.

"Well, that's good news isn't it?"

"I don't know. It ... it's very quick. I have unopened texts and emails from him so he may have been trying to tell me himself. It's just so final."

"Well, I think it's good news. It will be easier to get over him if you don't see him around the place."

"I know."

"But if you are having feelings for Simon Molloy, you need to find out what his plans are. Is he staying in Cork for good now? Does he even want a relationship or is it the comfortable option to fall back in with how things were between you two?"

Rachel sighed. "I don't need to know all that, it's just dinner, but you're right, it does feel familiar and comfortable. Maybe I'm being an idiot. I'm not the best person to judge a man at the moment."

"No, you are not an idiot! Look, if you and Simon get back together and he treats you like a queen, then I will sing and dance all the way down Patrick Street in celebration. I would absolutely love that for you, but I think you should just be cautious, you know. You've just come out of a relationship with a dickhead and the idea of starting over again with someone new is probably awful so of course it would be a lot easier to go out with someone you knew."

"You're right, it's probably the last thing I need."

"Just be careful, okay?"

"I will. Love you."

"I love you too. Now go and enjoy yourself but think about all that, okay? And grill the fucker, do you hear me? You need him to answer any questions you have before you move forward."

"I hear you."

"Okay, ring me tomorrow."

"I will. Goodnight."

Rachel threw her phone down on her bed. She was in great form before she rang Charley and was excited about going out with Simon but now her mood had dropped. Am I being naive here? That whole business with Craig was making her doubt herself now.

She looked over at the other two beds. The triple room was big and bright, and she hadn't seen the women all day. She knew Cathy was out with Bernie and Paula never said what her plans were.

They both seemed to like Simon a lot, which was nice, but Charley was right, there were a lot of unanswered questions. Was tonight the night to have that conversation or should she just go and enjoy being taken out? She didn't know. Looking in the mirror she tucked her T-shirt into her hiking trousers. She had tried on her jeans, but they wouldn't fit over her bandaged knee, so it had to be the hiking trousers. It was going to be a casual night.

Tying up her wavy ginger hair in a ponytail, she pulled a few loose strands down around her face.

Taking a deep breath, she picked up her crutch and went out to reception to wait for Simon.

Simon stood up when he saw her. He smiled and she could tell by his eyes that he was happy with what he saw.

"You look great," he said, walking to her and leaning in to kiss her cheek.

He smelled great. "Different day, different hiking trousers!" Rachel said.

"The look suits you," he said, opening the front door.

"So have you anywhere in mind?"

"Nuria booked somewhere for us – it's not far," he said, holding out his arm for her to link.

She hesitated for a moment before putting her arm through his and using it as support.

"So does everyone know we are going out to dinner together?" she asked.

"If you mean Nuria, my mum and Cathy, then yes. Are you okay with that?"

Rachel nodded. "It's hard to have secrets around here. So how is your mum today?"

"She had a great morning with Cathy and then she slept most of the afternoon. Tonight, the two of them are having an early dinner in the square. They are great friends now."

Within a few minutes, they arrived at Casa Teodora. It was busy with locals and some Camino walkers. The dining room had a quaint traditional feel. The exposed brickwork, yellow curtains, and tablecloths made it feel homely. They were seated by an older waiter who explained the menu to them. Everything looked delicious.

"*Hmm*, I know I'm only away from Ireland a few days, but those potatoes look so good," Simon said as plates of food were coming out from the kitchen.

"I was just thinking the same thing," Rachel said with a laugh.

They held each other's gaze.

"Drinks?" asked the waiter.

"Do you want to share a bottle of red?" asked Simon

"Sure, and some water, please."

The waiter took their food order and returned to pour them each a glass of wine.

"This is quite unbelievable," Rachel said, looking at Simon as she took a sip of her wine.

"Yes, the wine here is so good and so reasonable."

"I didn't mean the wine, I meant this, you and I having dinner, that's what's hard to believe."

Simon's mouth opened to respond but the waiter arrived with their food.

They both started eating in silence.

"So, I never asked what brought you here on the Camino," he said then. "I didn't have you down as a hiker."

"I'm not, clearly," Rachel laughed pointing to her crutch. "All my efforts in the gym didn't prevent this old injury from flaring up."

"So what did make you come here?" Simon said, tilting his head.

"*Hmm*, that's an awkward question." Rachel put down her knife and fork and took a sip of her wine. "The short story is that the person I was dating for two years, who I was about to open a legal business with and move into my home, let me down in the worst way possible, and now neither is happening. My business dream is gone, and the relationship is over."

"I'm sorry to hear that."

"It was, and still is, a huge shock. I needed to get away somewhere. I had never even heard of the Camino, but my boss Helen has done it a few times and she suggested that it might be the best place for me, to figure out my next step."

"And ... has being here helped?"

It was helping until you came along, she wanted to say.

"No. To be honest, it's thrown up more doubts."

"Like?"

"I've been planning on opening my own business for years, dreaming of it all my life ..."

"*Hmm* ... I know," Simon said, cutting into his food.

"What do you mean, you know?"

"The cottage, remember?"

Rachel gasped in surprise and her jaw dropped.

"Did you think I'd forget that?" said Simon. "You spoke about it all the time. You wanted to renovate a cottage in West Cork and run a tea shop or pottery workshop from it. You must have described it a hundred times to me."

Rachel could not believe it. She hadn't thought of that dream in such a long time. When she and Simon were hanging around his house or lying in a park on a sunny day he would say "Tell me about your cottage dream again" and she would describe every detail of what it looked like.

"I cannot believe you remember that. I haven't thought about it in donkey's years," said Rachel.

"It's etched in my brain," said Simon.

"Oh wow!" Rachel shook her head and went back to her food. "Thank you for remembering that. Well, I don't think I'll be buying a cottage, but I'm not sure I want to go back to my old job either. I had already handed in my notice when it all fell apart and, even though I have my job back, and I'm on one month's leave, I'm not feeling it anymore."

"What do you mean?"

"I don't want to go back to working long hours for someone else. Life is too short for that. So, I suppose the Camino has thrown that realisation up. I'm still waiting for a few options on what I will do. So yeah, to answer your question, I'm even more confused than ever. What about you? Any life-changing revelations?"

"*Em* ... well ..." Simon looked serious all of a sudden. "Bumping into you has thrown me in a bit of a spin, to be honest."

"Oh really?" Rachel felt herself blush, so she looked down, focusing on her food.

"In a good way," he said quickly.

He was looking at her now and she wasn't sure she wanted him to go on with this conversation.

"Rachel ..." Simon put down his knife and fork and leaned forward, placing both elbows on the table, his fingers interlocking under his chin. "I know you weren't happy to see me, and I understand that. I apologised the other day for the way it ended between us, and I would really like us to move forward, but I don't think we can until I have answered any questions you have about that time. So if there is anything you need to know or want to know I'm open to talking about it. Look," he said, taking out his phone, "it's on silent now so we won't be disturbed."

Rachel sighed. She knew he was right, and Charley too had said she had to get answers but right now she just wanted to enjoy her night out.

"We don't have to do this now, Simon."

"But if not now, when? It's the big elephant in the room and I know every time you look at me you still have some anger. I'm hoping if I can be one hundred percent honest with you and answer any questions you might have, that maybe then we can get past it."

She knew he was right.

"Okay," she said, putting down her fork. "When you broke up with me, you said that you needed space, and you wanted to go somewhere and try living on your own to figure out who you were. Was that true?"

"Yes. We'd been going out together since I was seventeen. I remember feeling claustrophobic. The flights were booked, and it was like my destiny was laid out in front of me. You booked the flights and organised the visas and I felt like I was going along for the ride. I felt detached from it all. I was also so stressed studying for the Finals that I just went along with whatever plans were made but inside I felt numb. I thought I was having a breakdown of some sort. And I was worried that I might get to Australia and feel the same and then if we broke up over there you would be on your own so we probably would have stayed together even though I wasn't happy."

"I see. You're making it sound as if I forced you against your will into going to Australia. But if I remember correctly it was you who wanted to go there."

"Yes, you're right. I'm not explaining this well. I know Australia was my idea but part of me wanted to escape, to run away as far as possible. I felt so intense and so drained from the exams but you were so happy and excited and, even though I went along with the plans, I was suffocating inside. So instead of dealing with it in Ireland, I thought I needed to cut all ties and go and find myself, I guess. But I know now that I was suffering from depression then and I just didn't recognize it."

"Okay I get it, I do. You had to do what you had to do for you. But at the time it seemed cold and selfish, and I had to deal with all the questions after you left. And then not a word from you. That hurt, Simon."

"I'm sorry. I didn't know how to handle anything right, so I ran away, and I now know that was very wrong."

Rachel picked up her fork, took another bite of her food, and a sip of her wine. It was now or never. She took a deep breath and looked straight at him.

"Tell me about your wife."

"Ah, yes." Simon picked up his glass and took a gulp of his wine before taking a deep breath. "When I got to Australia everything was bright and sunny and wonderful. I got a job straight away in an architect firm in Sydney and because I didn't know any Irish people over there, I filled my spare time going to the gym and that's where I met Gabby."

Visions of a tall blond slim gym bunny went through Rachel's head.

"She is a gynecologist and women's health doctor, very driven, very career-orientated. Things got serious very quickly and we moved in together after two months."

Rachel felt sick when he said that. She looked away and took a sip of her wine.

"Are you sure you want to hear all this?"

"Yes, all of it." Rachel had spent years wondering about Simon's wife and how he could move on so quickly.

"It was quick. I know that seems crazy and it was. I was high on life. I fell in love with Australia. I loved everything about it and Gabby was part of that picture. My visa was for twelve months, and I knew I wanted to stay. Honestly, at that stage, I didn't care if I never returned to Ireland. The lifestyle over there really suited me, and I thought it had fixed my low thoughts. After ten months, we got engaged. My job applied for a visa extension on my behalf and to help that visa process along, Gabby and I got married. I did believe that I was in love with her, but I think I was in love with Australia and the whole way of life out there just as much. You only need to register to get married one month in advance so it's not as big a deal as back home. So we were married in her parents' back garden in Melbourne and had a barbeque for the reception. It was very casual."

Rachel's eyes widened. "*Wow.*"

"I know it seems reckless as we were only together a year, and it was. Obviously, as we're divorced now, it's clear that it was not the best idea. But having said that, and in fairness to Gabby, at the time I thought that it was everything I wanted."

"So what went wrong?"

"I never talked to a doctor about my low mood and apathy while in Ireland, and I should have. I blocked it out and convinced myself that life was great. I kept myself so busy at work, in the gym, running, hiking, anything to not spend time on my own or thinking too much about things. And, as Gabby was a very impulsive person, we had a very busy lifestyle. But she is a doctor, and she recognised my depression long before I was ready to admit it. So we did argue a little about that and I got better at hiding it. Stupid, I know." He shook his head. "Anyway, Gabby was working in a women's clinic outside Sydney and about a year after we were married she was offered an amazing opportunity to work in the Australian outback. She always had an interest in improving the health of Aboriginal women and had worked on other projects out there before."

A modern-day Mother Theresa, thought Rachel, filling her glass with more wine.

"She rang me to tell me about this new opportunity and I thought we agreed to talk about it over the weekend, but she accepted the job before we had a chance to do this. Like I said, she's impulsive. But it was her dream, so I supported her, and off she went, and I stayed in Sydney."

"So, when did you see each other?"

"She got every second weekend off. The place was called Yuendumu, and the nearest city is Alice Springs nearly 300 kilometres away. I would fly to Alice Springs, and she would travel from Yuendumu. We did that for a while and things were still okay, but it was clear she loved the job and was doing really important work there. But all that time at home on my own didn't help my mental health. We talked about me moving to Alice Springs but there were no jobs for me there. Then she was offered a position that she felt she could not turn down, to head up her own clinic and recruit a team to work under her. The writing was on the wall, as they say."

"*Wow.*"

"Yeah. We tried to figure something out but couldn't, so we decided to go our separate ways. Once you apply for a divorce and live apart for a year, your divorce comes through after that."

"But if she had never taken that job," Rachel asked, "would you two still be together?"

"No. My depression came back, and I know our relationship would not have survived it. When we separated I was so tired from putting up a front that I crashed. Badly, actually. I missed days at work and missed deadlines and when I finally went to the doctor he admitted me to a special clinic in Sydney and I spent four weeks there."

"Jesus I ... never knew, Simon."

"Nobody did. Nobody does. My mum knows that I suffered with my mental health, but I never told her about the clinic. You and my job are the only people who know. My boss was brilliant about it and held my job open for me."

Rachel reached over and covered his hand with hers. "I'm sorry I blocked you. I should have at least read your messages."

"Don't feel bad. Honestly, it's best you didn't answer me. I'd caused you enough problems."

Rachel went to move her hand away, but he held on to it.

"I want you to know that when I started working with the psychiatrist she would ask me to go back to a time when I was happiest. It was always when I was with you."

"Simon ..." Rachel shifted uncomfortably.

"I needed to go through that phase and grow up and ask for help. And I got that help."

"How are you now?"

"Better than ever. I take my meds and I'm fine."

He was still holding her hand and they both looked at it.

"I'm back in Cork for good now. And I know last night I said I wanted us to be friends, but I would like us to be more than friends."

"Simon, I ..."

"Don't say anything now. I know I have no right to say that but, when I realised that my happiest times were with you, that's when I tried to get in contact. And, although you never replied, you have been in my thoughts since then. I wanted to come to Dublin to see you. I asked Charley for your address but, don't worry, she didn't give it to me."

Rachel smiled.

"But Seán did."

"What?"

"Yeah, I know, sorry. Don't tell her, she'd kill him." He smiled. "I went to Dublin, but I couldn't cold call on you like that. I spent the whole weekend hoping I'd just bump into you by accident like an eejit."

"Eh ... like a stalker?" Rachel said in pretend alarm.

"Yeah, that too. Look," he said, still holding her hand, "I don't think it's just a coincidence bumping into each other here, in the middle of nowhere where people move on every night. I mean, what are the chances?"

Rachel nodded. "It's a weird one alright."

"I felt something as soon as I saw you here and I would love if you would just consider that maybe ... I don't know, maybe not close yourself off to the idea? And this, tonight, it just feels right, doesn't it?"

Rachel took her hand away. "You're pushing me, Simon."

"I'm sorry. I don't want to pressure you."

"I need space to think. This is all ... a lot to take in. It's just not that simple, you know, and even if we did ... whatever ... reconnect, you live in Cork, I live in Dublin."

"I know. Let's leave it there. The last thing I want to do is make you uncomfortable or have you avoid me. Let's enjoy tonight."

"Sure." Rachel nodded.

Just then Simon's phone buzzed. "Sorry – I put this thing on vibrate." He took out his phone. "I have a missed call from Mum. Do you mind?"

"No, not at all, you go ahead."

"I'll take it outside," he said, getting up from the table.

Rachel watched him as he walked towards the door. What the hell am I going to do? I still hurt when I think of what happened with Craig. I certainly don't need to go from the frying pan into the fire. My head says to leave it and see how things go when we get home. My heart says go for it. But really the best thing, the sensible thing, would be to spend some time on my own.

Sitting here with Simon felt like putting on a familiar comfortable jumper. He was familiar, she was attracted to him, but had he answered all her questions? He left her and had a failed marriage behind him. Did he know what he wanted at all? Then, again, her own relationship history wasn't great either, but who got to forty without having some baggage?

She put her hand in the pocket of her hiking trousers and pulled out a two-euro coin. It had a number two on one side and a single harp on the other.

What's it to be, she thought, as she twirled the coin on the table. Carry on single or become two again? The coin twirled and twirled and then landed. The number 2. But with which one? She sighed and put the coin back in her pocket.

Rachel knew as soon as she saw him coming back that something was wrong.

"What is it?"

"It's Mum – she's not answering her phone. I'm sure everything's fine but I need to pop back and check."

"Oh, okay," Rachel said, picking up her crutch.

"No, you stay here. I'll be back in a jiffy."

"But I don't mind –"

"But I do. I'm really enjoying tonight, and we still have more wine to get through. Honestly, stay here and I'll be back. I just want to make sure she's taken her meds before bed."

"Sure, I can relax here and you're right, this wine is too good to leave behind." She smiled before taking another sip.

After he left, Rachel gathered her thoughts.

CHAPTER 34

He had been so open with her tonight. What more could she ask for? It was clear he wanted to be more than friends and it felt right too. But then it had felt so right with Craig. Rachel sighed. She thought she was in love with him and look where that got her.

That was just a few weeks ago and coming on the Camino seemed like the perfect place to escape from Craig and find space to take in all that had happened and figure out a way forward from that mess. And she still had feelings for him that weren't going to disappear overnight. But never in a million years did she expect to be hit with a face from the past and have feelings that were well buried rise to the surface again.

Would giving Simon a chance be another big mistake or would letting him go be the biggest mistake of all? Did I overreact with Craig? Could I forgive him and carry on with our dream? Or do I go it alone again?

Sighing, she took another sip of wine and wondered how Simon was getting on and if Bernie was alright.

Then her phone rang. It was Simon.

"Rachel! Mum's had a fall. The ambulance is here!"

"Oh my god, is she …"

"She's okay. She's sitting up and conscious but very confused. I gotta go. I'll message from the hospital."

Simon hung up and Rachel called the waiter for the bill.

"Is everything okay?" the waiter asked, seeing Rachel's worried face.

"My friend's mother is ill," she explained, "and she's had a fall, I'm afraid."

"Oh I am sorry," the waiter said and quickly went to get the bill.

Rachel stood up, picked up her crutch and got her card out. "*Eh*, you forgot to put the wine on the bill," she pointed out.

"No, the wine has been paid for."

"By whom?" Rachel said, looking around.

"Another customer. They are gone now but they saw that you two were pilgrims and wanted to pay for your wine."

"That's incredible."

"Not so much, it happens a lot on the Camino," he smiled. "We know that people on the Camino are making a special journey, and we respect that."

"Thank you so much, it's a beautiful gesture."

Rachel handed over her card and marvelled at how this Camino was throwing up so many emotions and tears and so many kindnesses too.

Heading back on her crutch, she saw an ambulance driving out of the same street as Pension Luis.

"Oh no, that must be Bernie!"

Walking as quickly as she could, she got to the pension and found Cathy, Paula, and Nuria standing in reception.

"Oh, Rachel!" Cathy said coming forward, "Bernie has gone off in an ambulance and Simon has gone with her."

"I just saw it. What happened?"

"She had a fall, in her room."

"Oh god!"

"She seems okay though," Paula said. "The doctor doesn't think anything is broken."

"I had just left her – we had a nightcap here," Cathy said, pointing to the tables. "I was just going up to my room when she rang me and said she'd fallen and couldn't get up off the floor. So I ran down and Nuria got the master key. When we got in she was lying on the floor. We didn't know whether she had fallen over something or perhaps fainted so we lifted her onto the bed as gently as we could. She's so light, she's skin and bone really. Anyway, Nuria called the doctor, and he was here so quickly. He checked her for broken bones or fall injuries and she was fine, but she was dizzy, and her blood pressure was very low, so he called the ambulance."

"Oh god, poor Bernie!" Rachel felt guilty, remembering that Simon had put his phone on silent when he began answering her questions about Australia.

"Don't worry, love," Paula said. "She was sitting up and talking. I think it's precautionary because of her condition and the meds that she's on."

Rachel nodded. "I'd better message Simon," she said, taking the phone out of her pocket, "Actually," she paused, "I think I should be there with him."

"Whatever you think," said Paula.

When Rachel opened her phone she already had a message from him.

At the hospital with Mum. It looks like low blood pressure made her dizzy and caused the fall. No bones broken, thank god. They are putting her on a drip as she may be dehydrated, and they are giving her something once they check the meds she's on. It may be a while. I'll keep you posted.

Rachel relayed the information to everyone.

"Oh, that's a relief! She should feel much better after the IV," said Paula.

"I feel bad that we had some wine at dinner – maybe we should have been drinking water," Cathy said, looking distressed.

"It wasn't the wine," Paula said, trying to comfort Cathy. "It was low blood pressure. She'll be fine but she may have to call a halt to the rest of her walking."

"She'll be disappointed if she has to stop walking now but there is no shame in taking taxis the rest of the way," said Cathy.

"Yes and we'll be here for her," said Paula. "She's part of our gang now."

Our gang, thought Rachel. Somehow, these strangers whom she didn't even want to talk to at the start of the week had become a gang, supporting each other, and confiding in each other. And now Simon and Bernie were part of that too.

She turned to Nuria. "Can you call me a taxi, please, and give him the name of the hospital they've taken Bernie to?"

"Of course."

"I have to go there," Rachel told Paula and Cathy.

"Of course. Let us know how it goes, will you?"

Rachel nodded.

"What are we going to do about tomorrow?" Paula asked.

"You guys go ahead. We're booked into accommodation in O Pedrouzo, so we have to get there, and you guys need to walk it to get your certificate. I'm going to be slow anyway, so you guys go as planned."

"I want to make sure Bernie's okay," Cathy said, concerned for her friend.

"Well, she was sitting up and talking when she left so that's a good sign," said Nuria.

"I'll message you from the hospital but please pack and get ready for tomorrow. Paula, will you let Carlos know what happened?"

"Sure." Paula blushed a little at how everyone presumed she had been keeping in touch with him.

"Taxi's here," Nuria said, going to the door.

"Good luck and keep us posted," said Cathy as Rachel headed out.

In the taxi, Rachel sent a text to Simon, saying she was on her way there. On reaching the hospital, she headed straight for the reception desk. Before she could ask a question she heard her name.

"Rachel!"

Simon was hurrying down the corridor.

"I had to come," she said.

He opened his arms, and she stepped into his hug, and they stood there holding each other.

"How is she?" Rachel said, pulling away.

"She's good. They are excellent here. They saw her straight away and ran all sorts of tests. Mum carries a list of her meds on her phone, so they just needed to look them up before treating her. Luckily no injuries from the fall but ..."

Simon turned away as his eyes filled up.

"Simon?"

"Sorry, it's just that ..."

"Hey, let's go sit down," Rachel said, leading him to a line of plastic chairs along the wall.

She sat down and Simon sat beside her and put his head in his hands.

"I just know that there is more of this to come. Over the past month, she has been getting weaker and she's losing weight."

Rachel put her hand on his shoulder and rubbed his back.

"I just hoped we'd get through these two weeks with no mishaps, and she has been doing great."

Rachel nodded.

"And meeting you guys has been the best thing ever for her. It has been great to see her so animated and to see her laughing at Paula's jokes and making a new friend in Cathy. And she loves you, of course." He put his hand on her knee.

She kept her arm around his shoulders and let him leave his hand where it was.

He looked up at her. "Thanks for being here."

Sitting up straight, he took a deep breath.

"Right, let's go in and see how she's doing."

He stood up, held out his hand and she took it as they walked down the corridor to Bernie's room.

The clinic released Bernie three hours later. The IV had rehydrated her and brought colour back to her face. While they were sitting at her bedside, Simon and Rachel checked the Camino Ninja app to check the route for the next day. Simon suggested a rest day and Bernie was happy to get a taxi to their next town, O Pedrouzo.

"That sounds great, love. My goal is to walk into that Cathedral Square in Santiago de Compostela so a rest day tomorrow should set me up for that walk the following day."

"We're almost there, Mum," Simon said squeezing her hand, "and you will walk into that square."

"And we'll be right there with you," said Rachel and Bernie's face glowed.

Rachel rang Paula and told her they were on their way home with Bernie and that she would be going straight to bed. Everyone was relieved that she was feeling better and that she was carrying on with her Camino.

Nuria, Paula, and Cathy had been sitting in the kitchen having a cup of tea when the call came in.

"So Rachel says we have to carry on as normal tomorrow and we are all staying in the same pension in O Pedrouzo, so we'll see Bernie then."

"Oh, that's a relief," sighed Cathy. "I was so worried for her. I hope she sleeps well tonight. I'm off to bed myself now," she said, standing up. "Now that everything is settled I want to try to sleep and get a good start tomorrow. Goodnight."

"Goodnight, Cathy. I'll just let Carlos know the story. He messaged me twice for an update," Paula said, picking her phone up.

Cathy went up to bed and Paula tidied up the cups and said goodnight to Nuria who went into her family quarters. As they were sharing a room, she wanted to give Cathy time to go to sleep before she went in, so once she was alone she sat in a comfy chair in reception and took out her phone. She needed to reply to Carlos. It was true that he messaged her, but he wasn't asking about Bernie – he was asking if she would like to go with him to visit a waterfall early in the morning for a swim. It was clear that the invite was just for her this time. She wasn't sure about this. She didn't have a swimsuit with her. Could she really go in her bra and knickers? Was it an innocent invite or something else?

Paula had been thinking about it all afternoon. To distract herself, she had messaged her kids who both replied with a thumbs-up emoji when she asked how they were and neither asked how she was. Kevin sent some pictures into the family group chat, but she didn't reply to them. She didn't want to engage with him right now. Any time she thought of him with Bloody Hiking Noreen, she felt sick. She added one photo to the group chat, a photo she had taken of her shadow in the forest.

She would have loved to pick up the phone today to tell Kevin about her chat with Sheila and the wonderful volunteer trips she organised but that was impossible. She couldn't even think about him now without feeling nauseous. Until she spoke to him face to face she didn't know if they had a future together. The fact was that on the same night he kissed Bloody Hiking Noreen, he had booked a double room in the name of Mr and Mrs Byrne while she was sitting at home in Dublin. She couldn't get her head around the fact that he returned home as if nothing had happened. Although they hadn't made love that week, they had shared the same bed and there was no strange atmosphere between them. Could he really share a bed with her after sharing one with another woman? It shocked her to think he could. It just wasn't the Kevin she knew. Who was this version of her husband? She sighed heavily. She had heard of so many women who hadn't a clue that their husbands were cheating. Am I one of them now, she wondered. Why am I not more upset or angry? Is it shock? Disbelief?

She didn't know how to feel. What she did know was that her husband kissed another woman and admitted it. And booked that double room. But if she hadn't asked for his phone that night she would still be in the dark.

She felt a pain in her chest as a tear rolled down her face. She needed to prepare for both outcomes after she spoke to him. Yes, she wanted something different in her life but she never for a moment thought that those plans would involve a future on her own.

What would he think about me going swimming in a waterfall with Carlos? It's not something a married woman should be doing. But then, there was that double room. And was he in a double room in Peru now with someone else?

Right now she wanted to believe that she and Kevin had a future. Maybe they could relight a fire between them back home. But did he even want to do that with her?

One thing she was sure of was that she wasn't going to feel guilty about feeling turned on by the idea of swimming in a waterfall with Carlos. If she and Kevin relit the fire of desire somewhere else, couldn't they work harder at home to create that excitement with each other? And would it do any harm if Carlos reminded her of how it could feel?

"You're being ridiculous," she said under her breath. Carlos had an opportunity to kiss her if he had wanted and he didn't do it. It was just a swim. When would she get an opportunity to swim in a waterfall again?

I'm going to do it, she decided, as she picked up her phone to reply to him. It will be my last time seeing him, so why not? Tomorrow after their swim, Carlos was delivering their bags to their pension in O Pedrouzo, and she would never see him again. Because of their two nights in Arzua, another driver would take their bags from O Pedrouzo to their hotel in Santiago.

After Santiago people had other plans and they would be getting different flights and making their own way to the airport. Carlos would be returning to his life in Madrid.

Carlos is a beautiful man, she thought. He sees me and he has been part of my experience here. He has confided in me and woken up some feelings in me that I haven't felt for a long while and I will enjoy my time with him tomorrow no matter what happens.

She smiled as she started texting him to arrange a collection time for the morning.

CHAPTER 35

It was still dark when Paula slipped quietly out of the room. She dressed quickly in the bathroom, using the light from her phone so as not to wake Cathy and Rachel.

Tiptoeing out of the room, she quietly opened the main door to see Carlos parked outside, leaning against the van. He smiled and stepped forward. He placed his hands on her shoulders and kissed her gently on both cheeks. Smiling, he opened the passenger door for her and Paula sat in. They drove to the corner of the street and then turned left onto the main street which was deserted at this hour.

Paula could smell his musky cologne as she turned to speak to him.

"So is it far?"

"No, only about 15 minutes."

"*Hmm ...*"

"It will be cold, very cold, but I think you will enjoy it. You have swimsuit?"

"No."

Carlo's turned to look at Paula with a shocked face but then a big smile crossed his face.

"Don't get too excited, "Paula smiled. "I didn't bring a swimsuit with me to Spain, but I'll be swimming in my underwear."

"*Aw*, too bad!" Carlos pouted and smiled again.

Paula began to feel hot. Did he really want to see her without her clothes on? Even the idea that he might, turned her on. Carlos turned off the main road at a sign for Fervenza das Hortes and they drove the short way through a wooded area to a car park.

As soon as they stepped out of the van she could hear the waterfall.

"*Wow*, that's loud already!"

"Yes, there was rain the last two nights so it will be perfect for a natural shower. It is the tallest waterfall in Galicia, so it is a popular spot but not at this hour."

It was light now and a mist was rising creating a canopy at the top of the trees. The smell of the eucalyptus forest was at its strongest and the sounds of nature waking up echoed around them. They walked to a wooden fence which was a viewing point for the waterfall. The car park was in an elevated position so looking up you could see the water fall over the rocky edge of the mountain as it cascaded down wild and fast to a plunge pool below. A set of wooden steps led all the way from the viewing point to the water's edge. Paula felt nervous now as she looked at the enormity of it and how powerfully the water was falling.

"Let's go," Carlos said as he held out his hand and she took it. With each step the sound of the waterfall grew louder.

When they reached the bottom, they put their bags down and looked around.

"It's beautiful," said Paula.

Carlos nodded as he closed his eyes and inhaled the morning air.

"Okay, are you ready for the waterfall?"

"I think so. It seems quite shallow here," she said looking at the pool beneath it, feeling a little reassured.

"Yes, at this time of the year, it is shallow, but the shower is strong under the waterfall. It will make you feel fantastic, you'll see."

Carlos put down the small backpack he was carrying and removed his jacket.

Oh god, thought Paula, feeling nervous. The morning air was cold, and the water would be freezing. But I can't just stand here and watch him undress, she thought, putting her own bag down and taking her jacket off.

As she removed her trainers and socks, her bare feet on the cold grassy bank sent a shiver up her body.

"It is cold, so it is best to move fast," Carlos said.

She turned around to reply to him and gasped to see him standing there, looking towards the waterfall, naked apart from a pair of small black Calvin Klein briefs. He looked magnificent. She couldn't help staring. Her eyes were tracing his body just as he turned around and caught her looking. A slow smile crossed his face.

"Come now!" He nodded towards the water.

Paula turned away and quickly removed her hiking trousers and T-shirt.

Well, here I am, warts and all, she thought, standing in her mismatched Primark underwear.

"Let's do this," she said as she stepped into the running stream. "Oh my god!" she gasped. "It's freezing!"

"We will move fast," Carlos said, taking her hand.

Her heart was pumping, and her body was tingling. She didn't know if it was from the icy-cold water or the electricity she felt holding his hand and walking so close to his almost naked body. As they neared the waterfall, icy splashes from the strong current made them yelp and laugh. He pulled her in towards the stream of water pouring from up above them.

Paula shrieked as the water crashed down onto them. She thought she had gone into shock. Carlos, standing just one foot away from her, threw back his head under the flow of water. He was still holding her hand. He turned back to look at her. Taking her other hand he pulled her to him. They held each other's gaze for a moment. The feeling of his firm chest against hers made her catch her breath. Before she could think his lips were on hers.

His kiss was gentle at first. He dropped her hands and cupped her face. He then stopped and looked at her. He nodded and she nodded back. This time his kiss was long, deep and passionate. Her head was spinning as she moved her hands up to his chest. He moved his hands to her shoulders, down her arms and around her back while still kissing her. All the time the cold water was crashing against their skin and flowing away.

"Oh my god!" Paula said when they broke away, but she couldn't hear her own voice over the noise of the water.

His mouth reached hers again. She savoured his kiss but this time she pulled away. He smiled and nodded before he took her hand and led her back out of the waterfall to the water's edge.

Opening her bag, he quickly wrapped her in her towel before retrieving his. Her skin tingled and she felt wide awake. Her head was still spinning as she quickly ran her towel over her body. Wrapping the towel around her, she quickly removed her wet underwear before pulling on a dry pair of pants. Picking up her hiking trousers she pulled them on, followed by her socks and sneakers.

She stood up and, turning away from Carlos, she unclasped her bra and removed it. The padding inside was soaking wet. As she twisted it to wring out the water she could feel Carlos' eyes on her. Not looking at him, she rolled up her bra and pants and put them in the bottom of her bag. She then took hold of either end of the towel and arching her back she dried it off. Then she turned to look at Carlos. His eyes were firmly on her bare chest, his mouth half open.

"*Ehem!*" he coughed, dragging his eyes away as he turned to pack his own towel.

Paula picked up her T-shirt and pulled it on over her still damp skin.

"Time to go," Carlos said, holding out a hand to her.

She took his hand and they climbed the steps back to his van. She felt her heart racing. She felt the chemistry between them had changed.

Carlos opened the back of the van and threw his bag in. He then turned to Paula and his eyes were once again drawn downwards. With her body still tingling from the cold fresh water and with her bra abandoned to the bottom of her bag, her hard erect nipples were very visible through the thin fabric of her T-shirt. When his eyes met hers, Paula threw her bag in the van and took one step towards him. Aroused by the lust in his eyes, she lifted her hand to his face and gently pulled him to her. This time their kiss was deep and slow. He placed his hands on her hips as she slowly ran her fingers through his hair.

Paula gasped when his hands touched the skin where her waistband and T-shirt met. His cold hands moved up her rib cage his thumbs circling her flesh slowly. Kissing him hungrily now, she moaned when his thumbs scraped across her nipples.

Then, pulling away for breath, she looked up into his eyes.

"I'm sorry ... I can't ..."

"*Shhh* ..." he said, placing his finger on her lips. "It's not a problem," he whispered, looking into her eyes. "Let's go, Irish Paula!"

Paula picked up her fleece from the boot and stood back as Carlos closed the van door. Pulling the fleece over her head, she went around to the passenger side and hopped in the van.

"Thank you, Carlos, you really are a wonderful person."

"And you are too, Paula," he said turning to look at her. "This has been a very good week for me because of you."

"I won't see you tomorrow, will I?"

"No. This is our last meeting. I won't see you in O Pedrouzo. Another driver will collect the bags tomorrow and I will go home to Madrid."

"You have woken something up in me, Carlos, that I definitely did not think I would experience on the Camino!"

They both laughed. Carlos patted her knee and leaned over for a final kiss before starting the engine.

Paula stared out the window as they drove back, her body still tingling. Maybe they were just two people who needed something at this exact time, who happened to meet here.

It was the second last day of this Camino and what an incredible and unexpected experience it was turning out to be.

CHAPTER 36

ARZUA – O PEDROUZO

When Paula arrived back at Pension Luis, Cathy and Rachel were up and getting ready to head out on the trail.

"You look wide awake," Cathy said.

"Yes, I've been up for a while," Paula said as she began fiddling with her backpack to avoid eye contact. She didn't want to give anything away. "What are your plans for walking today, Rachel?"

"My knee feels good this morning." Rachel was sitting on the side of her bed, rubbing anti-inflammatory gel into her knee. "I'm going to start easy and take my time."

"Good idea," said Cathy, packing up the last of her toiletries into her backpack. "I want to stop and take in the scenery – I haven't done enough of that the past few days as I was so eager to get to the next destination."

"Well, you probably had a lot on your mind like the rest of us," said Paula, looking at the Camino app on her phone. "I'm just looking at the app here and there is a breakfast place in As Quintas which is 4.9 kilometers away. Do you fancy walking together to have breakfast there?"

"I'd love that, but I wouldn't want to hold you up," Rachel said.

"I'm in no rush today," said Cathy, tying up her hair, "so I would love that."

"Great, we'll do that," said Paula. "And don't worry, Rachel, we'll walk at your pace, have breakfast, and see what happens after that."

The way Paula was feeling this morning she could have run the whole way to O Pedrouzo. Carlos had lit a fire in her that she had long thought had gone out. They'd both got something out of it and the question now was, could she re-ignite that fire with Kevin? Would she even want to after she heard what he had to say?

The road out of Arzua was busy with walkers. The clip-clop of walking poles on the cobbled streets died out as they reached and crossed a main road and followed the Camino signs and yellow arrows into a small forest.

The early morning dew enhanced the scent of the eucalyptus trees as they took their time enjoying the strong smell of the trees and the crunch of pine needles underfoot. The sun was rising now behind them, the rays casting long shadows of the three friends onto the forest floor.

"We have to get a photo of our shadows," Paula said, taking out her phone. "I'll get in the middle and you two hold up your poles."

The sunlight behind them and golden floor of the trail made for a great photo of them, their shadows stretched and their poles in the air.

"I'll treasure that," said Cathy as she peered over Paula's shoulder.

"I'll put it in the WhatsApp group when we're in a Wi-Fi area," Paula said, putting her phone away.

The forest incline was gradual so Rachel could manage it with very little difficulty, having replaced her crutch with the walking poles. She also had a strong support on her knee and had taken painkillers and anti-inflammatories. At the top of the woods, the trees thinned out and the path widened through fields and meadows. In no time at all they reached As Quintas and joined the queue of walkers ordering breakfast.

"Everyone seems in a happy mood this morning," Cathy noticed as they sat down at an outside table. They had been passed by many smiling walkers, exchanging *Buen Camino* greetings all along the way.

"I think it's because the end is in sight. Some of these people have been walking for weeks," Paula said as she set her tray down.

"Yes," Rachel said. "It must be especially poignant for the pilgrims who started their journey at the Start of the Camino Frances, nearly forty days ago."

"It must feel so strange returning to normal life after forty days of walking these routes. I'd say it takes some adjustment," remarked Rachel.

"Yes, and it's not everyone who can take time out of their lives to do this," said Cathy. "It really is a privilege."

"I wish I had taken more time to appreciate the quiet and the scenery at the start," Rachel said, putting down her knife and fork, "but, even in this short time, something has changed in me. In fact, my life has been turned upside down."

"Are you talking about Simon?" Paula asked. "I didn't want to say anything, especially with Bernie falling and all that, but have you and Simon got closer?"

Rachel smiled and then blushed. "Oh my god, I'm blushing!" she said, laughing. "Yes, things have changed between me and Simon. I wasn't looking for anything. Honestly, I'm still not. My ex is moving to London apparently, so he has moved on very quickly and I had no intentions of going near any man ever again! But this business with Simon ... I don't know ..." She shrugged.

"Well, I think there is something there," said Paula, "but you take your time."

Rachel nodded. "I swear to god, it's this place," she said, shaking her head. "If I had bumped into Simon anywhere else in the world, I would have hopped on a plane or a train and just left, but you can't do that here. And look what happened when I tried to run away – I got injured. This place, this Camino, you have to keep walking forward, you cannot run or hide from yourself. I think I understand now why people do this. We distract ourselves from our feelings and our thoughts too easily at home, but here you are stuck with yourself whether you like it or not."

Paula sat back in her chair. "I think that's the best description of the Camino I've heard. I still have some thinking to do. I have a feeling my life is going to change dramatically when I get home. I'm hoping that the more I walk the clearer things will get. How about you, Cathy?"

"I'm still figuring it out," said Cathy quietly, "but I realise that the people I am thinking about the most out here are the only people that are important to me, and that is making my choices easier now and it's also making me feel stronger."

Paula and Rachel nodded, both aware that this petite quiet woman had been through so much. Losing her husband only four weeks beforehand, she must be still grieving. But, unbeknown to them, Ted was not in her thoughts at all.

CHAPTER 37

O PEDROUZO

Paula arrived in O Pedrouzo by lunchtime. It was a small town, and the accommodation wasn't open for check-in until two, so she typed in a search for the nearest restaurant on Google Maps and headed there. Casa Santaia was located in what looked like an old farmhouse with beautiful brickwork. The waitress offered her the option of eating outside in the lovely garden, but as the sun was hot now and she was dusty from the walk, Paula was happy to sit in the cool dining room just off the bar area.

She was the only diner eating inside and felt a little out of place with dusty shoes and walking poles at a table with white linen and sparkling silverware.

I deserve a treat, she thought, and my legs are too tired to look for anywhere else. She ordered the set lunch menu, a bottle of sparkling water, and a glass of white wine.

The wine was served in a big wine glass and tasted delicious after walking under the hot sun. The sun shone all morning, and unlike other days, there wasn't a cloud in the sky. It was probably only twenty-five degrees but that was warm when you were walking nineteen kilometres without cover. Thankfully her UV sunhat had done its job so, although she knew her face was red, she knew it wasn't sunburnt.

After breakfast, the three women had decided to walk on at their own pace. Rachel was taking it easy and making loads of stops to rest her knee and Cathy had a list of churches she wanted to visit on the route. As Paula was energized from her waterfall visit with Carlos, she was full of energy and marched ahead. They had all agreed to go out to dinner tonight with Bernie and Simon who were making their way by taxi.

Poor Bernie, thought Paula. Cathy had said that her cancer was incurable and that she was just being treated for the symptoms. She was trying to fit in as much as she could without wearing herself out. It was clear that Cathy and Bernie had become close – they seemed to confide in each other.

It was hard to figure Cathy out. Her husband was only dead four weeks, yet here she was walking the Camino alone. However, Paula could understand her need to get away and grieve by herself and she seemed to be doing remarkably well. She didn't say much about him or the situation, except that it was a bad marriage and she and that she was trying to figure out what she should do next.

Hopefully, the Camino would provide the answers she was looking for. She had seemed so timid and lost when they met her first, but she was tougher than people perceived, and Paula could see her confidence growing as the week went on.

And then Rachel, who couldn't get away from Simon quick enough, seemed to have rekindled something there. The Universe certainly stepped in there, giving her an injury that forced the two for them to spend time together. It seemed like a very quick change of heart but then who was she to talk?

Her own friendship with Carlos had been so unexpected. He made her feel feminine and sexy again, and her encounter this morning ... well, he made her feel alive again and it was such a boost to believe she could be attractive to a good-looking man like him.

But it was Kevin she wanted.

I don't want a new man to come and sweep me off my feet, I want life to sweep me off my feet, she thought as she sat there.

If Kevin had sex with hiking Noreen, could she forgive him? If she told him about Carlos would he forgive her? She knew she should feel guilty, but she felt alive again for the first time in ages and feeling guilty would only ruin it. How did they even get to this ridiculous situation? She shook her head. She would have to wait and see what happened when she got home

She was glad in a way that she wouldn't be seeing Carlos again. She knew there was nothing in it, just two people who needed to feel hopeful and alive again. But what now for herself and Kevin? She had asked these questions as she walked the Camino over the past few days, looking for answers and then she met Sheila. If they stayed together and started afresh, her trips sounded exactly what she had been looking for and sounded like something they could both enjoy. She was meeting Sheila later for a pre-dinner drink so she would get her details from her then.

Still so much to figure out. She sighed.

When her food arrived, the beautifully presented scallops in scallop shells put a smile on her face.

"*Una copa mas de vino, por favor,*" she said to the waitress as she held up her glass.

Another wine, some lovely food, and then a siesta before dinner, thought Paula.

Just then her phone rang. She had noticed two missed calls from this Irish number earlier but didn't answer them as she didn't recognise the number.

"Hello?"

"Oh, hello there, am I speaking to Mrs Byrne?"

"Yes, who's this?"

"This is James from The Hikers' Inn in Killarney. You rang last week about your husband's charger."

"Oh ... yes, I did." What now, Paula wondered.

"Well, we found it. It was in one of the dorms after all. The cleaner had put it in the lost and found box but forgot to inform reception. I knew it was his because you mentioned it's one of those big international ones."

Paula's jaw dropped open. "*A dorm?* But when I rang last week you said he didn't stay in a dorm – you mentioned a double."

"Oh yes, my fault. We had another couple, Mary and Pat Byrne, regular hikers who stay with us, and they were in the double room. Your husband was sharing a dorm with Tony Clinch and the booking was under Tony's name so I didn't see your husband's name at first."

"And he definitely stayed in a dorm?" Paula asked, her heart pounding. "It's just that he usually hates dorms."

"Oh, I know. Kevin and Tony are regulars here. Our regular rooms were full but one of the dorms was empty so there was just the two of them in it."

"I see." Paula felt lightheaded.

"So we have his address on file here. Will I pop it in the post?"

"Eh ... yes ... please."

"Great, I'll do that and sorry for the confusion. Have a great day!" And, with that, cheery James hung up.

"*Sorry for the confusion?*" Paula repeated his words.

She sat staring into space, her mouth open in shock, as images of her and Carlos flashed through her mind.

Oh my god! This whole time I thought Kevin was with her in that double room! What the hell have I done?

"Is everything okay, madam?" The waitress appeared in front of her with a concerned look on her face.

"Yes." Paula swallowed hard. "*Em* ... I think I need another glass of wine, please."

"Of course."

Paula took a deep breath and let it out slowly. I may need the whole bloody bottle to figure all this out now, she thought as she sat with her head in her hands.

CHAPTER 38

Rachel arrived at her accommodation in O Pedrouzo. It was very quiet and there were no other pilgrims in the reception area, so she checked in and headed up to her room. She was happy to have a room to herself tonight as she had so much to think about. Dropping her bag on the floor, she took out her toiletries and headed into the bathroom. Her eyes widened when she saw that the bathroom had a huge bath in it. Everywhere else she'd been had showers in the bathrooms, so she presumed this was standard, but this was such a sight for sore eyes and sore limbs. And she gasped when she saw that the pension had supplied a bottle of Radox Muscle Soak bath foam.

This is going to be heavenly, she thought as she put the bath-plug in and turned the taps on. She walked back into the bedroom and pulled out some clean clothes from the backpack and retrieved her plug and charger. Her phone had died two hours ago so she needed to recharge it while she had her bath.

When she plugged in the phone it lit up and beeped four times. Glancing down, she could see that she had three missed calls from Craig and one text. She ignored the calls but opened his text.

CHECK YOUR EMAIL is all it said.

Hmm ... what does he want? She had kept an eye on some work emails but ignored any others filling her inbox. Sitting on the bed, she held the charging phone in her hand. She didn't want to deal with Craig now, but curiosity got the better of her and while the bath filled she opened his email.

Rachel,

I know from my many unanswered texts that you don't want to speak to me, but I hope you read this email. I apologise. I made a terrible mistake, and I dealt with it horrendously. I am a pig-headed fool, and I deeply regret what I did and how much I hurt you. I love you so much, but I know that words are not enough, so I hope that my actions will show you how much I want you back and how much I want us and our company to succeed.

These past two weeks I have been in talks with Howster & Howster. I know it has always been your dream that in 5 years' time, after we got our company off the ground, we would approach a big international company and offer partnership. Well, I have worked my ass off and I have convinced Howster &Howster to come in with us now.

Rachel gasped. Howster & Howster were one of the biggest legal firms in London with offices in New York and Sydney. It was her dream that one day they could partner up with them. This would put her company on the international stage, with the backing of one of the biggest legal firms in the world. This was part of their 5-year plan for the company and Craig had got it for them before they even opened for business. This was unheard of.

We have until the close of business on Friday the 14^h of July, just over a week away, to finalise this deal. See the attachment for the details.

This is it, Rachel, this is the dream, your dream.

Please forgive me and let's get back to being us again. I want you as my partner in every sense of the word. Let's put the unfortunate incident behind us and move on.

Yours

Craig x

Rachel sat with her jaw open, staring into space. The steam oozing out of the bathroom shook her back to reality. Jumping up, she ran to the bathroom and turned off the taps.

Oh my god, Howster & Howster, my dream company! He is basically giving me my dream on a plate!

She poured the Radox into the steaming water. Taking off her clothes, she lowered herself into the bath, careful not to displace any water over the sides.

He knew exactly what my dream was for the business, and he went out and got it for me five years early. How the hell did he do that?

She had everything she dreamed of within her reach but the price for that was forgiving Craig and letting him back into her life and into her bed.

"*What the fuck do I do now?*" she said out loud before lying back and submerging her head under the water.

Rachel wrapped herself in all the pension's towels and flopped onto the bed. Her skin was hot and red from the bath water, but the soothing effect on her muscles made it worthwhile. While lying in the bath, she realised that she needed to lay out the pros and cons of her situation. The journal she had brought with her had been very useful for jotting down her thoughts every night. So much had happened in such a short space of time. And now Craig needed an answer within a week and Simon was flying home to Cork in two days' time. She needed to give both men an answer either way.

Pushing herself up to sit, she swung her legs off the bed. Reaching for her backpack on the floor, she pulled out the journal and her pen. My brain is too busy to read that contract now, she thought. I need to do something practical instead.

I need to approach this like I would a case. I need to lay down the facts as they are and look at the pros and cons of both situations. Grabbing all the pillows, she propped herself up against the headboard and pulled back the duvet to swing her long legs in under it.

She opened the journal and started writing.

She put CRAIG at the top of the page with three columns underneath headed PROS, CONS, and POSSIBLE OUTCOME.

Then on the next page she wrote SIMON and, underneath his name, PROS, CONS, POSSIBLE OUTCOME.

And then, turning over a new page, she wrote another option titled GO IT ALONE.

And underneath, the same columns: PROS, CONS, POSSIBLE OUTCOME.

The truth was that everything was happening so fast, and she was, after all, a strong independent woman. I can go back to my old job with Helen and carry on as before, she thought, biting the end of her pen. This trip has shown me that I am stronger than I ever thought I was and more resilient than I knew. I can survive with or without either of them.

"So what's it going to be, Rachel?" she asked herself. "Craig, Simon or ... me?"

She had started writing in her own column when her phone rang.

"Oh my god!" she gasped as Craig's name flashed up on the screen. Her finger hovered over the decline button but, after ignoring his calls for three weeks now, she felt strong enough to hear his voice.

Taking a deep breath, she answered his call.

"Craig?"

"Rach! Thanks for picking up. Can we talk?"

Her heart ached when she heard his voice.

"Yes we can talk."

"Okay, great. Now don't panic but I'm here in Spain ... in O Pedrouzo actually."

"*What!* Are you serious?"

"Please don't freak out. I just arrived in Santiago this afternoon and I'm staying there tonight. I got a taxi to this place because I need to speak to you face to face. Did you read my email?"

Rachel was stunned.

"Yes ... I did. But who told you I was here?"

"Nobody told me."

"But how ..."

"Your location is on the Find My Phone app. Remember that time in New York when you lost your phone and you put the app on my phone to find it?"

"Oh my god!" She couldn't believe it. Craig had known where she was all along. "Where are you now?"

"I'm sitting outside a Mexican café on the main street. My taxi guy is hanging around and I'll be going back to Santiago tonight, I promise."

"Okay. Give me fifteen minutes."

She hung up.

"*Wow!*" she said out loud, putting her head in her hands. "Craig is here? In Spain?"

She checked her watch. The rest of the gang were getting an early night so hopefully she wouldn't run into anyone. She dressed in her well-worn hiking trousers and matching T-shirt. She always liked to look her best for Craig and they both liked to dress sharp for work and social occasions. I don't think he's ever seen me look like this, she thought, looking at her reflection in the mirror.

Picking up her eyeliner, she leaned into the mirror and then stopped. No, let him see me as I am, she decided, and threw the eyeliner on the bed.

Taking a deep breath, she picked up her key and headed out to meet him.

The Mexican café was only a five-minute walk away. She had passed it earlier and popped in to get one of their amazing stamps for her pilgrim passport. They let you choose a coloured wax and then they melted it, added glitter and stamped your pilgrim passport with different Mexican symbols.

Turning the corner onto the main street, she spotted Craig immediately and, despite herself, her heart flipped. Among the tables of hikers sitting out finishing their meals, he stood out by a mile. He looked like a movie star, sitting at a table wearing chinos, a sky-blue polo shirt and his favourite Cartier sunglasses even though it was dusk. Rachel almost laughed at how out of place he looked.

He didn't move as she walked towards him and then she realised that he didn't recognise her.

"Craig," she said, stopping at his table.

"Rachel!" he said, jumping up and pushing his sunglasses up onto his head.

"Did you not recognise me?" she said, smiling.

"I was miles away and you do look very ... different." He leaned in and kissed her on the cheek.

He smelt amazing. Craig loved his expensive brands.

"Let me get you a drink," he said, raising his hand. "You look great, by the way."

He held her gaze and she had to pull her eyes away from his as she felt her mouth go dry.

You are just here to listen to what he has to say, she reminded herself.

The waiter arrived and Craig ordered a glass of red wine for himself and Rachel ordered a glass of white.

"The wine is beautiful here and so reasonable," Rachel said, trying to dispel the awkward atmosphere between them.

"Well, I just arrived so I haven't had much time to enjoy it," he said, smiling.

"So were you surprised to find out where I was?"

"I was very surprised. I hadn't got you down as a walker, never mind a pilgrim," he said, shaking his head. "It's not really you, is it?"

"I don't know what me is anymore, because my world was turned upside down," Rachel said, getting irritated now.

"I'm sorry," Craig said, holding his hands up. "And kudos to you – it's one hell of a walk."

"It's more than just a walk, Craig, but I'm not here to talk about that."

The waiter arrived with their wine and Rachel took a large gulp of it

"Why did you come here?" she asked.

"As I said, I needed to see you, face to face."

"To talk about the Howster deal?"

"Yes, there is that, but I want to talk about us, Rach. I have missed you so much, I really have, and I'm willing to do whatever it takes to get us back on track."

Rachel felt herself welling up.

Craig leaned across the table. "I fucked up, I know I did and I'm sorry. You have to believe me."

"I do believe you but it doesn't change what you did. You broke my heart, Craig. We had everything going for us."

"And we can still have it all, but even better now. You were very clear that you didn't want to hear from me so I gave you the space and I know actions speak louder than words so I set up this Howster deal. Just let me explain it."

Rachel nodded, taking another sip of her wine.

"I pulled in a few favours to get a person-to-person meeting in London with the CEO, Clifford Howster. I explained about our new business, our vision, our five-year plan, and how they were our dream company to partner with. He agreed to look at our business plan and I emailed everything to his people. I then flew to London again for a more in-depth meeting with his team."

That's why Helen thought he was moving to London, Rachel realised.

"And, a few days later, the offer came back. Did you get a chance to read through it?"

"I read the email an hour ago but I didn't open the attachment."

"The deal is exactly what we hoped we could get in 5 years' time. This is your dream company. They will send so much work our way and our partnership with them puts us on a world stage. In time we'll need a proper office away from the house and we may need to take people on but ... they want both of us."

"I guessed that."

"There is no deal otherwise. And we would be working long hours beside each other so I don't think we can do that if we are not together. In fact, I know we can't."

Rachel squirmed in her seat. He was right. There was no way they could do this, sit side by side, and present a united front if they were not back together. It would be too uncomfortable for both of them.

"This will only work if we are together. We have a week to confirm the deal." Craig sat back in his seat and looked at her.

Rachel looked down into her glass.

"Well?" Craig shrugged. "What do you think?"

"I'm just getting my head around it."

Craig nodded and looked away. She noticed his jaw tensing.

"It's a great deal, Craig. It's a lot to think about..."

"I thought you'd be more excited about it. Howster & Howster is your dream company."

"I know." He was giving her everything she wanted for her business but it came with a big price tag.

"Okay," Craig said, his face softening. "I've thrown a lot at you, turning up like this ... you think about it, yeah?"

He picked up his glass and finished his wine.

"I'm going to head back to Santiago now," he said. "I have a suite in the Parador – it's stunning by the way. Here's the address." He reached into his pocket and passed her a business card. "Why don't you ring me when you're done walking tomorrow and I can come pick you up?"

He raised a hand and Rachel saw his taxi approach. It pulled up and the taxi man opened the door for him.

"Until tomorrow?" Craig said as he bent down and kissed her head.

She shivered as he ran his hand over her hair and down her back.

She watched him get into the taxi. He turned and smiled and she waved back. And, just like that, he was gone.

Rachel let out a deep breath. Her head was spinning. She needed a few minutes to process their whole meeting.

He wants another chance. He looks great and he's worked so hard to get a fantastic deal for the company. So why am I not excited about it? Is the price of taking him back, to forgive and forget, too high a price for having my career dreams handed to me on a plate?

She sat there as the sun went down behind the mountains, going over the pros and cons of the decisions she had to make. She tried to listen in to her gut but she just felt nauseous. No answers were coming.

I have no idea what to do, she thought as darkness fell, and the tears ran down her face.

CHAPTER 39

The final walking day

O PEDROUZA TO SANTIAGO

The sun rose over the Galician mountains as Paula prepared her backpack for the last time. The last day of the Camino.

It's hard to believe that I only started this seven days ago, she thought, and so much has happened, incredible really.

She'd woken up about twenty times last night, going over everything in her head. She came away thinking that Kevin had spent the night with Noreen. Now it turned out that wasn't true and that he was telling the truth about the dorm. He still kissed her though and they did need to work things out but, oh my, after what she had done with Carlos she felt she could happily let things slide about Noreen.

Meeting Sheila for an early drink last night just confirmed to her that the Ethical Volunteering Adventure group was exactly what she wanted to do. She tried ringing Kevin to tell him about it, to see what his reaction would be, but his phone just went to voicemail. She really wanted to hear his voice now. She had sent some pictures yesterday while walking, to the family WhatsApp group, and although the kids replied, Kevin hadn't.

She realised, on yesterday's walk, even before The Hikers' Inn rang her, that she missed him. She missed telling him her news. Even if it was boring things that happened in school that day, he always stopped what he was doing to listen to her. And he had been so patient while she ranted and raved about feeling uneasy and unfulfilled. She hoped he didn't think it was because of him but then again she never told him it wasn't. She didn't ask him if he had any retirement plans as she was so wrapped up in her own frustrations. No wonder he was flattered when he got attention from Noreen.

When he went away on hikes at home, she was happy to have the house to herself and never missed him because there was always something to distract her like housework, visiting her parents who lived nearby, or catching up on her reading.

Now she was desperate to talk to him and see his face. He had told her that he would be out of coverage for a few days on this trip, but she couldn't remember when that was.

Taking out her phone she, decided to send him a text so he could see it when he was back in phone coverage again:

Hi, it's me. Last day here. 19 km to Santiago! I am so excited. I can't believe I will have walked over 100 km. I have met so many wonderful people and I can't wait to tell you all about it. Can we video call today? I would love to video call you when I reach Cathedral Square. I know it's the middle of the night where you are but I'm meeting my gang at a fountain in Santiago as we all plan to enter the square together, which is the official end of the

Camino. I'll message you then and maybe we can Zoom or video call. Love x

Tucking her phone away, she took a minute to reflect on today. Over one hundred kilometres. How on earth did I do that?

Sitting at dinner last night, the group decided that they would meet in Santiago at a fountain in Plaza Cervantes and they all put the location into their phones. Pilgrims coming in from the many different Camino routes passed through this square before walking on to the cathedral.

As today was the last walking day, everybody agreed to walk on their own and at their own pace.

Simon and Bernie were getting a taxi but planning to walk the last kilometre through the old town of Santiago to the square.

It will be emotional for both of them, Paula reckoned as she zipped up her bag and looked around the room to make sure she hadn't forgotten anything.

She had come on this trip looking for answers and unbelievably she found them. In hindsight, it was a blessing that Jill couldn't come. She had needed the time alone to think and meet the people she did. And her friendship and connection with Carlos would never have happened if Jill had been here. Everything happens for a reason and so many people say the Camino provides, she thought. Although she didn't really believe that at the start, she did now.

CHAPTER 40

Cathy woke up to the sun streaming in the window. She had deliberately left the curtains open to let the natural light wake her.

The last day, she thought. Who would have thought that I could do this, walk one hundred kilometre on my own, meet new people, and leave with a new confident idea of the life I want to live? Ted would have never believed I could do this.

"You can't do anything on your own. You're a worry wart, afraid of your own shadow. Do you really think you could cope without me doing everything for you? You have everything handed to you on a plate here. That's your problem, spoilt rotten!"

Cathy shivered remembering the words he taunted her with for years. How long would they still haunt her, she wondered.

"Well, look at me now, Ted!" she shouted out loud. "*I can do it, and I can have the life I want now, without you!*"

She felt so empowered shouting those words out loud. She had become so quiet in that house, not bothering to give her view because it would be ridiculed, that she had almost forgotten what her voice sounded like when she shouted.

"I'm going to live somewhere where I can shout at the top of my voice and dance to loud music if I like, without anyone around to criticise me," she decided. "If my dream comes true."

She had mixed emotions today. The last day of walking was huge for so many, especially people who had started weeks before. The others at the dinner table last night were so excited and she would be happy too when she met them at the fountain where they agreed that they would walk into Cathedral Square together.

"How lucky am I to have met such wonderful people!" she sighed happily.

But there was one thing hanging over her, one thing that she had come all this way to do. She had to go to Confession.

A special Pilgrim's Mass was held every day at noon at the Cathedral de Santiago de Compostella and some days, if you were lucky, the enormous, famous Botafumeira incense burner might be swung from the ceiling over the congregation. This was the only place in the world where this happened, and everyone was wondering last night if they might get lucky at their Mass tomorrow.

But Cathy wasn't too interested in that. She had arranged to meet with Father Eduardo and the prayer group an hour before the Mass for prayers and the Stations of the Cross. Then, following the Mass, he was going to find a priest who would hear her confession in English. It was a very popular thing to do, to finalise your Camino journey. But for Cathy it was something she had to do to complete her Camino journey. Then she could leave the old Cathy behind, and the new Cathy could move on.

Lying on her bed now, thinking back to the nervous shy awkward person she was when she arrived, she would never have believed that the mix-up with the accommodation on the first night would have led to meeting people that she cared about, and they seemed to care about her.

Everything is amplified on the Camino, she thought. Relationships form quickly here. Father Eduardo and the prayer group provided familiarity and comfort for her in those first few days. Then Paula and Rachel included her in everything and seemed to genuinely like her. And what a gift it was to meet Bernie. That woman could see into her soul.

These strangers have made me feel like I can be myself and that I am an okay person. I didn't know what I was looking for when I came here but now I do. They say the Camino provides and it provided these people who believe that I am normal and, without knowing, have given me the confidence to believe that I deserve to lead the life I want. She reached up and held her Miraculous Medal.

Sitting up in bed, she looked out the window as the sun rose over the hills and then at her rucksack in the corner.

"Time to get moving," she said before blessing herself and hopping out of bed.

CHAPTER 41

Rachel wrapped a towel around her as she stepped out of the shower. She hoped a cold shower this morning would somehow ease her pounding headache. She gave up counting how many times she woke up during the night going back and forth with the pros and cons of the decision she was about to make.

How did I end up with this crazy dilemma, she wondered, shaking her head.

Wrapping her wet hair in a towel, she applied moisturiser and sunblock to her face. Looking in the mirror, she marvelled at how different she looked compared to how she looked on the flight out. Then she'd had her hair blow-dried and had applied some daytime make-up before she left the house. Now, when she looked in the mirror a bare, fresh, freckled face looked back at her. She hadn't worn any make-up on this trip apart from some eyeliner and lip gloss when she went out to dinner with Simon. And her hair, which she normally kept under control with a straightener at home, was back to its wavy self after a week of walking in the open air.

What would they think of me in work if they saw me now, she wondered. She looked different on the outside, but had she changed inside? *Am I really that different to the person I was coming out here?*

Before closing her backpack, she stood at her window and watched the sun's rays peek between the trees in the mountains surrounding O Pedrouzo. Despite the beautiful view, the same thoughts that kept her awake all night were going around in her head.

If I go back with Simon will it be the biggest mistake of my life? And if I don't, will I regret it? And then there is the distance. Could she leave Dublin after building up a career there and start again in Cork? And to do what there?

Craig still loves me and wants me back. He has somehow negotiated my dream contract for the business in order to prove how much he wants us both to move forward. But was the price for that dream too high? Could I forgive him and move on? Or do I go it alone? Take some time to figure out what I really want for me?

She sighed loudly. I never asked for any of these problems. Maybe the only person I can rely on is myself.

"Well, I won't find the answers looking out this window," she said out loud and went off to dry her hair.

Leaving her rucksack at reception she headed out with her small backpack and her walking poles. Her knee was much better now, and she had left her crutch in a local pharmacy the day before to hopefully help someone else. As long as she took it easy today she should be okay. She was going to take her time. They were all meeting up at the fountain to walk into the Cathedral Square together. She was delighted to do this with these strangers who had become friends so quickly.

But this is where the Camino ends, and she needed to give Simon an answer today and Craig was in Santiago waiting to hear from her.

Craig or Simon or me?

One way or another, after walking all week, she had just nineteen kilometres to decide what her future would be.

CHAPTER 42

O PEDROUZO – SANTIAGO

The Camino Trail from O Pedrouzo to Santiago started at the familiar Camino stone bollard with the yellow scallop shell on a blue background, the yellow arrow underneath and today's distance of 19.136 km carved into a copper plate.

Less than twenty kilometres! Cathy smiled as she stopped, took a photo and sent it to Father John, Sophie and her cousin Maggie with the caption: **Last day of walking!**

These were the three people who mattered most to her and the only people she had sent photos to on this trip.

Over the week she could see texts and emails had been sent from Patsy and Mark. It is probably driving them mad, me not replying, she thought, but I have nothing to say to them.

The route today was a continuation of yesterday's forest walk. The tall trees blocked out the sun, making the atmosphere dark and cool. The morning air enhanced the smell of the forest and the familiar sound of people walking and poles tapping was a comfort at this hour of the morning.

After ten minutes Cathy passed a long wall, and some movement caught her eye on the other side of it. It was two huge black Spanish horses. They were slowly walking through the trees. They looked so beautiful, so mystical, that she filled up as she watched them. She decided not to take a photo but to just stop and watch them as they moved with grace quietly on their way. This trip has been such an emotional journey, she thought, as she took a deep breath of forest air before moving on again.

Others had said that a good portion of the route today was by the side of the road as they were entering a big city, so Cathy wanted to enjoy this bit at the start, walking in nature, gathering her thoughts before the reality of her life was upon her again.

Paula walked in silence this morning. Coming out of the forest, the landscape opened out into fields, some with crops and others were meadows of beautifully coloured mixed wildflowers. The red poppies and blue cornflowers were stunning against the yellow rapeseed flowers. She wanted to cherish this walk today. She felt happy, her heart was full. All the rage she arrived with seemed to have eased. People smiled as they passed each other, uttering a quiet *"Buen Camino"*. Imagine how the people who started in St Jean maybe forty days ago must feel, she thought. How strange to go back to the real world after so long walking with your thoughts.

Paula saw the first sign for a café in the traditional farmhouse-style building she was used to now. God, I'll miss stopping at these beautiful places for my first *café con leche* of the day, she thought.

She ordered a croissant and coffee and the bartender gave her the first stamp of her day with a friendly *'Buen Camino'*.

When she carried her tray outside, she nodded to a table of people she recognised from meeting along the way but chose to sit at a table away from them, outside in the garden. Today was the final day she could enjoy the peace of the Galician countryside before the big arrival in Santiago de Compostela.

Rachel stopped to take some photographs. The sun, now high in the sky, cast its light across the fields, turning them golden. The path was busy now. Today was a big day. It was the end of the Camino for everyone.

After the fields at the start of another forest walk, she passed a shrine. She had passed a few shrines on the route, but this one stopped her in her tracks. It was a beautiful green shrine to an Irishwoman who died peacefully in her sleep having completed her second Camino.

That is so sad, thought Rachel, feeling tearful. Life is so short – this woman was only fifty-two years of age. She looked around and behind her was a field of wildflowers, so she picked a bunch of flowers, a mix of reds and blues and yellows. Taking down the elastic holding up her hair, she arranged them in a bouquet and laid them down at the shrine of her fellow Irishwoman. She stood for a few moments thinking of her, before walking on.

The Camino Way continued through forests and open fields but pretty soon the sounds of nature were replaced by the sounds of traffic and modern life.

Time for one last coffee, thought Rachel as she stopped at a roadside café just before the bridge into the city.

"*Una tarte de Santiago y una café, per favore,*" she ordered from the waiter as she sat down in the shade. I'm going to miss my Tarte de Santiago, she thought, having had a slice nearly every day since arriving in Spain.

As she sat there enjoying her coffee, her phone buzzed.

It was a photo of Simon and Bernie, smiling, looking into the camera with the fountain behind them – with the words **See you soon**.

She smiled and took a deep breath. She had made up her mind and knew exactly what she was going to do.

CHAPTER 43

SANTIAGO

Cathy walked alone and in silence. The forest, the fields and the meadows were behind her now, exchanged for concrete, traffic and the business of modern life. She was almost there.

When she reached San Moras on the outskirts of the city of Santiago, she saw people pose for photos at a very large modern sculpture.

As she leant in to read what it was called, an older pilgrim, with his big backpack on his back, pointed to the sign.

"It is called Monte do Gozo," he said.

"Mount of ... I'm sorry ... my Spanish isn't great," said Cathy.

"It means Mount of Joy. And do you know why?"

Cathy shook her head.

"Look!" The pilgrim came and stood at Cathy's side and pointed.

She gasped. "Oh my goodness!"

"Yes," he said, smiling. "This is the first point that you can see the Cathedral de Santiago and your face is full of joy."

Cathy was smiling from ear to ear and her eyes filled with tears. There it was. The spires of the Cathedral de Santigo rose out of the city skyline and sparkled in the sunshine.

The pilgrim placed his hand on her shoulder. "You are almost there," he whispered. "All will be well now."

Cathy turned to thank him, but he had walked on. She felt so emotional as she watched him walk away. An old man, a stranger, carrying his belongings on his back, had spoken the words she wanted to hear at the end of her Camino journey: *"All will be well now."* How beautiful was that!

She allowed the tears to flow as she carried on putting one foot in front of the other.

She had watched the movie *The Way* so many times and been so moved by it and now she was about to enter Santiago. Father John always said that she'd get there one day, and he was right. He was right about a lot of things. He told her that one day she would be free of Ted. He said when she was strong enough, she would leave, and he would be there to support her. He told her everything would be okay, and he was right. She trusted him completely.

Soon after leaving the busy outskirts, she entered the old town. The narrow streets led her through the beautiful timeless medieval town as all the yellow arrows pointed to the one destination, a path that pilgrims religious and otherwise had walked since 44 AD, to witness the tomb of St James. Cathy started to cry again at the enormity of it all.

It was a lot to take in that the path pilgrims walked today was the same that pilgrims had walked for thousands of years. Despite modern life and motorways being built, the route crossed these things and carried on in the traditional way. The Camino de Santiago still passed through the same villages, climbed the same hills, crossed the same rivers, visited the same churches and monuments as all the pilgrims in centuries gone by.

It is quiet overwhelming to think about it, thought Cathy, but this is the magic of the Camino.

The streets of Santiago were very busy as pilgrims from the many different Camino routes through France, Spain and Portugal all arrived on the same pathway that led to the Cathedral de Santiago. Tradition had it that the pilgrim must come here to the tomb of St. James, kneel down and thank him for his protection on this ancient route. Cathy couldn't wait to get there.

She took out her phone as she got closer to the square and saw the photo of Bernie and Simon. They were there, smiling and waiting for her. Her new friends. Her heart swelled as she put her phone away and carried on.

Paula followed the yellow arrows and the pilgrims ahead of her. She could feel the excitement build as other pilgrims followed each other through Santiago's old streets. She smiled when she saw the photo of Bernie and Simon waiting for them. Local shop owners called out *"Buen Camino!"* as she and others walked by.

Following the directions on her phone, she arrived at the fountain in Plaza Cervantes.

"Paula!"

Following the sound of Bernie's voice, she turned and saw her sitting at a table with Simon ... and beside him ...

"Kevin? Kevin!" Paula's jaw dropped open in disbelief. "Oh my god! How ..."

As she rushed over to him, he stood up. One arm was in a sling.

"What on earth ...? What happened?"

Kevin stood there. "Have you a hug for your poor injured husband first?"

"Yes ... of course."

Paula carefully hugged his good side and stepped back to look at him. He looked so good, she thought as she felt butterflies in her stomach. And so handsome. She started to cry.

"Are you crying? Hey ..." he said, smiling as he put his good arm around her and kissed her tears.

"It's just so good to see you, that's all," Paula said, wiping them away. "I am so happy to see you," she said, smiling, looking into his eyes. He smiled back and she leaned in to kiss him.

"Let's sit down," he said, holding her hand.

"Yes, and tell me what happened your arm and ... how are you here?" she said, looking from Kevin to Bernie and Simon. "And how did you guys meet? I'm so confused!"

Kevin went on to explain that he tripped on a particularly stony part of a hike in Peru and came down hard on his elbow. After hours of getting to a town and finding a medical clinic, an X-ray showed a chipped bone in his elbow which meant that the trip was over for him.

"I insisted Tony carry on and then instead of flying home and sitting on my own in an empty house, I looked up flights from Peru to Spain and came here instead."

Paula watched as he told his story, and she felt so proud of him. I have taken him for granted, she thought.

"I hope you don't mind me surprising you like this," he said. "I know it's something you wanted to do yourself."

"I am so happy you are here! Really I am." Reaching out, she put her hand on his. "And how did you come to be sitting here with Simon and Bernie?"

"Pure fluke. You said in your last message that you were meeting your Camino friends at a fountain and that you were all walking into Cathedral Square. So using your last message as a guide I calculated how long it would take you to get here and then I walked from the Cathedral this morning to see which fountain that might be. Once I calculated that, I sat here until I heard Irish voices of which there are tons, I can tell you! But only two sat down. So I introduced myself as the very proud husband of Paula Byrne and we have been here for an hour waiting on you."

Paula leaned across and kissed him. "I just can't believe you are here. I'm so happy."

"I am so glad to hear that." He lowered his voice and leaned in close to her. "I was a little worried that you mightn't want to see me, especially after that stupid Kerry incident. I realised when I was away just how hurt you must have been and I'm so sorry about that. If I never go hiking in Kerry again I don't care as long as we're okay. I love you, only you, and I am so proud of you. I really wanted to be here for you."

Paula started crying again.

"Hey, don't cry," Kevin said, wiping her tears away again with his free hand.

"I'm sorry, it's been such an emotional experience." There was no way she was ever going to tell him about Carlos, she decided. What happened happened, and it would do no good to tell anyone about it. She would lock that memory away as a reminder of how easily things could fall apart. She now wanted to work hard at keeping her marriage together.

"You better brace yourself," said Kevin. "There are lots of emotional people in Cathedral Square, I can tell you."

"*They're here!*" Bernie called out and waved as Rachel and Cathy arrived at the same time.

They hugged everyone and then pulled over some chairs as they were introduced to Kevin.

Simon pulled out a chair beside him for Rachel.

"Can I have a word with you for a second?" Rachel asked Simon.

"Yes, of course," he said, standing up. "Let's go over here."

They walked around the other side of the fountain to a closed doorway.

"Simon, as you know, I came away here after a break-up with someone I was planning a future with. My world as I thought it was going to be got turned on its head. Well, he showed up last night."

"Here? In Spain?"

"Yes. And I met him and he wants me back. He wants us to go back to how we were."

"I see," said Simon. "And what did you say?"

"I told him I couldn't give him an answer and ... I am saying the same to you."

"Right, well, that's clear enough then," Simon said, looking away.

Rachel touched his arm. "No, Simon, I just need more time."

"Do you still love him?"

"I still have feelings for him. Two weeks ago we were planning a future together. It's not easy to switch those feelings off."

Simon nodded. "I understand that."

"But I have feelings for you too, Simon, feelings I never thought I would have for you again. So I need to be on my own for a while. I know that's not the answer you wanted but ..."

"Rachel, I'll wait. I'll wait for you to make that decision and whatever that decision is I'll respect it."

"Thank you," she said, her eyes filling up. "I'm going to say my goodbyes in the square. I've decided to get a bus to the coast for a few days."

"You're not staying for dinner tonight then?"

"No. I need some time now completely on my own."

Simon leaned in and gently kissed the top of her head. "I will wait for you, Rachel O'Brien," he whispered.

Rachel wiped away a tear. "Okay, we better join the others," she said, looking up into his beautiful green eyes before heading back to the table.

They sat and Rachel turned to Kevin.

"I thought you were in South America?" she asked him, happy to have the focus on somebody else.

She nodded as Kevin recounted his story, not really taking anything in. She had done it. She had told both men she needed more time to be on her own and both had accepted it. She had been so nervous when she'd called Craig at her last stop. He sounded so happy to hear her voice but then disappointed when he heard that she wouldn't be joining him in his suite.

"I just need more time on my own. I thought I'd have it on this trip but for various reasons that didn't happen."

"Howster wants an answer by Monday, Rachel, but I can explain that you are away, and I'll push them back."

"Thank you."

"But Rachel, deal or no deal I want you back. I'm miserable without you. I just want you and me back to the way we were, even if it means going back to our old jobs and me staying in Roger's for a bit longer."

"You mean that?"

"Of course I do. You are the best thing that has ever happened to me. I'll see if I can push the deadline back by a week, okay? And I'll text you to let you know."

"Thanks, Craig."

"Hey, it's you and me that matter more than anything. I love you, Rachel, just remember that."

Rachel agreed to ring him when she got back.

She googled bus times and booked one for 5pm from Santiago's bus station and hoped that one week would be enough time for her to come to a decision.

"Right, shall we do it?" Bernie said and everyone nodded.

Simon helped Bernie up and put his arm through hers. Rachel took her arm on the other side. They led the way, and the others followed. A long trail of walkers, carrying their sticks, were ahead and behind them. The atmosphere was of nervous excitement.

As they neared the Cathedral they heard a piper playing, the sound making its way up the old town streets. As they approached the archway that led into the square, the lone piper was there, playing. It was a tradition to have a bagpiper welcome the pilgrims to Cathedral Square and the end of their Camino.

Cathy started to cry and so did Paula. A single tear ran down Bernie's face as they helped her down the steps and then there they were. Opening out in front of them was Cathedral Square.

Their jaws dropped as they walked toward its centre. All around them other walkers were hugging, taking photos and many were openly crying with happiness. Others were sitting or lying down, resting on their backpacks, looking up at the spectacle that is the Cathedral of Santiago de Compostela.

The cathedral itself looked magnificent and together with its cloisters on both sides of the square and the Palace of Rajoy on the opposite side, the square was complete. Everywhere they looked they saw magnificent architecture from Baroque to Gothic.

"It's breathtaking," said Bernie, tears running down her face.

Simon put his arm around her. "I'm so proud of you, Mum," he said, kissing her on her head.

"Okay, well, seeing as I'm the only one not crying, how about I take the photos?" said Kevin and they all laughed as they handed him their phones.

"*Cathy!*"

Cathy turned around to see Marta and Father Eduardo waving as they came towards her, arms outstretched.

"You did it!" Marta said, hugging her.

"I am so proud of you!" Father Eduardo said, coming in for a hug too.

"Okay, everybody, another photo with the padre!" Kevin said and they all huddled together for a group photo with the magnificent cathedral as their background.

They stayed in the square for an hour, taking photos, talking to other pilgrims, and taking photos for those who travelled solo.

"Time to get the certificates," Cathy said, "before they close."

"And then time for a rest for me," said Bernie.

"Why don't we meet up later for dinner and to celebrate? Is everyone free?" Paula asked.

"I won't join you. I'll say my goodbyes here. I have a bus to catch to Finisterre," Rachel announced.

"Oh, I didn't know you were leaving," said Bernie, looking confused.

"It was a last-minute decision," said Rachel.

"Well, let's have a group hug for Rachel," Paula said, drawing everyone in.

Tonight would have been their last night together as a group but now Rachel was moving on already.

Bernie and Simon were staying an extra night in Santiago. Cathy mentioned something about getting a train somewhere for a few days. Paula was due to fly home the next day but now that Kevin was here they might stay a few extra days in Santiago. Neither of them was in a rush home.

"Okay, well, Kevin and I can look out for a place for dinner on our way to the hotel if the rest of you would like to join us?"

They all agreed.

"Great. I'll book somewhere and stick it on WhatsApp," said Paula.

Everyone hugged Rachel one last time and then she made her way across the square and through the crowds.

Simon walked with Bernie to find their hotel while Cathy, Paula and Kevin headed for the certificate office. Paula took Kevin's hand and squeezed it gently. She felt so full of love for him showing up like this that she didn't want to let his hand go.

He smiled and squeezed her hand back as they strolled across the square in the beautiful Galician sunshine.

CHAPTER 44

Cathy hesitated as she stood beside the sign that said 'ENGLISH'.

The confessions were held in highly decorated alcoves, like tiny churches themselves with ornate paintings, at the sides and back of the main altar in the cathedral. Although the priest sat at an angle, Cathy had not expected that he could see her face.

"Are there more traditional confession boxes available?" Cathy asked Father Eduardo who stood at her side.

"Not in English – only in Spanish today. But you can move your chair so as not to look at him if that is more comfortable for you," he said, placing his hand on her shoulder. "But remember he is there to listen and forgive, not to judge."

Cathy felt sick.

"I will leave you now and you have my number if you wish to talk afterward. I will be around here for a while."

"Thank you. Thank you for everything," Cathy said, her eyes filling up.

"Please stay in touch and we will send you the details of next year's trip. We would all love to see you again, Cathy," he said as he hugged her.

"I would love to join you again. You all mean so much to me now."

"Go easy on yourself," he said, and she knew that he sensed she had been through something big on this Camino.

"Goodbye, Eduardo."

Cathy felt an emotional wreck. Saying goodbye to Marta and the rest of the Spanish group, who had accepted her and helped her more than they would ever know, was so hard, especially after the emotional Pilgrim's Mass that moved everybody so much. And when the Botafumeira incense burner swung over the congregation, people were ecstatic. There was an outpouring of crying and joy that Cathy had never experienced in a church before.

Then last night she had said her goodbyes to Paula, as she and Kevin had decided to get a bus to Muxia on the coast and walk the ancient Camino route to Finisterre. It was a one-day walk, and they were then staying in Finisterre for a few days before flying home. Paula wanted to give Kevin a feel for Camino walking. It was lovely to see that they were so happy to see each other and were so loving towards each other after all their years together.

That's all I ever wanted, thought Cathy, but I never got it, well, not from Ted anyway.

"Next!" the official standing at the front of the line motioned for her to step forward.

"This is it," Cathy whispered as she took a deep breath and walked towards him.

Cathy briefly looked at the priest's face and he at her, before he nodded and motioned for her to sit down. He turned his head so that the side of his face was facing her.

"Bless me, Father, for I have sinned. It is about six months since my last confession."

The priest nodded and Cathy swallowed hard.

"I'm here today looking for absolution. My husband died last month, and ... I could have saved him, but I didn't."

She glanced at the priest to see his reaction. His brow furrowed and he leaned in more towards her.

"Go on."

"I didn't kill him, Father, or anything like that, I just didn't do anything to save him."

The morning that Ted died, he shouldn't have been there. He was supposed to have left the house for work. He always left the house at seven. He was a stickler for routine.

Every morning he woke at six-thirty and showered for three minutes only – he had a timer installed in the shower so that she wouldn't waste water – and then he quickly dressed in the clothes he'd laid out the night before. He always had a bowl of porridge that he made in the microwave, and one cup of tea, and at seven on the dot he left the house. He had done this for all the time she lived with him, but not that day.

Cathy remembered checking her watch when she heard him go back into the bathroom for a second time and her heart started to pound. He was supposed to go straight down the stairs and leave the house. But he returned to the bathroom, and it sounded like he was throwing up. He had complained about feeling unwell all week but wouldn't go to the doctor.

"Waste of money," he always said and there were times that Cathy had to borrow money from her mother to go to the doctor herself without his knowing.

The sound of him vomiting in the bathroom panicked her. She stood behind the door of the box bedroom in the house where she had her packed suitcase, ready to go, under the bed.

Oh God, please let him leave! she prayed, kneeling down at the side of her bed.

She had written Ted a letter and had planned on leaving it on the hall table before leaving the house for the last time. She was leaving him today and all the details were in there. She had taken advice from a Women's Aid helpline that she telephoned anonymously six months previously and they had given her the name of a female solicitor who would help her. Women's Aid were very kind and had helped her see that the things that happened to her were not her fault. It took six months of phone calls with them before she had the courage to leave, and today was that day.

The plan was that she would leave the house and get a train to Dublin and then to Cork and stay with Maggie. When he got home from work he would find the letter explaining her absence. She couldn't leave without leaving the letter, otherwise if he came home and she wasn't there he would be ringing everyone including Sophie and she didn't want Sophie to worry until she could tell her herself in person.

Cathy closed her eyes and held her breath as she heard the toilet flush and Ted closing the door and walking down the stairs. She put her ear to the bedroom door and let out a sigh of relief when she heard the front door shut.

Relieved, she took her suitcase from under the bed, thanked God and blessed herself before opening the door and placing the suitcase on the landing. Taking the letter out of her handbag, she hurried down the stairs and placed the envelope on the hall table. She took a moment to stand it up facing the door so that it would be the first thing he saw when he came in from work tonight. Happy that it was in the right place, she went back upstairs to pack up her toiletries from the bathroom and take one last look around upstairs to check that she had everything.

She was putting her toiletries bag in her case when she heard his key in the door and the door slam.

"*Oh Jesus!*"

Surprised to see her standing at the top of the stairs he stopped, looked at her, then the case and then as if in slow motion his head turned to see the envelope with his name handwritten by Cathy, on the hall table.

"*What – is – this?*" He picked up the envelope and waved it towards where she was standing.

Cathy's mouth opened but no words came out. Her heart pounded in her chest as he opened the envelope, and her breath quickened. She couldn't move.

His eyes scanned the letter and then turned to her.

"*Who the fuck do you think you are!*" he shouted as he marched up the stairs. His knuckles were white as he clenched the letter.

Cathy couldn't breathe. She looked around but she knew she had nowhere to run to.

"I ..." was all she could splutter, putting her hands up in front of her.

He was on the landing now. His face was red with rage.

"*You stupid little bitch!*" he spat as he roared in her face.

He's going to kill me, she thought as she tried to back away.

He pinned her up against the bathroom door.

"*You? Leave ME!*" He laughed – a manic laugh full of rage.

Oh Jesus, please don't let me die this way, she prayed, closing her eyes and bracing herself for what was to come.

"*Open your eyes, you little bitch, you whore! I would rather do time for killing you than let you leave me to be a whore!*"

Sweat was rolling down his face now. He tore up the letter about an inch from her face. Grabbing her jaw, he shoved the torn pieces into her mouth. She tried to turn away, but he put his hand around her throat. She couldn't breathe.

"*Happy now, are you!*" he shouted. "*Look at what you have driven me to!*"

He shoved another piece into her mouth, and she gagged and gasped for breath.

He is going to kill me. Oh, sweet Jesus, help me! she begged, as her eyes watered and her vision blurred.

And then it stopped. His hand left her throat and instead went to his chest and then his arm.

Cathy coughed and spat out the paper, grabbing the landing banister to steady herself as she gasped for breath.

Ted stumbled backward, clutching his chest, his face turning a purple colour.

"Heart ..." he wheezed, reaching out to her.

She froze to the spot.

He looked at her, confused, as he stumbled again and then a look of horror came over him as he fell backward over her suitcase, falling down the stairs, unable to stop himself until he crashed headfirst into the heavy hall table that she always hated.

The house went silent.

Cathy got her breath back. She was almost afraid to look. A low gurgling sound was coming from him as he lay there motionless in the hall. Moving slowly to the top of the stairs, she looked down. His body was twisted at the bottom of the stairs and a pool of red-black blood was forming around his head. She took a few steps down the stairs and paused. Then she took a few more. His eyes were half open. He tried to speak but the only sound that came was a gurgling sound and then blood oozed out of his mouth. It sounded like choking. His hand trembled towards her and his bulging eyes stared at her in disbelief.

He was going to kill me, but God saved me, she thought. *This is just a terrible accident.*

Calmly, she turned around, walked back up the stairs, and picked up the suitcase. Taking it back to her bedroom she unpacked her clothes and hung them back up in her small single wardrobe. Walking out to the landing, she picked up all the torn-up scrunched-up pieces of the letter he tried to choke her with, carried them into the bathroom and flushed them down the toilet. Picking up a flannel, she ran it under cold water and wiped her blotchy tear-stained face, repeating until the redness calmed down.

Returning to the bedroom, she put on her coat, picked up her handbag and walked down the stairs.

She bent down to look at him. His eyelids were twitching but the gurgling sound had stopped.

"Goodbye, Ted. I have to go now, or I'll be late for work," she said.

Picking up her house key from the bowl on the table, she left the house, closing the door securely behind her.

Jesus saved me, she thought as she walked out into the sunshine to start her long walk to work.

"So, Father, as you can see, it was a terrible accident, in the home, but I'm afraid I didn't do anything. I could have called for help, but I let nature and God do what was best. I have prayed and prayed for forgiveness, and I can only hope that our Lord Jesus can forgive me now, through you."

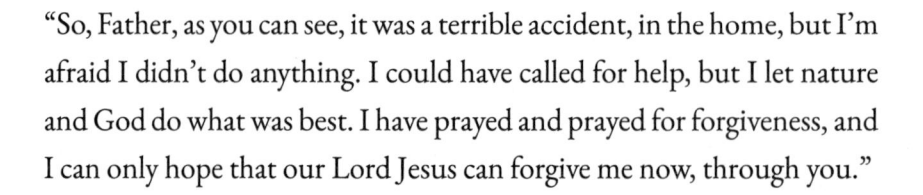

The priest looked very tense. He sighed as he rubbed his hand over his head, rocking slightly, taking time to gather his thoughts on what he had just heard.

They both sat in silence for a few minutes.

Then he cleared his throat. "Only God knows what is in our hearts and what are our true intentions," he responded gently, not looking at her. "He is the only one to judge our actions or lack of actions. So we look to our Mother Mary as an example of love, compassion, and forgiveness. For your penance, say five Hail Marys and reflect on her life." He then paused. "May God grant you pardon and peace. I absolve you of your sins."

Then, lifting his hand in the air, he made the Sign of the Cross. "*In the name of the Father, and of the Son, and of the Holy Spirit. Amen.*"

Cathy sighed deeply. "Thank you, Father."

"Go in peace," he said and then, without looking at her, put a closed sign up, took out his rosary beads and started praying.

Cathy left the cathedral, feeling lightheaded and elated.

She checked her watch and made her way to their arranged meeting point, behind the cathedral in the Platerías Square.

"Cathy!"

She turned and smiled. "I would never have recognized you," she said, leaning in to kiss him. "You shaved your beard off!"

"Yes, but I can lose the sunglasses and baseball cap too when we board the train," he said, pulling her in for another kiss. "Anyway, there are too many Irish people here. I could easily bump into a parishioner! But the villa I have booked for us is deep in the mountains so we can truly be ourselves there." He smiled down at her, giving her goosebumps.

"What time is the train?"

"Four o'clock."

"That gives us just enough time to collect my bag and ..."

"And?"

"Well, I have been absolved of all my sins now so ... clean slate and all that."

"*Hmm*, I like your thinking," smiled John. "Let's go."

"Oh, there is just one last thing I need to do before we go," Cathy said, reaching deep into her pocket.

Taking out the stone she brought from her garden at home, the home she vowed never to return to, she held it in her hand. Then she flung the stone representing all the guilt and shame she had felt for years, into the fountain behind her.

"I'm ready now," she smiled, linking John's arm.

As they walked through the crowds, Cathy felt her heart swell with joy, finally free of her guilt and with a man who truly loved her. God would always be his number one, but she felt blessed to be his number two, a secret for just the two of them and nobody else.

EPILOGUE

Five months later

November 2023

"Five minutes more?"

"No, absolutely not! We have guests arriving, our first guests."

"They won't be here for hours!" Simon tightened his grip around Rachel's waist by throwing his leg over her in their big wide bed, pinning her to the spot.

"Hey, you!" Rachel laughed. She still couldn't believe her luck, waking up beside this gorgeous man every morning.

"I just want to look at you up close for as long as I can," Simon said, pushing her long hair away from her face.

"Can you believe this day is here?" Rachel said, snuggling into his tanned chest.

"No," he said, kissing her forehead. "But I know now it's what my heart wished for. When I thought of you over the years, one of my vivid memories was you describing your dream life and I remember thinking, if only that had could come true. It's incredible how it all came to be in the end."

"Hey," Rachel said, kissing him on the lips to stop him talking. "Two Golden Retrievers will start barking soon to be let out, so why don't we see what we can do with limited time?" And she winked.

Simon pulled back the patchwork quilt in different shades of nautical blues. His eyes lit up as he took in Rachel's nakedness. She stretched her arms over her head and spread her long athletic legs to each corner of the bed. Simon moaned as his body reacted to the vision before him.

"Oh my god, you are stunning," he whispered as he moved down the bed, placing himself in the space between her legs.

Keeping eye contact, they moved together slowly at first before upping their pace. Rachel held on to his broad shoulders and let her hips do the work, giving Simon a view that he relished.

As the pace quickened Rachel could not hold out any longer and let out an uncontrollable yell. Simon soon joined her, followed by the howling of two Golden Retrievers on the other side of the door. At that, Simon and Rachel crashed together in laughter.

"We need ... to keep .... those two locked up in the kitchen," panted Simon before lying beside Rachel, holding her close and kissing her gently.

I never knew love could be like this, she thought as she smiled at how wonderful things had turned around in such a short time.

Hartley House B&B in the coastal town of Schull, County Cork, had been closed for over two years when Rachel and Simon went to see it.

As soon as they drove up the driveway to view it, they knew it was the house for them.

"It's ... perfect." The tears rolled down Rachel's face as she tried to take it all in.

From the front it looked like a regular, white-washed dormer bungalow but a double extension on the back of the house added six extra bedrooms, all ensuite, an extra living room downstairs and a big open kitchen.

So much had changed for Rachel in such a short time. Despite agreeing to give her time to figure things out in Finisterre, Craig had called her after just two days claiming that Howster would not give them the extension and that they needed an answer within 24 hours.

He sounded more irritated on the phone now when she said she needed more time so she claimed bad phone coverage and hung up on him. When she went back and read the contract she could see no deadline so she emailed the contact on the form who replied that the deadline of Monday only applied to Mr Callaghan's contract of employment in their London office. She quickly rang Craig back.

"Rachel!"

"Yes. I'm a bit confused."

"Oh yeah?"

"Well, maybe you can clarify why the deadline just applies to your contract, Craig? The one that says you will be working in their offices for six months?"

"Oh, that."

"Yes, that."

"Well, it's simple enough. If and when we sign the main contract to collaborate with Howster, I will need to work in their office in London for six months. It's part of the deal."

"Six months! And when were you going to tell me this?"

"When you agreed to come back. There was no point in telling you otherwise."

"Don't you think that you moving to London affects me? Affects us?"

"London isn't that far and we have to think of the bigger picture. Six months is nothing."

"You said you wanted us to go back to the way we were and already you are hiding this from me? If I say yes to this contract you move to London and I stay in Dublin. How does that help our relationship?"

"We're stronger than that. As far as I'm concerned this is the best move for us. I've already being looking at apartments there so I need an answer, Rachel."

"You've what? Craig, are you moving to London anyway?"

"Rachel, I want to do this with you but I can't hang around waiting for an answer. If this deal falls through I have other options in London. I need to move on with my life."

No talk of love, no talk of missing her. His patience had run out and his mask had slipped. He was going to London with or without her.

"I won't hold you back any longer then, Craig. My answer is no."

"*Rachel, you are making a big mistake.*"

"I don't think so. Goodbye, Craig."

She had a big cry when she put down the phone but then felt relieved. She walked to the seafront in Finisterre just as the sun was setting and sat on the rocks, feeling a huge weight lift off her shoulders.

She didn't hear from Craig again after that last phone call. So much for needing her in his life. When she got home to Dublin she heard through the grapevine that he had taken a job in London, out of her life forever hopefully.

Simon and Bernie returned to Cork after the trip and, although Rachel wanted to take things slowly with Simon, she contacted him and they began messaging each other and spoke every night on the phone. By the end of the week, when his mum was settled back into her routine, he drove to Dublin to see her.

Once she let her guard down and surrendered to her true feelings, she couldn't deny that she was mad about him. He had promised to never hurt her, and she had chosen to believe him.

This would never have happened if she had not gone on the Camino. That trip broke her down but also broke down the walls she had spent years building up. She just surrendered to whatever the future would bring. She wanted the fairy tale and believed she could have it with Simon. She was tired of putting up a tough image, it was exhausting. She could never forgive herself if she didn't give him a chance. So that's what she did.

The next time Simon came to Dublin he told Rachel he loved her. She didn't hold back either and they sealed their love in her little townhouse. Simon divided his time between Dublin and Cork but Rachel felt unsettled in Dublin now. This was the house that she and Craig were going to live and work from. She wanted a fresh start and to leave the ghosts behind.

When she suggested to Simon that she sell up and move to Cork, he could not believe it.

"Are you sure?"

"Yes, I'm done with Dublin. Honestly, I don't have the same appetite for the work life here and this house ... has too many memories. You need to be in Cork to look after your mum and ... I need to be where you are."

Simon swept her up in his arms and spun her around. "That is the best news I have ever received!" he said, stopping to put her down.

Taking her head in his hands he kissed her gently on her lips, her eyes and her nose, making her laugh.

"I promise you I will do everything I can to make your dreams come true."

"I don't know what I'm going to do for work but I have this crazy idea of doing something completely different."

Simon's eyes lit up. "You can do whatever you set your mind to. What do you want to do?"

"It's crazy and I have no experience but I keep thinking about the pensions on the Camino and how happy the hosts were, meeting new people and taking care of them."

"Okay ..." Simon said, looking at her quizzically

"Is it a crazy idea to open a Bed and Breakfast with no experience?"

"Tell me what you see?"

"In an ideal world, I can see me and you running a Bed and Breakfast Guesthouse near the sea in West Cork, Schull maybe. We could be busy all summer with guests and then in the winter maybe just the two of us. We could even have writers groups or artists to stay over the winter but mostly I see you and me running our own business."

Simon stood with his mouth open

"Say something!"

"I love you."

"What?"

"I love you, Rachel, and if I could spend my days running a guesthouse by the sea with you, that would be a dream come true for me. I would be the happiest man alive."

"So you don't think it's crazy?"

"Yes, of course it is but so what? We can definitely do this."

And that's what they did.

"They're here!" Simon called to Rachel and she came rushing down the hall from the kitchen.

"This is it. Our first guests," she said excitedly.

Simon opened the front door and stepped out to greet them.

"Paula," Simon stepped forward to hug her. "And Kevin! Great to see you."

"What a place you have here," said Kevin, shaking his hand. "I'm sure I could get a group to come and stay here for a hike."

"We'd love to have them. Come inside."

"Rachel!" Paula hugged her.

"It's so good to see you both, come into the heat." Rachel linked Paula and brought her into the big drawing room at the front of the house where their two Golden Retrievers sat warming themselves at the roaring fire.

"Oh this is beautiful, Rachel," Paula said, looking around.

"We're really happy with how it turned out."

"Now can I make anyone a hot port? It's Baltic out there," said Simon.

"I wouldn't say no," Kevin said, approaching the fire and rubbing his hands.

Just then another car pulled up.

"There's Cathy now," Paula said.

A car door shut and the front door was opened. Paula heard Simon greet Cathy and take her coat before leading her in to the others. Rachel and Paula both gasped when they saw her. Although they had kept in touch through WhatsApp, Cathy didn't have an Instagram account so they hadn't seen any recent photos of her. Gone was the lank mousy-brown hair, replaced with a chunky layered bob. They had only ever seen her in loose-fitting clothes and her hiking gear but today she stood there in skinny jeans, high-heeled black boots, and a red cashmere jumper.

"You look fantastic, Cathy," Rachel said, coming forward to hug her.

"Amazing," Paula said, joining them. "You look so well, Cathy."

Cathy blushed, still not used to taking compliments. "It is so good to see the two of you."

Simon arrived with a tray of hot ports.

"Please, sit down everyone, and get one of these into you to heat you up."

"Your house is beautiful," Cathy said as she sat down on a light-brown leather couch with soft Avoca rugs thrown over the ends.

The colourful rugs and the red walls added a warmth and luxury feel to the big drawing room. The floorboards had been stripped back to their original colour and a big cream rug kept the retrievers comfortable as they stretched out in front of the fire.

"We had to get a cream rug in here because of these two," smiled Rachel. "Anything else would have shown up how much they shed." She joined Cathy and Paula on the couch. "So tell me all your news."

"Oh, a lot is happening with us," Paula said, putting her hand out to Kevin. He came to where she was, sat on the arm of the couch and held her hand. "We've put our house on the market! We are downsizing."

"That's a big move," Rachel said, surprised.

"Our kids have flown the nest and I was very restless, knocking about in that big house. The Camino made me realise that we need very little in our lives now. So after a lot of persuasion, Kevin agreed."

"It did take a lot of persuading," said Kevin, smiling.

"And have you found somewhere to move to?" asked Simon.

"No, not yet. We are looking at apartments as well as small townhouses. Something that needs very little work as we plan to be away a lot."

"Oh?"

"Yes. Remember Sheila?"

"Yes, of course," said Cathy. "The woman who runs the ethical volunteering trips?"

"Exactly. Kevin and I are going to Vietnam next week on one of her trips."

"That's so exciting. How long for?"

"Three weeks," said Kevin. "One week sightseeing down the south in Ho Chi Minh and touring around there, one week volunteering, and one-week sightseeing and hiking up north."

"That sounds incredible," said Simon.

"My wife came back a changed woman," said Kevin, "and I'm delighted that we can do these things together now. I'm taking time off work for this trip but the next one falls over the Easter break so that works well for me."

"The next one?" Rachel asked.

"Yes," said Paula. "We're booked on a Bali trip for next Easter, visiting various islands and then helping turtles on an island called Nusa Penida."

"You guys! Is that all because of the Camino?" asked Simon.

"Pretty much. I don't think I would have come across Sheila otherwise. Downsizing the house means we will have more funds in the bank to keep exploring."

"It sounds so exciting," said Cathy.

"It is and it's an adventure we can have together," she said, looking up at Kevin, and everyone could see they were still very much in love.

"How about you, Cathy?" asked Paula "I know you were talking about selling your house too. Any word on that?"

"Yes, there is. What if I told you it only took twenty minutes for me to get here today?"

"Twenty minutes?" said Rachel. "Are you staying in the area?"

"*Hmm*, kind of," answered Cathy, looking around at everyone. "I didn't want to say anything because I was still finding my feet but ... I moved into my new house four weeks ago. I've moved to Durrus, here in Cork, so we're kind of neighbours now!"

"Durrus! But that's only down the road," said Rachel. "That's wonderful news – congratulations!"

"I'm so happy for you, Cathy," Paula said, moving over to hug her.

Cathy didn't want to bore everyone with her story, but as soon as she got back to Mullingar from the Camino trip, she stayed in her parents' house. She only returned to her own house to take any documents she might need and bag up any clothes belonging to herself and Ted to give them to the local charity shop. After that, she asked the solicitor to organise the sale of the house.

As expected, Patsy was on the phone, disgusted that she had to find out from a stranger that her brother-in-law's house was up for sale. But Cathy didn't care. The Camino had given her a strength she had forgotten she had and with John by her side to confide in and support her she continued to carry out her plans. She handed in her notice and stayed with her cousin Maggie in Cork City while she looked for a new home.

"This is great news," Rachel said. "How did you decide on Durrus?"

"Well, I wanted to be near Sophie and also my cousin Maggie who has been so good to me so I knew it had to be Cork and, after the Camino, I just craved a quiet space. When I came across a small two-bedroomed bungalow in Durrus, I fell in love with it. It's a short walk to the village and it's elevated so I have a view of Dunmanus Bay from the front windows. The front garden is a little overgrown but I like it that way and, as it fitted my budget, I bought it as quick as I could."

What she didn't tell them was that the overgrowth prevented people from seeing when she might have a visitor over to stay. A visitor who would leave his priest's collar in the car before entering the cottage as John.

"That is amazing, I'm so happy for you. It's beautiful out there," said Simon.

"Well, the house needs a lot of redecorating and there is very little furniture in it but I'll get there. I just need a little job to keep the money coming in and there might be a cleaning job going in the holiday cottages in the village so I'm going to enquire about that."

"A cleaning job?" Rachel asked, looking surprised. "But you worked as a receptionist, didn't you?"

"I know but I don't want to do that type of work anymore. I want a quiet life and if I can get a cleaning job a few days a week I will be happy."

Rachel and Simon looked at each other.

"Eh, would you work here?" Simon said.

"Here?" Cathy said, looking from Simon to Rachel.

"Yes, here. We literally sat down today to write an ad for the local shop's noticeboard. We are looking for a local woman to come in maybe three mornings a week or more in high season to clean the bedrooms. Simon and I can manage the cleaning everywhere else. Would you be interested?"

"Yes, that sounds perfect. But are you sure?"

"Of course we are. It's much better for us to have someone we know. It will probably include a weekend day. We won't know for sure until we see how busy we are. Could you be flexible with the days?"

"Yes! That sounds perfect."

Sophie sometimes visited on midweek for dinner as she was busy with friends at weekends and John had Masses to do in Mullingar so he never came at the weekend. This was ideal.

"This calls for a celebration!" Simon said. "I was saving the champagne for dinner but I think now is the perfect time."

Returning with two bottles of champagne and a bucket of ice, Simon put them down on the sideboard while Rachel took the champagne flutes out from a glass cabinet in the alcove.

"I can't believe this," Cathy said. "Thank you both so much."

"This is great news for all of us." Simon popped the first champagne bottle.

"*Who started the drinking without us?*" A shout came from the hall.

"Oh, they're here!" Rachel said. "I didn't get a chance to tell you all who would be joining us. Come in, you two!"

"Don't you dare start without us!" Bernie called from her wheelchair.

"Bernie!" Cathy said, rushing forward and hugging her friend.

"Jesus, we got here just in time, Bernie," said a short blond woman with a cheeky grin.

"Everyone, this is Charley, my mad friend!"

"Jeez, thanks!" Charley laughed as she took off her coat.

Cathy helped Bernie out of the wheelchair and took her coat off, then sat her in an armchair by the fire.

"I'm delighted to meet you all!" said Charley. "I've heard so much about ye."

"Did you tell them?" Bernie whispered loudly to Cathy.

Cathy smiled, nodding.

"Wait a minute – did you know Cathy was moving to Cork?" asked Rachel.

"I might have – we've kept in touch since we came back – and isn't it just great news?" beamed Bernie.

"It is and, even better, she's coming to work for us," Simon said.

"Really? Oh, I never thought of that. That's just perfect!"

"Paula, let go of that handsome man of yours so he can come over and give me a hug," Bernie said, waving them over.

"Hello again, Bernie," said Kevin, bending down to hug her. "How have you been?"

"Well, I'm so glad I did the Camino when I did. My legs started to give me bother when we got back and I have to use this bloody wheelchair now but ... I'm still here and I'm hanging on for as long as I can. Maybe these two might give me a reason to hang around," she teased, looking at Rachel and Simon.

"Well ..." Simon said, looking at Rachel.

"I can't believe nobody noticed!" Rachel beamed as she held up her left hand.

"Oh my god!" Charley was first over to hug her. "I'm so happy for you, girl!" And she started to cry.

"Stop that crying or you'll start me off now," said Rachel, tears of happiness welling up in her eyes.

"Let me see," said Bernie.

Rachel knelt down beside the wheelchair to show her sparkling engagement ring to her and she started crying too.

"This is .... the best news ever," Bernie said between tears.

"Congratulations!" Paula and Cathy stepped in to hug Rachel, and Kevin shook Simon's hand.

"To the bride and groom-to-be!" said Kevin, raising his glass and everyone joined him in raising their glasses.

"There was definitely magic under those Camino skies," Bernie said and everyone nodded.

It changed all their lives, that one week in June. A week to remember.

THE END

Also published by Poolbeg.com

The Weekend Break

RUTH O'LEARY

Four friends, four secrets, one explosive weekend break that tests their friendship.

VIVIENNE'S perfect life is a façade, and she at last wants out. She needs a divorce fast.

HELEN'S nightly glass of wine has become a bottle or two, and her drinking is threatening her marriage.

CLARA feels she must lie to her husband to save her sanity and reach towards some freedom.

MIRIAM, wanting to change her life, does so in the most dramatic way possible. Her friends are supportive when she tells them, but she knows there is still a hidden truth that can never be exposed.

Their time in Galway has life-changing consequences. As the weekend unfolds and their secrets are laid bare, will it be too much for some to cope with? Will their friendship and loyalty to each other survive the weekend break and its painful aftermath?

ISBN 978-178199-698-0